CW00832760

Hexad

The Chamber

(Hexad Book 2)

Copyright © 2015 Al K. Line

Sign up for the author's newsletter for new release
announcements and flash sales at www.alkline.co.uk

All rights reserved. This book or any portion thereof may not be reproduced or used in any manner whatsoever without the express written permission of the author except for the use of brief quotations in a book review.

This is a work of fiction. Names, characters, businesses, places, events and incidents are either the products of the author's imagination or used in a fictitious manner. Any resemblance to actual persons, living or dead, or actual events is purely coincidental.

Digging

Present Day

"Who the hell are you?" Dale felt beads of sweat pricking his skin in rolling waves, shivering over his body like he was lying on the shores of his own sanity, a cold madness trying to drag him under.

"Huh? What do you mean Dale? It's me, Amanda. Go to sleep, you just had a bad dream." Amanda put her head back on the pillow, hair cascading over onto his side of the bed.

What's wrong with me? This doesn't feel right; this doesn't feel right at all.

Dale looked at the face of the already sleeping Amanda, then glanced over at the clock, a retro Bakelite gift she had got him when his old one broke, orange curves making it as much a work of art as a functional object.

His head felt funny. Everything felt funny, even reality, and the woman beside him definitely felt wrong. What was going on? Ah, the booze, that was it. The wine from the night before, and the conversation. That damn conversation.

What had they talked about? Time travel, that was right. They'd gone totally off on one about how crazy it would be if in the morning they went and dug up proof that time travel existed from under the apple tree.

It's messing with my head, that's all.

Dale knew he wouldn't be able to get back to sleep, and besides, his head was hurting and he needed a glass of water. Overriding all else however was the undeniable fact he was in desperate need of a pee.

Mind clouded by confusion and alcohol, Dale staggered to the bathroom and relieved himself. He drank water from the tap until he felt like his belly would burst, then popped a couple of paracetamol before creeping slowly back into the bedroom, dread crawling up his back like his cerebrospinal fluid had been replaced with liquid nitrogen.

He got dressed quietly, taking surreptitious glances at the sleeping form in the bed. What was wrong with him? How could this not be Amanda? It was that time travel talk, it must be. Putting stupid ideas in his head, mixing everything up until it made no sense and all he could think of was different timelines, different universes — realities where anything and everything could happen and he could have just this minute gone off, changed his own reality, so that he now had no concept of a future he had once lived but would now never come to pass.

Ugh, it was enough to make your head split open, and the pills certainly weren't going to help if he kept thinking such strange thoughts.

Dale took one more look at Amanda before moving closer and kissing her on the temple — it didn't help. There was that fragrance again. That wasn't her, not what she smelled like. He knew her scent anywhere. He knew what she smelled like when fresh from the shower, after love-making, when sweaty from exercise and any other possible situation.

This wasn't her.

With a head feeling like cotton wool, Dale went into the kitchen. He needed coffee; lots of it.

~~~

Somehow he found himself out in the garden, grabbing a trowel from the shed. Feeling very embarrassed and like a first class idiot he began to dig a hole three paces to the right and one back from the old apple tree that already had tiny fruit growing amid the cascade of dense green foliage.

A squirrel watched with interest from the safety of the hedge Dale had neglected to trim, and the resident robin chattered impatiently from the apple tree then decided to risk it and landed quickly on the pile of excavated earth, snapped up a worm, and took off again.

Christ, I'm such a muppet. If Amanda wakes up and sees me doing this she's never going to let me hear the last of it.

Dale dug deeper, jeans damp from the morning dew on the lawn that really needed a mow. He'd get to that later, after he'd finished with his idiocy.

"I wouldn't do that if I were you," said Amanda.

"Hellfire, you scared the life out of me. Thought you were still sleeping?" Dale looked up at Amanda, shading his eyes from the early morning sun — it promised to be a glorious day in suburbia.

Amanda's shadow darkened the patch of bare earth where he had begun to dig, highlighting his idiocy. Amanda said nothing, just carried on staring down at him, as if waiting for something more than for him to simply admit he was feeling rather embarrassed.

"Okay, look, I know, all right? But I couldn't get it out of my head. I just had to do it." Dale was expecting her to burst into laughter, to mock him and never let him hear the end of doing such a daft thing, but instead she simply stood there, shifting slightly from one foot to the other.

Dale was starting to feel really uncomfortable, as if he knew the day was just going to get more weird than it already was, not to mention that Amanda was being way too intense. Normally she'd be totally making fun of him by now. Maybe she was still annoyed at him? After all, it's not every day you get woken up and are accused of not being you.

Dale got to his feet, brushing the mud from his knees, realized his jeans were soaked through so wiped his hands on them, giving it up as a lost cause.

Amanda was still just standing there, hands on hips, head tilted to the side so her long golden hair hung like a flag without a breeze, as if accusing him of something. Something really wasn't right. She must be seriously annoyed with him.

"I'm sorry okay? I just woke up and felt weird; you felt weird. Not felt, just smelled different. I'm sorry." Dale waited. "What, you not going to say anything? You not going to make fun of me for digging for time travel proof like a total idiot?"

"You mean like this?" said Amanda, pulling a strange silver tube-like device from a pocket in her thin cotton jacket.

Where did she get that from? He'd never seen it before.

"What's that?" Dale got the feeling he really didn't want to know. It was the booze, it must be, playing with his head. He needed coffee. Maybe life wouldn't seem quite so surreal once the caffeine hit.

The strange object seemed to be flashing blue on its domed top, and Amanda was holding it out like she expected him to recognize it. Dale just shook his head, trying to get some clarity.

A gentle breeze lifted Amanda's beautiful hair — how she'd got it fixed so quickly this morning was a bit of a mystery, normally she took forever to get it just right.

The breeze tickled Dale's face as it passed, carrying that all-too-familiar scent of the woman he loved more than anything in the world.

Hey, wait a minute...

"Amanda? It's you, isn't it?"

Before Dale knew what was happening Amanda was clutching him tight like she hadn't seen him for a lifetime. He hugged her back, cupping the back of her head in his hand.

Is she crying? She is, she's crying.

Dale pulled back. Her face was soaking; she looked totally distraught.

"It's you, isn't it? Not... not the you in the bedroom? Ugh, what's happening? I think my head's gone funny."

"Oh Dale, I've missed you so much. I love you."

"I love you too honey. That was weird this morning, right? Your new perfume must have thrown me, sorry about that."

"Dale, I haven't got new perfume, this is me. That isn't." Amanda pointed to the bedroom window — the curtains were still pulled tightly shut, as if she hadn't got up, had a shower, done her hair and then come outside.

"What? What's going on?" asked Dale tentatively, knowing that he really wasn't going to like the answer one little bit.

"I think we better have a little chat. But I've missed you so much."

"Haha, don't be silly, I saw you ten minutes ago. Now, if you'd just tell me how you can get showered and dressed so quickly we could probably make a million."

"Dale, that woman, that woman you woke up to, it isn't me. This is me, right here."

"Very funny. You know not to try and pull that kind of stuff on me. I know I'm digging up the lawn but it doesn't mean I'm that gullible."

"Go and take a look then, but don't wake her, don't you dare," warned Amanda, more serious than Dale had ever seen her. "This is too important to mess up... again."

"This isn't funny anymore. I'm going to make some coffee." Dale headed back to the house before turning and saying, "You know, I'd prefer it if you just made fun of me, not acted so weird and like I've done something wrong. This was just me being stupid." Dale pointed at the half-dug hole.

"Just go and look. I'll be waiting."

~~~

Dale wandered into the kitchen feeling cross. Why Amanda was being so strange he had no idea. He knew he'd acted odd himself when he first woke up, but c'mon, he was just out of sorts from feeling hungover and got a bit weirded out. But something wasn't right. Her scent was different, that was for sure, but now it was right again, so it was just one of those tricks of the mind that happens when you first wake up and are a little confused... wasn't it?

Dale flipped the kettle on and put a spoon of Nescafe in two mugs, then stood there tapping his foot, willing the water to boil so he could clear his head and hopefully just get on with the rest of the day normally — no digging like an idiot. Although, what if...? Maybe he would finish his digging after all, just to be sure.

"Ugh, you muppet Dale. As if."

Then it hit him. What was Amanda holding? What had she said? 'I wouldn't do that if I were you.' What did she mean by that? It wasn't exactly just her mocking him, was it? It was almost as if she believed he'd find something.

Dale tiptoed down the hall of the bungalow and quietly opened the door to the bedroom, shaking his head at his own actions, feeling stupid to be so sneaky when she was outside. God, what a way to start a Saturday morning.

Dale's heart skipped a beat, ice clawed up his spine and froze his brain as he heard the gentle snoring of Amanda from the bed, something she refused to admit she did, but was what Dale awoke to most mornings.

Dale glanced at the windows, still covered by the drapes. Could she have run around the house and got in through the window then closed it, got into bed and pretended to be snoring so quickly? He ran back into the kitchen, peering out through the window.

Bloody hell, she's still stood in the same spot.

In a daze, Dale poured the coffee and took two mugs outside — he'd forgotten the milk.

He handed Amanda a steaming mug; he had the distinct feeling this was not going to be a relaxing day of mowing the lawn and maybe having a beer over a long lunch.

"Thanks," said Amanda.

"Um, your welcome." *How am I not running around screaming?*

Dale sipped his coffee, burning his lips without the cooling effect of the milk. "Bugger. Hot."

"Dale? Hold my hand?"

"Sure honey." Dale went to put his mug down.

"No, keep hold of it, you'll need it."

"Um, okay." Dale reached out to the offered hand and felt the soft, familiar skin of Amanda. She fiddled with the object she had in the other, having put her own drink down on the grass.

"Hold tight."

The world collapsed around him as Dale's reality became nothing more than a cosmic joke, then it was all over.

Dale was aware of the morning chorus of the birds, eager to start their day and check whether or not Dale had remembered to fill the feeders hanging from the apple tree he and Amanda were stood under.

Morning chorus? That would make it about five in the morning. It was eight thirty when he'd got up.

A Confusing Morning

3 Hours 19 Minutes Past

Dale slurped his still-hot coffee, numb to the heat as it slid down his throat, thinking burned lips were better than the weird after-effects the night before were clearly having on his brain — he definitely needed to give up drinking. That, or have a few more right now, just to eradicate the woozy feeling in his head.

"We need to talk," said Amanda, releasing his hand, putting the strange device back in her pocket.

"I think you may be right. What just happened?"

"I took you away from digging up proof. It's a slippery road that I don't want repeated yet again."

"Proof?"

"Of time travel."

Dale gulped his coffee. One of them had to have their wits about them and Amanda was clearly still hammered from the night before. Or was she?

Dale tried to relax, to let the caffeine work its magic. It was going on for nine, now it was first thing in the morning. He hadn't, had he?

"Did we just, you know, time travel?"

"We did. Mad, eh? Now look, we have a lot to talk about. You ready?"

Dale slumped onto the lawn, the grass much damper than it had been, his jeans thoroughly soaked through now — he didn't even notice. "As ready as I'll ever be. Be gentle, I'm having a bad day."

"You think you're having a bad day? Wait until you hear about mine."

Amanda was right, she was having a much harder time of it than him.

~~~

As soon as they'd jumped Dale knew that Amanda was different, it just didn't quite register as it wasn't something that was possible. But now that he could see her properly — as earlier she had purposely placed herself in front of the sun so all he saw really was her silhouette without getting a proper look at her features, it was obvious that she was older, older than the woman he'd woken up to that morning, or would wake up to in a few hours.

The whole concept was already messing with his mind. Was he really in bed asleep right now? Well, not him obviously, he was here. But how? How could that make any sense? He couldn't be thinking these thoughts but still be in bed asleep at the same time, could he? That would mean there were two of him. If he went in right now and woke himself up then would it be like he had a perfect clone?

"I know what you're thinking. It won't work."

"What do you mean?" asked Dale, shifting uneasily now he realized his bum was soaking wet from the early morning dew.

"If you go into the bedroom and try to wake yourself up then you won't be able to. Something will happen to stop you, and even if you did succeed, what do you think it would do to you: waking up to find yourself peering down at you? You'd have a fit, probably have a heart attack right then and there, then there would only be this you left alive and you'd have a dead you to try to get rid of. That or the paradox would be too great and both of you would simply blink out of existence like you were never born. I wouldn't want to find out either way. You know, whole universes have been destroyed then reborn because of this stuff, because of what we did, what we will do."

Amanda waved away the seemingly meaningless difference. "In any case, we have a problem. But Dale, I missed you so much, it's been horrible, so horrible I can't explain. I don't know whether to be angry with you and slap you so hard, or kiss you."

"Um, kiss me?" prompted Dale. He got up and stared into eyes that had seen much more than the woman he went to bed with the night before. Much more. He pulled her to him, kissed her lips softly, then hugged her tight again. "I think you better tell me what's going on."

~~~

"No way. You're telling me that you were taken and I just left you there, wherever there is? I wouldn't do that, no chance."

"I didn't think you would either, but you did. I don't blame you though, not really. The Caretaker explained it all; you didn't really have a choice."

"Caretaker?" said Dale, confused. Although it wasn't like anything was making any kind of logical sense anyway.

"Long story," said Amanda. "I'll tell you later. First I need to get you up to speed on what's been going on since I last saw you."

"Okay. Um, a question. Just how old are you? You look different. Sorry, not being rude, but you are older, right?"

"Ten years older," said Amanda, nodding her head. "We waited for ten years for Hexads, these devices." Amanda pulled the device from her pocket, waved it about then put it back again as if she didn't trust herself, or Dale, with it. "We waited, then we dug up a hoard of them from the garden, then all hell broke loose. Again."

Dale led Amanda down the garden to the seating area and slumped into a weathered Adirondack chair. "Tell me all about it, don't hold anything back."

Amanda looked around guardedly, then said, "Well, if you're sure?"

Dale just nodded. What choice did he have?

~~~

"We did what!?"

"Told you it was kind of crazy. Who would have believed it, right? Us, responsible for breaking time, the death of universes, then we, well you and the other Amanda, fixed it. Almost. You killed all the other Amandas that were housed in that terrible room, and then it was all fixed, everything went back to normal. Like none of it ever happened."

"Except not quite, right? Otherwise you wouldn't be here, you wouldn't have ever existed."

"Exactly. You and the other me made one huge mistake."

Dale didn't like the way this was headed. "And what's that?"

"You didn't kill me. Now there are two of us, when there should only be one. I shouldn't be here, or her, as it means there is a continuity of what went on in the past. Well, the future to be more precise, but it doesn't matter."

"So, um, why are you here? Sorry, that sounded like I'm not glad you are, but all of this is a bit hard to take. It sounds made up."

"I know, but I am here, you have the proof this is real. I am here to kill Amanda, the other one, then we will be all right. I think."

"You think! What, we just go in there and stick a knife in her?"

"No Dale, not we. You."

It Gets Worse

3 Hours 19 Minutes Past

"That sounds like the craziest piece of logic I've ever heard. There is simply no way I'm doing it. None." Dale folded his arms across his chest, resolute.

Amanda burst into tears. "Dale I've missed you awfully; it's been so lonely, and terrible. The things that happened, it was too much, too much to take. And besides, you've done it before, hundreds of times."

"So you said, but I don't believe it. There is simply no way that I would go around killing anyone, let alone you, or versions of you. Certainly not over and over again."

"Well that's what happened."

"But you didn't see it, did you? This is just what this Caretaker told you has happened, will happen. Whatever." Dale waved it all away, it was the stuff of nonsense, gibberish spouted by people locked in asylums for their own good.

"Yes, and I believe him. Look, I've lived through all that happened, I was a part of so much: finding the Hexads, us digging up that damn note under the tree, being chased by Laffer, all the stuff I've told you, it's all true."

"Okay, okay, so you say. Even if I believe every word you've said it doesn't mean I can do it. How can you ask this of me?"

"Because it's all still going on. The mess. We didn't solve a thing, not really."

"Because The Caretaker told you?"

"Not really, no, although he did. But it's because I'm still here, still have a Hexad, know where I can get lots more. It's all going to repeat itself over and over. There's another reason too..."

"Come on then, tell me." Dale could sense that Amanda was holding things back and there was a lot more to this incredible story than she had told him so far.

"Because, well, because you aren't my Dale. I'm sorry."

Dale got the now all-too-familiar icy feeling creeping up his spine, making him think of the room Amanda had described, feeling like he too was on a hook, spinal fluid draining away along with his sanity. Resigned, he said, "Okay, spill it."

"I've searched and searched, but you aren't my Dale, not the one I have lived with for so long. I'd know you anywhere."

"The scent?"

Amanda nodded. "The scent. It's off somehow, this isn't you."

"I don't understand. After all you've told me, how can I not be me? Of course I am."

"Well, yes, of course you're you," said Amanda, like she was speaking to a child. "Just not the you that I lived with. You're a different one. You aren't the one that had all the adventures with me, you are a Dale that woke up one morning after getting very drunk and thought he was with a different version of the Amanda that he thought he knew."

"I am, aren't I?"

"Yes, and no."

"Bloody hell Amanda, this is doing my head in. What are you talking about?"

"I didn't want to do this, tell you this, but that is your Amanda in your bed, you just had a weird dream when you woke up, you were just confused, everything would have been all right. A few hours later and you would have forgotten all about it."

Dale was having a really hard time trying to get things straight in his mind. "I don't understand. You said—"

"I know what I said. I lied."

"You lied. Why? You wanted me to kill her! Kill you."

"I know, I know, I had no choice Dale. Honestly."

"Tell me."

"I'm lonely Dale, so lonely. I've searched and I've searched, jumped into countless alternate universes, and we aren't together in any of them, not any more. When you, you and the other Amanda, when you killed all those versions of me, then that was it, you repaired the damage, set the universes right, but it meant that I wasn't a part of your life then in any of them. You killed me in most of them before we ever met, or before we had a proper future together anyway. And in the few where we managed to have a life then it ended badly, or I was killed, by you, or by the other Amanda. Or the detective."

Dale felt his palms beginning to sweat. "What detective?"

"It doesn't matter for now. But I'm sorry, I need you."

"Just tell me one thing, is she my Amanda, the one in bed?"

"No Dale, she isn't."

"So that part was true, that she is the one that came to help sort things out?" Amanda just nodded. "But you are my real Amanda aren't you? You have to be, you smell right."

"Not quite Dale, but it's so close that it may as well be us, the us that were always together."

"But we're not?"

"No. Yes and no. Look, this us here, we lived, or would have lived, lives so similar to the ones we do that it makes no difference, not really. In all the places I've been, not just in time but in parallel universes, you are the only one where we stay together, where we have a future."

"And how do you know this? No, don't tell me, because you've jumped to check, haven't you?"

"Yes, I have. If you let me stay then it will work, if we do what we're supposed to do. I need you Dale, you're my only hope."

"But I'm not your Dale. How can you be happy with that?"

"I can get over a little change in your scent Dale, that's the only difference. There aren't any Dales that remember what happened because of the Hexads, all that changed when the last Amanda was killed that was in the room, but it doesn't mean there aren't still countless other versions out there. But none of them are your true Amanda, and do you want to know why?"

"No, not really." Dale watched as Amanda began to cry. It was just getting worse by the minute but he had to know. "Okay, get it over with."

"Because, Dale, you are dead."

"What do you mean I'm dead?"

"I mean that the Dale that had all the adventures with me until we got split up, he died. The Universe set things right when you finished in that room, and then you vanished. Poof, gone."

"But I'm here, right here," protested Dale.

"You are, but you aren't him. All those things that happened, they didn't happen to you, they happened to him. Then when things were reset you were gone. I went to find you, but you'd never existed. It all became too impossible after the mess we made of things because of the Hexads. When we repaired it all then the timeline you had been a part of was still too convoluted, so you simply popped out of existence. You were never born."

"If that's the case," said Dale, head dizzy, the caffeine nowhere near enough to keep him straight, "then I have no part in this. It wasn't me that did any of it."

"Like that matters. The version of you that did it all wouldn't remember even if he had ever existed. As soon as reality was set straight then it stands to reason that you would be back in your own present, having no idea any of it had ever happened. You're all I have left Dale, I want you back."

"But I never existed, so how could you want me back? You shouldn't be able to remember me at all if I never existed." Dale thought his reasoning made sense, as much as was possible with such a bizarre conversation.

"I know, but I do. I was away from it all when it happened, when you and the new Amanda solved the problem, so for some reason I remember. And I've hunted for you for an age Dale, and you're the only one that is like my original Dale."

"Apart from the fact I smell different and aren't really him?"

"Exactly."

"And you can live with that? Live with the knowledge that I'm not really, truly your guy?"

"Yes, and do you know why?" asked Amanda, eyes moist yet Dale could tell she was refusing to cry. Dale shook his head. "Because apart from that one thing then you are him, you really are. And I love you Dale, I love you so very much."

"I love you too Amanda, but you aren't my Amanda, you said so yourself. Not that I get it if I'm not the one that did any of those things anyway. How can I not be with my Amanda if it wasn't me that did any of what you have been saying?"

"Ask her," said Amanda in shock, but seemingly resigned to what she appeared to know was happening.

"Dale? What's going on?" said a sleepy Amanda, coming out the door in her green silk dressing gown, staring blearily at Dale and Amanda sat at the table.

"Oh shit. This isn't good, is it?"

"No. In fact it's very bad."

"Don't come any closer, stay right there!" shouted Dale.

Amanda kept on walking, shock spreading across her face as she looked at Dale and then at... herself.

"Dale, what—"

Amanda vanished. She was gone, just disappeared from where she had been walking towards them. Dale turned back to Amanda. "You knew, didn't you?"

Amanda looked him in the eye, sad, but at the same time determined, resolute. "I'm sorry, I was so lonely. I had to be with you again. I'm sorry."

Dale put his hands to his temples, trying to stop the pounding that felt like his head was going to split in two.

He just wanted to mow the lawn and have a chilled out Saturday.

A Wakeup Call

3 Hours 19 Minutes Past

"Change it back, right now."

"I can't," said Amanda. "I'm sorry."

"Just get out your thing, your Hexad, and jump us back a little, before she woke up."

"It doesn't work like that Dale. If I do that then all that would happen is that we'd be sat next to that version of ourselves and then we'd probably all disappear, or one version of us anyway, and on and on it would go. She's gone, there's no changing it. It's for the best."

"For the best? For the best! Are you kidding me? I just watched her disappear and you're saying it's for the best?"

"Yes, because she wasn't your Amanda. You might be a Dale that never did time travel and have the things happen to him that my Dale did, but that's only because I came here and stopped you digging that hole, changing everything. But the rest is true. If I didn't come then everything that has happened would have happened to you and that wasn't your Amanda."

"But none of that did happen to me, or will, not now, will it? So how could I have woken up to be with a different version of you?"

"Because of the paradoxes. Some things just can't be put properly right."

"And now they are?" Dale was furious, yet at the same time it didn't seem real. How could it when he was sat across from the love of his life? Even if she did have crow's feet forming at the corners of her eyes. It was still his Amanda. It felt right; it was her. "So what are you saying? That wasn't her even though because of what a different me did it should have been?"

"No," sighed Amanda. "It wasn't her because you would have done it all if I didn't return, so you would have woken up next to a different Amanda once everything was set right, so you did. That's the best I can do. It's happened, all that I told you, it's simply that it wasn't exactly you that did it, or, well, not did it once everything got put right."

"Makes no sense at all. I need coffee; this can't be happening." Dale picked up the mugs and went into the kitchen to make coffee.

He opened the cupboard door. A simple, familiar act.

Dale blacked out, falling hard onto the tiles Amanda had said would be a good investment though he never understood how tiles could be seen as an investment. Bloody expensive, yes. An investment, no.

The two mugs Dale had placed on the counter top were still where they had been before he'd taken them out of the cupboard to make the coffee. It seemed that mugs didn't follow the same rules as people in terms of being able to be in the presence of each other, were Dale's thoughts before he hit the ground.

He never did see the mugs disappear into thin air just before they hit the tiles and cracked into a million pieces, just like his mind.

~~~

Dale woke to find himself in bed, head pounding. Amanda had an arm over his back, clutching him like she never wanted to let him go, like she hadn't held him for years.

Dale shot upright, thoughts a mess, trying to shake off his sleep. Was this a dream? Had it been a dream? Must have been. It didn't feel like one though.

Amanda shifted at the sudden motion and sat up next to him. He turned, fearing the worst, happy to see her smiling back at him, hair disheveled like it always was first thing in the morning.

"Morning love."

"Morning Dale," said Amanda happily.

Dale stared at her face. Since when did she have crow's feet?

Dale thudded back on the pillow. Maybe if he just closed his eyes it would all go away and life would be uncomplicated once more.

It didn't work.

Strangely, and it proved that he really had lost his marbles, the first thing Dale thought was how could he be in bed if he'd traveled back in time. Surely he'd be lying on top of himself, or there would be one of those paradox things and the other him would have disappeared. No, that couldn't be right either, as if the other him disappeared then he wouldn't have gone on to have the kind of morning he'd had. Would he?

"You didn't, did you?"

Amanda looked at him, questioning what he meant, then realization dawned. "No, gosh, of course not. I love you Dale. It's early afternoon, we've gone to the pub."

"Um, okay. How? If the other you disappeared then surely I can't be at the pub with her."

"You're not, you're there with me, well, your Amanda, like you would have done if none of what I told you happened. Imagine if I never came here, you just woke up like normal, dug up the garden, began down the rabbit hole that I told you about — that's what's going on with them. We're intruders, of sorts."

"Christ Amanda, this is too much. This is totally messing with my head you know?"

"Well imagine how I feel. I saw a room full of countless versions of me all lobotomized, or whatever it was. Hung up like meat, being milked to power time travel devices. Not to mention being chased through time by a giant, searching for you through the ages and the universes, going to the future and seeing it empty, running around foreign lands, visiting Venice after it had been taken over by cats and—"

"Okay, I get the point. So, now what?"

"Now you give me the shagging of my life and then we get dressed."

"Um, okay."

~~~

Amanda had been intense in bed, yet Dale somehow felt like he was cheating. It had been exciting, wild, and... how could he explain it? Different. Like he was having an affair with his own lover. Was it that she was older now? No, that wasn't it. It was because it was Amanda yet it wasn't. That wasn't right either.

It was like coming home. It felt like the most normal thing in the world as it was the woman he loved, the only woman he had ever loved.

Amanda.

As he showered and toweled himself dry he tried to get his new life straight. He couldn't.

As far as he could make out then he wasn't the Dale that Amanda had gone through so much with only for that Dale to then get sent back to when it all began and have no memory of it. According to her that Dale was gone. He couldn't help wondering what he had looked like. Was he a clone or did he have a different eye color? Different hair. Was he fat? Bald even?

Maybe he'd ask Amanda. On second thoughts maybe he wouldn't.

He had another idea, and padded barefoot back into the bedroom, where Amanda was sat on the edge of the bed brushing her still damp hair.

Dale dropped his towel.

"Busy?"

Amanda turned and stared at him, eyes widening as her gaze traveled lower across his body. "No, but I can be."

~~~

What is wrong with me? This feels so good, but so—

Dale's reveries were interrupted by Amanda saying something. "What's that?"

"I said we have to go, we'll be home soon."

"Huh? Oh, right, the other us that is me and a different you. Of course, how silly of me."

"No need to get sarcastic," pouted Amanda, face still flushed from their bedroom antics — the third time.

"Yeah, well, I'm having kind of a hard time here."

"I know, I can see," said Amanda, pulling back the bedsheets. "No time for that though. Come on, get dressed."

Dale did as he was told, feeling terrible about himself, but really rather good at the same time. He stared at Amanda — she really did look radiant. Could this be real? And how come he was fine with her having not long ago made another version of her drop out of existence?

Because she was still with him, that was why. It meant that nothing else seemed real, not when she was here and it felt so right. It still made no sense to him that for her he wasn't the right Dale but for him she was the right one, but then, if you thought about time travel even for a moment all it did was leave you confused, confounded, and you'd do anything to take your mind off it — even give your girlfriend, that wasn't really your girlfriend, the best rogering, or three, that you'd had in your entire life.

Dale got dressed.

Time to Run

3 Hours 19 Minutes Past

Dale stared in horror at the festering lump on the kitchen table — a steaming mass of flesh that he was sure had a human eye embedded in the misshapen flesh, covered in veins thick and bloated.

Amanda was already heading out of the door.

"Ignore it, we'll clean it up later."

"We? What? Oh, you mean the other we, right?"

"Yes. Come on, we have to go, and we have to go now."

"What's the rush? What's so urgent?"

"Dale, why do you think I'm here?" said Amanda, turning and staring at him quizzically.

"Well, you know, for me I guess."

"Yes, for you. But you know me, am I really that selfish?"

"Shellfish? Yes please."

"Haha, very funny. Seriously, we have to go."

Damn, she always liked that joke. "Okay, what's going on?"

"We have to save the world, of course."

"Oh. Right." Dale grabbed his satchel, or went to. It wasn't there. "Hey, where's my bag?" Amanda just stared at him like he was an idiot. "I took it when we went out?" Amanda nodded. "Bloody hell this is confusing."

"You haven't seen anything yet, not a thing."

Dale thought Amanda said that a little too ominously, being dramatic as usual. "Okay, let's go. Where to?"

"You'll see."

They wandered out into the garden and Amanda stood with her face to the sun, then turned to admire the views over their well-stocked garden. Both of them loved spending time out of doors, buying new plants and experimenting with various color schemes and plant groupings in different areas of their quite large garden.

"You okay?"

Amanda turned and smiled. "Fine, I just missed it is all. It's good to be home."

"Hey," said Dale, putting an arm around her shoulder, "you sound like you aren't going to see it again."

"Maybe I won't." Amanda sighed, pulled the Hexad out of her pocket and began to turn dials that ran around its circumference.

"Wait!" said Dale, realization dawning.

Amanda looked at him impatiently. "What?"

"This isn't making sense. You said that you had to get rid of the other Amanda to set things right. Well, she's gone, so if that worked then there are no more chances of Hexads, or any of this stuff having ever happened, so how come you aren't surprised by any of this? You should be either really freaked, or, um, maybe not even knowing any of what you said happened actually happened. In fact it shouldn't have happened."

"Dale, it isn't that simple. She had to go, so it's just you and me out of the countless versions of us that were ever involved with this."

"But I'm not," protested Dale.

"Of course you are. Right this very minute you are off being involved in this. Are you forgetting that we aren't in the present? We jumped back almost three and a half hours. The you in the present for him is involved, playing out what happened countless times before."

"So we can't do anything? We have to let that happen before we do anything at all?"

Amanda sighed. "Dale, it simply doesn't work like that. Besides, we won't be in this version of the universe anyway, so it doesn't matter."

"So why did the other Amanda have to go? No, wait, ugh, I can't think straight. You said another version of me and her were at the pub. So is she gone or not?"

"She's gone, gone from this universe, but it's a big place out there. Look, there are other Amandas, just not ones that ended up in that horrible room. It's infinite, but not. Please, trust me, I still don't understand this stuff very well, all you do is go around in circles until you want to pull your brains out through your ears and lie down in a dark room and cry."

"Okay, let's go." Dale knew he couldn't even begin to get his mind around what was happening, so resigned himself to just going with it for now until he could try to think it over quietly, calmly.

Dale noticed a flashing 3 on the top of the device and was about to ask about it when Amanda grabbed his hand and said, "Ready?"

"Where we going?"

"Just wait." Amanda held out the Hexad and said, "Press the dome, so it pushes down."

Dale nervously pushed down on the top of the Hexad.

~~~

2817 Years Future

Less than a split-second later Dale was staring at a wall of Hexads in a room he would imagine was furnished by a man with an awful lot of spare cash lying around — he'd never seen anything so opulent in his life.

"Bloody hell. Are they all Hexads? The time machines?"

"They are, but they're not really time machines as such, more like devices that allow you to travel through time."

"So, exactly like a time machine then," stated Dale. He really couldn't see the difference.

"No. Yes, sort of. It doesn't matter."

"Where are we? And when are we?"

"It's a little hard to explain but we are in the future, but not our future. Things have got rather confusing after you, or a you almost the same as you, put an end to all the trouble and set things back to being right. Me and you are from different timelines and it used to be it was very hard to jump from one universe to another, now things are mostly right it seems that it's not so hard any longer. You used to have to have a special Hexad, now that there aren't many people jumping, only me really and a few others, then it's simple to jump between the gaps so to speak."

"And...?"

"Sorry, just trying to explain," pouted Amanda. "And it means that we are in the future but also in an alternate timeline where things happened differently to how they did in the worlds we both came from."

"And...?"

"And it means that there's a problem."

"Amanda, will you please just tell me what the hell is going on here? In case you haven't noticed this is all somewhat of a shock to me. You may be used to all this," Dale signaled with his head at the dark wood-paneled wall where row after row of shiny Hexads stood like miniature sentries watching over the end of the world, "but I certainly am not. So what is all this really about? What's happening and what are we supposed to do about it?"

"Maybe I can answer that."

Dale spun around to find an elderly gentleman wearing a rather stylish brown hat standing next to a small drinks table, lifting the stopper from a decanter and pouring himself what looked like whiskey.

I could do with one of them right now, but hell, it's probably a bit early. Or is it?

"Dale, this is The Caretaker," said Amanda respectfully.

"Pleased to meet you Dale, although I must say this is far from the first time we have met."

Dale tried to remember ever meeting the man before, then it clicked. "Ah, you mean other versions of me?"

"Well, I wouldn't put it quite like that, no. After all, that would mean you are nothing but another version of them. No, you are your own man, just as the countless other Dales are too. But no matter," the Caretaker dismissed the notion with an elegant wave of the hand, the effect ruined somewhat as his drink sloshed in the angled glass, "we have more pressing matters to concern ourselves with I'm afraid."

"You know, I think my head is seriously just about to explode. Can we please take this from the beginning, and slowly? I need to understand what is going on and what the hell I have to do with any of it. And also why Amanda is not really the Amanda I have known so long, but apparently she is, but isn't."

"Help yourself," said The Caretaker.

Dale looked down at his hand, then at The Caretaker's, and realized he had taken the drink from the old gentleman and was pouring it down his throat, the familiar burn settling his nerves a little, but nowhere near enough. "Oh, sorry. It's been a rather odd day so far."

"I can imagine. Now, let's all take a seat and I'll see if I can explain all of this so it makes some kind of sense."

Fat chance of that. This is like a nightmare, but one that feels nice in parts, like the bits in the bedroom.

Dale sat down in a comfortable, entirely too opulent chair. Amanda and The Caretaker joined him, taking seats that looked just as comfortable, all arranged around a large, low table.

It took a while.

~~~

At the end of a rather long, and seriously messed up explanation as far as Dale was concerned, he felt that he at least had some kind of a grasp on the situation.

Sort of.

As Amanda and the strange man named The Caretaker, who told Dale to call him Tellan, went off to talk and give Dale some time to reflect on what they had told him, Dale went over and over the story in his mind, trying to make some kind of sense of it all, trying to understand what it was that was now expected of him.

He also tried to come to terms with the guilt he felt for the loss of Amanda, the one he woke up with. Even though she didn't really feel like the one he loved he still felt a terrible weight of responsibility, or maybe it was just guilt? But it wasn't quite tangible — how could it be when there she was, looking a little older, sure, but Amanda, his Amanda, was definitely in the room so it was hard to truly feel as guilty and dirty as he knew he should.

Again he tried to put the story into order, to get up to speed on exactly why he was in the situation he found himself in, thousands of years into the future by all accounts.

What a mess.

They told him that because of some impossible-to-get-your-head-around quirk of time travel, it was actually him and Amanda that had started the whole thing off by telling themselves that there were devices known as Hexads. It set in motion a chain of events that led to themselves sending a Hexad, then crazy stuff happened and they found out how they were powered. It sounded nightmarish and Dale could certainly understand why the rest of the story was so mad after such a discovery.

Then they waited ten years, and this new Amanda, his real Amanda, but not quite, was taken out of action while he and another one, the one that disappeared earlier, although it wasn't quite her, not really, along with some detective, went about destroying countless versions of her to put the universes back in alignment — or something like that. The reasoning seemed dubious to him, killing all those almost identical women so that Hexads could never be put into production, but it also made sense in a convoluted kind of way.

They were killed so Hexads were never in the world, which set everything back to normal, meaning they were then still alive in their own universes.

Simple.

If only it was.

Dale was still finding it very hard to accept the fact that as this Amanda had basically got rid of the one that wasn't quite right from earlier, then Dale too had sort of jumped back to his correct universe where right now he and his Amanda were going about having the crazy adventure she'd told him about, even though what they had done to stop everything going wrong had succeeded — almost.

Was that right? No, it couldn't be, so what was he, the other him, doing?

Don't think about it Dale, you'll be a gibbering wreck if you do.

The only issue was what now? If it had worked then what was he doing in this strange place? Had it all been for nothing?

He knew Amanda was the woman he loved, even if it wasn't quite her, and found that it really didn't matter — at the end of the day it was her, she felt right. But she'd said that she had to get rid of the other her to set the remaining problem straight, but that wasn't true — she'd simply wanted to be with him, so took the other's place.

If it had solved the problem then he didn't see how he would even know about any of it anyway. No Hexads then nada. He would have just woken up and dealt with his hangover and would be mowing the lawn about now or maybe having an afternoon pint.

Dale decided one very important thing: it was all bollocks.

He got up from his chair, feeling sleepy from the whiskey and the information overload. He grabbed the edge of the wingback as he stood, the sudden movement sending his head spinning. It cleared in a few seconds and he walked across the impossibly opulent room to Amanda and The Caretaker. They turned as he approached, halting their conversation.

"Why don't you tell me what's really going on? All these stories, it's nonsense. You aren't telling it to me straight, none of it." Dale waited, Amanda and Tellan exchanging subtle, yet clearly futile glances. "TELL ME!"

"You aren't going to like it," said Amanda, grabbing his hand and squeezing tight.

"Why doesn't that surprise me one bit?"

Bit Pointless
Then

2817 Years Future

Dale felt sick. Sick, scared, and way out of his depth. It was fine for Amanda and Tellan, they knew what the hell was going on — kind of, anyway. He was sure that Tellan wasn't even telling Amanda the whole truth, and it was clear by the way Amanda was acting that she was feeling the same.

"So it was all a waste of time then? Everything we did?" Amanda began to interrupt. "Okay, not me and you, a slightly different me and this you, but basically me if you hadn't come and ruined my morning." Amanda just nodded. Dale could see tears beginning in the corners of her eyes. "Hey, hey, it's okay." Dale hugged her; it felt so good.

"No Dale, it's not okay. It's awful. The things that we did, the things that happened to me while you and another Amanda tried to save everyone, it was too awful."

"What did happen? You haven't said."

"And I never will, but that's over now, and it's better than being dead. But I'm sorry, I really am."

Dale knew she loved him, he could feel it like a physical link between them. So what if they weren't exactly the couple they were? They loved each other. Even if the other Amanda, and countless others... Dale couldn't think about it any longer, there were even more wacky things to deal with.

Tellan coughed politely. "If I may?"

Amanda and Dale nodded. Amanda was clearly as eager as Dale to hear it explained again, and she must have heard it a good few times before from Tellan too.

"I understand the complexities of time travel," said Tellan, "I understand them only too well. I think it best for the pair of you to really think of it as being you that went through everything that has been talked about so far—"

"But—"

"Yes, yes, I know," said Tellan, interrupting Amanda just as she had him. "I know it was a slightly different Dale, but the fact remains that if you hadn't gone to him then the life he lived, the things he did, would have been almost exactly as it happened to you Amanda. And the same thing would have happened, he would have woken up back in his own present, the other you beside him, and then you would have started it all over again, changed it all, by going back and disrupting the whole process."

"But I had to," protested Amanda. "There were no other Dales left. Not ones that were like mine. Like him." Amanda pointed at Dale. Not accusingly, but it still felt like she was blaming him.

"Hey, hang on, you could have come back to when I was your age."

"I couldn't, because then everything that happened would have happened, and we wouldn't have changed a thing."

"But we, you, haven't anyway, have you?"

"No," said a dejected Amanda.

"That's not true. Haven't you been listening to anything that I've been saying?" said Tellan. "It worked, it really did. In most timelines, or universes, the same thing really, what was accomplished was entirely successful. The plans for the Hexad were obtained, thanks to Dale's friend Peter, and then the old man tried to replicate them, but failed, as he couldn't get hold of the Amandas he wanted. So everything returned to normal. Timelines reset, Hexads never existed, lives were lived without time travel, the universes were happy and everything clicked back into place."

"Just not here," said Amanda.

"Just not here," agreed Tellan.

"Here in the future you mean, or in the past?"

"All of it. It makes no difference. Past, present or future, all of it is wrong. The last parallel universe where things didn't reset as they should have, and that's because of you Amanda."

"I know. I'm sorry, but I had to go somewhere. I could remember it all, after everything that happened, and I could somehow feel that things were put right. I still remembered, so I hunted for Dale, and this is my Dale, wrong but right. The man I love."

"I understand," said Tellan, Dale taking the opportunity to grip tightly onto Amanda's hand. He could feel her fingers twitching nervously even as she clutched him tighter. "But this leaves us with a slight problem. Namely, you are here, and you have Hexads, and look at this place. If you don't put it right then the whole mess of everything will pour through the cracks and humanity will disappear once more as the universes simply will not put up with such convoluted realities."

"Don't blame them," muttered Dale. "My head can't take this either. It's too much, I don't see how time travel can possibly work."

"And that's what space/time thinks too. There must be order in the chaos, and people coming and going all over the place, warping endless realities, will simply not be allowed. So we must put an end to it once and for all, and this is the only remaining universe where we have a problem."

"Because of me," said Amanda.

"Yes," said Tellan. "Your existence is certainly necessary, that's a given now after what has happened, but you must correct everything or it will spread and we will forever be stuck in a loop of repetition and emptiness. And apart from all that it means my life will always be interrupted by you two, and much as I do think fondly of you I do have other things to do. I am The Caretaker after all."

"About that," said Dale. "What exactly does that mean: The Caretaker?" Dale shifted uncomfortably as they both stared at him like he was an idiot. "What?"

"He's The Caretaker," prompted Amanda.

"And...?" said Dale.

"I'm *The* Caretaker," said Tellan, putting his hat on, adjusting it carefully, clearly getting ready to leave.

"Um, okay. Of what?"

"Well, what do you think?"

"Dale thought about it. "Hey, you don't mean—"

Tellan was gone, Dale didn't even see him use a Hexad.

"Did he mean... You know?"

"What do you think?"

"I think I want a lie down."

"Dale?"

"Yeah?"

"Can I have a hug please?"

Dale stared at Amanda, really, truly seeing her for the first time as the new her.

Shit, I'm being an idiot.

Dale wrapped his arms tight around her, the embrace promising he would always be by her side, would never let her go even when his arms weren't wrapping her tight. How could he have been so blind? Missed such obvious hurt? After everything she had told him, everything she had been through and shown him, it should have been obvious: she was terrified, distraught, alone yet no longer alone, worried if he would accept her and completely and utterly bewildered at the same time.

"I'm sorry, I'm here now. I'm here."

Amanda pushed him back and stared deep into his eyes, her own eyes questioning as much as they were full of hope. "Promise?"

"I promise honey. I promise."

Amanda cried. And cried, and cried. Great wracking sobs that broke his heart and made him resolute — whatever the hell was going on then he would help as best he could, do what had to be done so that Amanda, the first, the only love of his life, could be happy.

Explanations, of a Sort

2817 Years Future

"Oh boy, did I need that," whispered Amanda, wiping away the tears, running her hands obsessively through her hair.

"What, even more than the hot sex?"

"Much more, although that wasn't bad either." Amanda laughed, then smiled coyly.

Here's my girl, no mistaking that smile, or that scent.

"Okay, what now then?"

"Now we save the world. Again."

"Hey, be gentle, it's my first time you know?"

"Oh yeah, right. Sorry, I forgot. But to be honest it's mine too, all joking aside. I was... away, when, um, a Dale and Amanda did what they did."

"So we're both saving the world virgins then?"

"Kind of, although after what I've been through I wouldn't exactly say I'm inexperienced."

"No, it didn't sound like it. It all just sounds crazy. Look, what happened? Where were you then when it all went down?"

"Dale, it was too, too bizarre. Let's just say I was in the company of The Caretaker and leave it at that. If you think time travel sounds impossible then you don't even want to think about him, let alone know the kind of life he leads. Let's just get on with this. Please? For me?"

"For you, anything. What do I have to do?"

"That's just it, I'm not sure. I think me even being here has messed everything up, but I'm not sure how. I really thought I was doing the right thing, making the other Amanda disappear, but clearly it didn't make any difference... Actually, I knew it wouldn't."

"What do you mean?" Dale got a sinking feeling, a familiar feeling yet new, like... like he'd felt it in a different lifetime, maybe a different him, cracks in reality? He shook it off. "Tell me."

"Okay, I wasn't lying when I said that you and the Amanda I got rid of were in the pub, remember?"

"Yeah."

"Well, if I made her vanish then that shouldn't have happened, right? But I've seen it, gone back, got there late and saw you and her go to the pub. Then I came back to when you saw me and you know the rest."

"So, maybe she isn't there now?"

"If not, then where were you? You wouldn't have gone alone if I, her, suddenly disappeared."

"You know what? I fucking hate time travel!"

"Ha, don't even get me started. Look, I'm sorry, I don't know what's happening."

Dale thought for a moment. "So let's go find out. First, why don't you show me how these things work?"

~~~

3 Hours 9 Minutes Future

Dale was on the verge of totally freaking out. It was too surreal, too damn surreal for words. It was one thing seeing two Amandas earlier in the day, quite another to be confronted with himself. Not only that, but now there were three Amandas.

He watched as he and Amanda walked into the pub — did he really look so scrawny? He could imagine the gruff greeting from Steve behind the bar, the usual sticky table and the crap warm beer. That was bad enough, but he could also see Amanda, the one beside him, on the opposite side of the street, trying to act all casual and peeking out from behind a lamppost like the worst detective you could possibly imagine. He had to look at Amanda beside him just to make sure she was really there. She was.

"Well I'll be... This is mad." Dale had a strong urge to run up to the pub, grab a beer and go sit at the table with himself — it was almost an impossible urge to resist. But he had no plans on testing out paradoxes. Not now, not ever.

Dale fiddled with the Hexad nervously, then grabbed hold of Amanda without a word and went, "Whooooooooooooooooooooosh," for some strange reason, before they vanished from outside the fish and chip shop much to the confusion of a bull terrier tied up outside, sitting and vibing them in the hope that they had some spare food for him. Dale was sure he heard it yelp before he found himself falling into an abyss, sure his life was at an end.

Action Stations

67 Years Future

"I forgot you were really bad at this," said Amanda, picking herself up off the floor.

"Oh my god, I thought I was dead for sure. What happened?"

"You have, had, will have, ugh..." Amanda shook her head to stop the confusion, blond hair dancing gently. "Anyway, you have a habit of not really focusing and you end up making the jump without really thinking clearly, so we end up just a little above the ground. It's really off-putting."

"You can say that again, haha. Phew, that wasn't fun." Dale stared around him, then checked the Hexad. A 4 flashed blue on the dome. He checked the dials, realizing that in his haste he hadn't really cared about when they went — he just had to get away.

Sixty-seven years. Wow.

Dale took in his surroundings. It was, to put it mildly, rather unexpected. "Okay, before I even ask about this place, can you explain how the other Amanda is still alive when you made her disappear?"

"I've thought about it and the only thing I can come up with is that the Universe, or rather, the universes, are making sure that what happened will happen." Dale raised an eyebrow, showing he had no clue what she meant. "Look, her, and you, the other you, do all the stuff I told you, or a version so close as to make no difference. I guess it would have played out similarly in a number of different timelines. So for us to put the mess right it means that all the things we did had to happen. So as soon as I got rid of Amanda at home then everything kind of just jumped a little so things could carry on being set right. The real hundred-percent-right Amanda would then have replaced her, just so things were totally as they should be."

"Except they aren't, are they?"

"No, not quite. But in most realities they are, just not in this one, or this sort of convoluted one anyway. But that's better, and makes more sense according to the rules of time, than for all realities to be messed up. It's just this one."

"So even though you are here, she is still here too, doing what you have already done in the past, or the future, whatever, to make sure that most futures happen? That people carry on living?"

"Exactly! So let's just sort out this one and we are done."

"But how?"

"Easy, we just have to ensure that we stay in this reality, and stop Hexads from being available here. As soon as the other versions of us begin all their crazy running around, well, they jump universes anyway, so chances are that none of what they do will matter here, it was all so jumbled up. The Caretaker said this is kind of more like an oversight than anything else, that this reality was sort of just overlooked because of all that went on."

"Okay, enough. Let's agree on one thing from now on."

"What?"

"Let's just do what we have to do and not talk about all this bloody timeline and universes and reality stuff any more. I haven't even got a clue what the difference is between all those words anyway."

"Easy. When I say timeline I mean—" Dale just stared at her. "Sorry."

"Right, so, what do we do? And more to the point, where the bloody hell are we?"

Amanda explained as best she could what they had to do, at least what The Caretaker had hinted at in his usual cryptic way — she had pieced together the rest herself. It all came down to one thing: doing all in their power to ensure that Hexads were never a part of this world. She chose her words carefully, skirting around the issue of divergent realities and parallel universes, and stopped whenever Dale gave her a dirty look for talking about infinite versions of them where every possible future played out in slight variations.

The plan sounded simple: they had to stop time machines being in the world. Dale began to get confused, which he didn't think was at all surprising, but Amanda made it easier for him by saying that as it was obvious that what the other version of them did in the world ended up with the problem being solved everywhere but here, then they had to let all of that happen and act in such a way so as not to interfere with the saving of all other realities.

"Sorry, I didn't know what other word to use."

"It's okay, I'll let you have one. So how do we do it? If we have to let them do it here then surely the point is moot? What happens will happen regardless, as we can't interfere with anything they do if we want the rest of it to work out."

"I think we have to go somewhere where we won't interfere with what happens, but where we can still make a difference to the outcome."

"And that is?"

"No idea. You?"

Dale just put his head in his hands. He needed time to think, and he really needed a drink.

A strong one. Very strong.

~~~

Present Day

Dale decided that rather than try to force some kind of a solution to what was clearly not just a simple problem, they should take advantage of where they were now that Amanda had cleared up the mess that he'd made of their jump. She'd grabbed him and made a jump of her own, and as he whoooooooooooooooooooooosh'ed his way to an unknown location he was vastly relieved to discover that he landed with his feet firmly on the ground.

Amanda explained to him that he really needed to focus on that, but more importantly that he needed to be specific with his thoughts concerning exactly where he wanted to jump to — the less of an idea you had, the more likely you could end up anywhere. Like in the middle of the sea, ripped apart by a plane, shot as you appeared in the middle of a police station, decapitated by a samurai warrior. That kind of thing, or worse. Dale didn't know what was worse, but he didn't ask either.

He'd actually jumped to the top of a building that they had both been to when on vacation years ago, only problem being that he had no idea that Venice was kind of overrun by cats by now, and that the buildings were less than stable. Just before the entire thing collapsed around them she'd jumped them to a much better, and altogether more exotic location.

With nerves frayed as he watched the ancient building crumble beneath his feet before he inexplicably made his jump noise — how weird was that? — he was pleased that he could relax, sort of, in the beautiful setting he found himself in.

Just sitting there was proof enough that Amanda knew him only too well. It was perfect.

Dale turned, just to look at her face — still as beautiful as it had ever been despite there now being an age difference. They had been through so much of their lives together, and every day he still felt himself inordinately lucky to have met and kept such a great woman. Her profile was strong and proud, her face, paler than usual — as she obviously hadn't been spending her time sunning herself lately — was lightly dusted with freckles that were always a surprise to him for some reason. And that hair — stunning.

"What?" asked Amanda, turning to him and smiling. A relaxed smile, like the day so far had never happened.

"Nothing, just looking." Dale smiled back, then looked out at the still, turquoise ocean.

The beach was busy but not crowded, and they had jumped to a quiet corner where nobody noticed their rather sudden arrival. Further up the sand, closer to a number of rustic, but he knew would be expensive, palm thatched huts, fish was cooking on a charcoal barbecue, the smoke wafting down to them and mingling with the tangy salt spray cooling them slightly as a gentle breeze blew in from the ocean.

The Bahamas. Perfect.

Dale lay back in the white sand, letting the warmth seep into his bones and burn away the crazy day like it was nothing but a sun-induced dream as he fell asleep listening to the gentle lapping of the waves on the idyllic shoreline.

But that wasn't the case, not really — as much as he wished it was he knew that life for the foreseeable future was going to be anything but tranquil.

Still, there was the moment, and Dale was going to do his best to make the most of it. He took off his battered boots, pulled off his socks, then rolled up his jeans to just below the knee. Standing up he let out a "Hot, hot, hot," dancing around like he was walking across red-hot coals as the burning sand made it impossible to stand still.

Amanda started laughing at the sight, and all Dale could manage was a "You coming?" before he dashed for the shallows in an attempt to cool his feet down.

It's nearly as hot as the sand.

Dale stood with the water halfway up his shins, amazed at the temperature. It was like getting into the bath rather than the cool sea he was used to in England, but he'd been abroad enough to know that he shouldn't have expected it to be cold. Still, it was better than the sand.

Amanda joined him, and for a moment there was nothing but the sound of the waves, the shouts of the cook touting for business for his freshly cooked fish, and the sun sparkling white off the ocean.

Perfect.

"Dale, what are we going to do?"

The spell was broken, reality inescapable. Dale wished the moment could have lasted forever but it was wishful thinking. He was surprised he'd been able to put the day behind him at all, but maybe the totally bizarre nature of it was too much to take so he'd simply been able to block it out as something that had happened to someone else, not to him?

Damn, there I go again. This stuff could seriously mess with your head.

"Dale?"

"Sorry, just trying to hold onto this." Dale took in the beautiful view with a terrible feeling that it would be a long time until they got to relax again. "Let's go somewhere where we can sit and have a drink. We need to talk."

Amanda looked at him worriedly, but turned back toward the beach. "Okay, but I don't have any money. You?"

Dale checked his pockets but knew he never carried money in them. His cash and cards were always in his wallet, a wallet that the other him had taken to the pub. "Nope."

They dried their feet in the sun for a few minutes, used their socks to brush the sand off before covering up, and then they both said at the same time, "Home."

With a smile Amanda set the Hexad and they jumped back to the only place either of them really wanted to be.

No matter how beautiful it was on the beach, there was no place like home.

Time for a Plan

3 Years 11 Days Past

"Where are we?" asked Dale.

"Home, of course."

"Um, no, I meant... them. The other us. Ugh."

"Oh, we're on holiday in Venice, so we have the place to ourselves," said Amanda smiling.

"Damn this stuff is confusing. How the hell are you supposed to make sense of it all?"

"That's the point, you aren't. Cuppa?"

"Yes please, but there won't be any milk will there." Dale really hated his coffee without milk.

"Well, if what happened in my version of events happened in yours, then there will still be half a bottle in the fridge. Remember? You forgot to throw it out before we left and it stank when we got back."

"Haha, I remember."

Damn, this is too mental for words.

Amanda busied herself in the kitchen, and Dale sank back into the sofa, skin feeling dry from the salt of the ocean, toes itching from the inevitable sand that was impossible to eradicate for days after a trip to the beach.

It was strange being back in their rented accommodation — in Dale's present they had only been in their home for just over a year, seeing the rather squalid state of the rental came as quite a surprise.

Dale popped his head around the kitchen door and told Amanda he was going to have a quick shower.

Once he was finished he got dressed and remembered the strange mystery that they'd had when they returned only to find clothes and sand in the laundry basket he never remembered putting there. Well, mystery solved.

Amanda showered too while he sipped on his coffee in the living room, trying to make sense of things, to come up with some kind of a plan. He drew a blank. Although Amanda had gone over the events that he, or a version of him, had been involved in — no, it was him wasn't it? — anyway, what he'd been told made sense once you accepted the whole premise, but it was still just a story, not actual fact for him personally, so it was hard to really get deep into the problem that now faced them, and everyone else in his world it seemed.

He tried to make a list in his mind, making a sequence of events up until the present, but it fell apart before he could even get started. How could you make such a list when there were multiple versions of everything going back and forth, countless realities and the converging of multiple versions of the same people all tied together, acting out events that had already happened, just so they would happen in the future?

Finally, knowing he would be waiting a while for Amanda to finish her beauty regime, he decided once and for all that none of it mattered. How could you take responsibility for things that happened in other versions of a reality you had no experience of? What had been done to eliminate the existence of Hexads in all other possible timelines had succeeded, right? So all he had to focus on was doing what he had to do in his own world to ensure that the future was a good one for him and Amanda.

He thought about the fact that there was another him and her, in this world, that would put into action everything that he had been told had taken place, and that they were successful, apart from here. So what was the answer?

Sacrifice one world for many? Billions of lives for countless trillions? He didn't think so — at such numbers it all became meaningless, mere digits, not real live people. No, he had to think of the here and now, or, well, the future anyway.

So the solution was...?

Dale decided there was only one answer: somebody was lying to him. Either Amanda or The Caretaker. Maybe both.

He was no time travel expert, heck, he'd only been doing it for one day, but there was no escaping the fact that if what he'd been told was true concerning what had been done to eliminate Hexads and had succeeded, then it would have succeeded in his own world as well. Surely?

"Hey Dale, you okay? You seem worried." Amanda appeared looking like a new woman, hair glossy and shining, clothes clean but casual as always: a simple cotton dress that set off her complexion. The only thing ruining it was the frown of concern as she walked across the threadbare carpet.

"Are you lying to me?"

"About what?"

Is it me or does she look nervous?

"About what? About everything. You said you hunted high and low, jumped about all over the place, and although you only found me, or as close to me as possible here, you said that all other versions of events meant that there were no Hexads, right?"

"Right."

Something was clicking with Dale, something important. He just had to let it come, let the knowledge crawl up from his subconscious.

Here it is.

"So how did you do that?"

"What do you mean? With the Hexad of course."

"But you only get six jumps then you're done. And apart from that, if we succeeded then there shouldn't have been any, should there?" Dale really hoped Amanda wasn't lying to him, and why would she?

"Let me think, but I promise you, I'm not lying to you Dale, everything I have told you is true."

"Okay then, so where did you get the Hexads to do all the jumps?"

"From that room we were in. The room I told you the detective made: Cray. It's full of them."

"And that room is in this world, in the future?"

"Yes."

"But nobody else knows about it, as everywhere else it won't exist?"

"Yes," said Amanda, clearly getting exasperated.

"Right, come on, we have someone we need to go and see." Dale stood, ready to jump immediately.

"Dale, Dale, calm down. What's going on? Where are we going?"

"We are going to see this Caretaker of yours. He's lying to you, lying to us."

"Wait, what do you mean? And Dale, we can't go to see him, or I won't anyway. Don't you get it? That's where I was while all the craziness was going on. I can't go back there, I won't."

Amanda was in tears, visibly shaking, like a dog that had been locked in a cage all its life and was now expected to go for a nice walk in the park.

"Tell me," said Dale.

Amanda told him all about it.

~ ~ ~

By the time it was over Amanda had regained her composure, but Dale agreed that it was no kind of place to go to voluntarily. In fact he was amazed Amanda had come through such an experience with her sanity intact.

But one thing was for sure: things were not as they seemed, and the fact remained that if Amanda had been diligent with the truth then The Caretaker had been playing with her. For what reason neither of them could figure out, but it left only one course of action and one possible explanation: Amanda had ruined everything and The Caretaker hadn't told her. Why?

For the first time since he'd been with the new Amanda it was him doing the explaining.

Dale had finally figured it out as they sat talking — it should have been obvious.

Everything Amanda had told him had been true, right up until she jumped and found him and told him not to dig up the garden. So he hadn't, had he?

"And that's it, none of it happened. None of it. You stopped it all."

"No, wait, that can't be right. We saw us going to the pub, like we did before, and I jumped everywhere and everything was back to normal, apart from in this world."

"Everything was back to normal because I never dug up the note in the first place, and if I never dug it up and then a Hexad appeared in the kitchen, blah, blah, blah, then none of the rest of it would have happened. We didn't need to go off and have all those crazy adventures as there was no note, no Hexad, so no us in the future doing what had already happened so it would play out that way. Everything was just normal."

"So how did we see you at the pub if you are here with me?"

She was right, he wouldn't have been, as Amanda interrupted all that. *Damn, you muppet Dale.*

"Because that was a different timeline we jumped to."

"Damn! Of course, you're right." Slowly it was all making sense to Amanda, Dale could see that now.

Amanda spoke, trying to get her thoughts straight. "So everything that happened had to happen, and we stopped the problem, but me coming back here, stopping you digging up the tin, that means that none of the rest of it happened anyway, not any longer. Everything's cool and right with the world. Worlds?"

"Exactly."

"Except..."

"Except now we have to stop the damn thing playing out anyway as we now have Hexads and the whole thing will happen all over again, somehow, and will warp reality again and we'll be right back where we started."

"Dale, I can't go through that again, not all of that. Not that room, not any of it. It's too much; I won't cope."

"Don't worry, you won't have to. Look, forget everything that has happened, everything's normal everywhere, peace is restored. All we need to do is get to the heart of where these damn things really came from. Stop them and it's all over."

"But I explained that Dale, it was a self-fulfilling prophecy. We did it, we made them happen because of the paradox."

"Bullshit." Dale was certain that there was someone else at the heart of it all, there had to be. "Look, I know what you told me, but you can't invent a time machine by saying you will invent it in the future so in the future you will send it back to yourself. That's just too far-fetched."

"But that's how it works," protested Amanda.

"Not in my mind baby, not in my mind."

"Okay," sighed Amanda. "Fine. But you do know that all of it is going to happen, or has happened now, don't you? This world is empty in a few years and the whole cycle will repeat over again."

"No, it won't. Not in the same way anyway."

"How can you be so sure?"

"Because I promise you this Amanda: I will not dig up any Hexads. I will not make them appear, I will not dig up the tin, I will not send notes to myself, I will not get Peter to release the plans, I will not go into that roomful of lobotomized Amandas, and I will not go hurtling through time and space killing versions of you. So, that version of events is done and dusted. I will not do it so it can't happen."

"So what will?"

"I guess we just have to go find out, now don't we?"

"Guess so," said Amanda, resigned.

"One question," said Dale, as it had been playing on his mind. Amanda raised an eyebrow. "Why here? Why this dump rather than, you know, home in the present?"

"I got scared Dale, I don't know where the other us is, or even what 'the present' is any more. What's present for me? For you?"

"Good question. Very good question."

Dale really was hating time travel more than he thought possible.

The Future's
Bleak

47 Years Future

With a short detour to get a leather satchel Dale had to admit was pretty cool even if it didn't have that worn-in feel of his long-time accessory, they jumped forward to the roomful of Hexads, grabbing as many as they could before making a jump to forty seven years in the future to see what the world was like.

This time they chose Rome.

It was empty. No slow-crawling traffic inching through the congested streets, no beeping of horns and fume-filled air, just a pleasant warm day, them, and silence.

It was the spookiest thing Dale thought he had ever experienced.

They knew the place well, having visited a number of times over the years, often coming just for long weekends as it was only a three hour flight from England. They wandered the streets for the day, one part of Dale relishing the chance to experience the ancient architecture unhindered by tourists and people offering their services as guides, or hawkers trying to get them to buy trinkets that would be put in a cupboard and never seen again.

It was like visiting for the first time. As they held hands and walked the ancient streets, marveling at the architecture, he felt like he had never truly seen it before — it was beautiful. Such accomplishments, such pride and skill, it made him proud to be a part of the human race. And that was exactly what made it all so wrong: without people, without the hustle and bustle, the noise and inconvenience, it all just felt so pointless.

One thing was for sure, however it had happened, and Dale was certain it wouldn't have played out like it did for Amanda, Hexads were a part of life and at some point the Universe had enough and simply got rid of people so they couldn't screw things up any longer.

The only questions remaining were how it happened and who started it all off. Dale was adamant that it wouldn't be him — he wasn't about to repeat the same mistakes a version of him made, so he kept that firmly in his mind, vowing that he would do none of the things Amanda had told him, ensuring that there would be none of those stupid paradoxes where you went around in circles until nothing made sense and you ended up thinking you'd invented time travel just by digging up a bloody tin.

No, that was nonsense, he was sure of it. There was somebody behind the whole damn thing, and as far as he was concerned he had a very good idea who it was: The Caretaker.

There was something off about the guy, something he was hiding, even if he did act like he was only there to make certain everything went smoothly.

Caretaker of what? Dale was fed up asking. But it couldn't mean...? No, that would just be stupid.

Dale figured he'd try again. After all, he didn't have anything to lose by asking, right?

They were sat outside what would have been a very swanky and expensive cafe, too pricey for them for sure, now little more than a dirt-covered hovel, the sign fallen, the tables and chairs in disarray, the door locked. It was weird, sitting there not able to people-watch, just him and Amanda, nothing more.

"Amanda?"

Amanda turned, looking at him seriously. "Why do I get a bad feeling about this?"

"Well, um, probably because you know what I'm going to ask."

"The Caretaker?"

Dale just nodded.

"Go on then, ask."

"Look, I won't ask you to go there, wherever that is, I can see it's too traumatic for you, but, well, could it be him? That's responsible, sort of, for all of this?"

"Dale, he came to us to solve the problem. Said it was us that started it all, that we had to save the world."

"Yes, yes, I know all that. But look, someone had to invent the bloody thing, right?"

"We've been through this, it's the—"

"I know, the paradox. I don't believe it. Somebody, somewhere, at some time, made Hexads and we got caught up in the middle of it, making it a self-fulfilling prophecy, but it had to have a beginning. Fragments."

"Not when it comes to this kind of madness it doesn't." Amanda pulled a Hexad from her bag, a 5 flashing in familiar bright blue on its dome.

"It has to, don't you see? It's technology and that means it has to have been made. I know what you said about Hector and his production plant, but he got the plans that I told Peter to send, and that means somebody designed it initially and then it all kind of unraveled. So, could it have been him?"

Amanda took a long time to answer, biting the corner of her lip in that cute way of hers while Dale tried not to rush her.

"Maybe," was the answer when it finally came.

"Okay, wait here then. I won't be a minute." Dale checked his watch, and before Amanda could reach out an arm to stop him he slammed his hand down on the top of a fresh Hexad and disappeared.

"Dale. No!"

Amanda was shouting at empty air. Dale hadn't even gone Whoooooooooooooooooooosh.

Bad Idea

Past, Present and Future

Dale knew he'd made a serious mistake as soon as he hit the Hexad's dome. A really bad one. As with all jumps it had been an instantaneous transfer from one place and time to another — it never really felt like there was a delay or any sense of hurtling through the cracks in reality — you were just somewhere else, disorientated sure, maybe even freaking about falling to your death if you didn't think strongly about landing on terra firma, but there was no pause in the jump, you simply appeared somewhere else, and sometime else.

This felt different. This felt like everything you imagined it to be when you watched a movie about people spiraling through vortexes and being ripped apart molecule by molecule then put back together again, never really sure if you were the same person again or if somehow bits got mixed up, wires crossed, brain reconfigured just that little bit differently to how it was before.

Dale felt all that and more. He felt like he had been spinning out of control for eternity, winding his way around the universes, falling apart at the seams and stitched back together an infinite number of times until he wasn't even anything resembling himself any longer.

The most bizarre part of it all was that he was just in a beautiful garden full of brightly colored flowers of all shapes, sizes and hues, with birds singing loudly, bees buzzing as they bumbled from one source of nectar to the next and butterflies danced in the clear, heavily perfumed air.

Yet he knew it was wrong, understood that this was not a place he should be, for it was no where and no when. This was the home of The Caretaker.

He'd made a bad error of judgment. More: a terrible one.

Dale saw The Caretaker, Tellan, walking toward him angrily from out of a large bed of ruby-red ripe tomato plants over two meters tall, lined up like soldiers, the canes they were staked to as straight as the backs of the perfect sentry.

"Shit, shit, shit. This is bad."

Dale fiddled nervously with the Hexad and mouthed a silent *whoosh* before pressing the dome and vanishing.

~~~

47 Years Future

"Ugh."

"You okay?" asked Amanda, staring at Dale suspiciously.

"Yeah, I think so. You were right, that place is weird. Well, weird and not weird, if you know what I mean?"

"I know exactly what you mean. It's like you are somewhere and nowhere, right? It just doesn't feel... normal."

"I bottled it, sorry. I jumped straight back from there, but he saw me, and he didn't look happy. I'm amazed I got there actually, I set everything on the Hexad to zero and just thought about him really hard, and the ground, of course."

"Um, Dale, you actually didn't look like you went anywhere, all that happened was that one second you were you, the next you were, well, older."

"Haha, I bet. I feel like it scared me into old age."

"I think it did. Sorry, look, you shouldn't have done that. It's his place. It's not for us. When I was there I felt wrong the entire time, like I was going against everything that was normal. But look..."

Dale opened the compact that Amanda held up for him, staring at his face like he was looking at it for the first time. He looked different. She was right, he did look older. There were the beginnings of faint lines around the corners of his eyes, nothing noticeable unless you really looked, and his stubble had grown a little. What was more worrying, as he really did like his dark shoulder length curly locks, was that he was now streaked gray at the temples.

"Damn. I got old."

"Not as old as me," said Amanda, eyes crinkling slightly as she smiled.

"Well, I won't be doing that again." Dale sank back into the chair, trying to calm himself, his heart racing like he'd been running hard.

"Damn, that looks weird." Dale studied himself from each side — the gray seemed to just be beginning. He wasn't looking too bad, not really.

"It's kind of distinguished. I like it." Amanda studied him some more as he handed back the compact.

"Really? Well, that's something. Nothing like that happened to you while you were there then?"

"No, but I had an invitation, it was different. You didn't."

"Yeah, well, I had to do something. It's all tied up with him, I just know it is."

"I guess you can just ask him," said Amanda, looking extremely worried.

Dale turned in the direction she was looking and watched as a rather angry looking Tellan walked towards them down the empty road.

He doesn't look happy, not one bit.

"How did you get there?" asked Tellan without preamble. "That's my private home, you aren't supposed to be there. It's my home."

"I'm sorry, I really am," said Dale, hands up in supplication. "But I wanted to talk to you, and as you weren't here I figured I would come to you."

"Well don't. I come to you when I need to, you never, ever come to me. Understood?"

"Yes sir!" barked Dale, saluting smartly.

"Don't try to be clever, it really doesn't suit you Dale."

"Well why don't you tell us what's really going on then? All this nonsense about us causing the end of the world, it happening over again, but just here, and everywhere else is fine, that's all nonsense, I know it is. Amanda coming back, coming back because you let her, it's just started the whole thing again from scratch, except it will happen in a different way, that's all. What's really going on? And more to the point, what have you done so that somebody, somewhere, has been draining out the life force of countless Amandas so they can power these damn Hexads?"

Tellan sank into a chair and placed his hat carefully on the table. "I think we better have a little chat."

"I think we better," said Dale.

"Tellan, what's going on? Is he right? Is this your fault really?" Amanda looked like her faith in the man was broken — their time together had obviously impressed her a great deal, now it looked like all the memories were exposed as nothing but lies.

~~~

Tellan, a.k.a. The Caretaker, told them a long, convoluted tale, yet at the same time he gave so little away that Dale was sure he must have been a politician in another life. He told of time, and of non-time, and he told of a man: Detective Inspector Cray. Dale interrupted him at that point, as he'd been told little of the man by Amanda, but Tellan told him that he would learn a lot more, that he'd meet him soon enough. It seemed that Tellan had encountered the man in various incarnations, some good, some bad, some neither, just complicated, and in some of those worlds he invented the Hexad, a machine that he sometimes used the right way, other times the wrong way, usually keeping it secret and never telling a soul. That was fine, that was allowed, it worked in the world, all of them actually.

But when there were many? Well, all bets were off, and things got complicated, very complicated indeed. Reality got skewed, Tellan's own reality warped and twisted and he found it hard to keep everything straight, in order, how it was meant to be.

So he stopped him, time after time after time, until the man was no more, gone, eradicated or left to live peacefully if his intentions were good, but often they were not. A single twist in one's life and a good man could turn out bad, especially when there was the possibility of absolute power — everyone knew that was the way to absolute corruption.

"What's that got to do with us though?" said Amanda, asking what Dale was thinking.

"Why, isn't that obvious? Each version of him involves a version of you two. It stands to reason doesn't it?"

Dale and Amanda exchanged glances.

Shit, of course.

"Because of Amanda, right?"

Tellan merely nodded, raising an eyebrow as if teaching a child that refused to learn.

"Me? Oh, the... the fluid?"

"Exactly. But not to worry my dear, it's nearly all taken care of. This is it, the last obstacle to freeing the world of Hexads. You just need to stop him one more time, in this world, and there will be no more such headaches for me."

Dale stood angrily. "For you! What the hell about us? What about Amanda and this loon that ends up causing people to hang her up by hooks and drain the life out of her? What about that, eh?"

Tellan had reverted to his usual calm self now, seemingly happy to have unburdened himself. "That was an anomaly, I can assure you. In most timelines they synthesize it, that was rather unfortunate."

"You could say that again," mumbled Amanda.

"So was it Amanda coming back that caused all this to spark up again or not?" asked Dale, getting more and more frustrated.

"It was. Is."

"So, um, no offense or anything Amanda, and I wouldn't have it any other way, but why the hell did you let her come back when you knew it would result in this happening again?"

Tellan fidgeted rather awkwardly, the first time Dale had seen the man anything less than composed. Even when angry he still somehow kept his cool — it was more like being disapproved of by your father than someone losing the plot. "I like her."

"Oh."

"Do you? Do you really?" asked Amanda brightly.

"Of course my dear." Tellan took her hand and held it affectionately.

"Hey, no funny business."

"I am a little old for 'funny business,'" said Tellan. "Now, if you will excuse me, I have tomatoes to pick."

"Wait, you can't just leave us. You have to tell us how to set things right," protested Dale.

"I'm afraid I can't," said Tellan, adjusting his hat.

"Why not Tellan?"

Is she fluttering her eyelids at him? She is!

"Because I have no idea what you are supposed to do. This is a new one on me, so I'm afraid you're on your own. Toodle-oo. Oh, one more thing..." He turned to Dale and said, "No more unexpected visits, or a little bit of gray will be the least of your worries."

Dale got the feeling he really didn't want to know what he meant, and had no intention of finding out either.

He was gone.

"Well, guess the holiday is over then," said Amanda, smiling weakly.

"Guess so."

"Can we please go home?"

"Can we? What about the other us?"

"Dale, weren't you listening? That was their time, remember? In our real home, this world, just in the present, then this is us now, us here. There is no other us going about doing things, as we are here."

"Oh yeah, right, forgot. I was thinking we would bump into ourselves. Well, not you, not since you... you know?"

"Come on, let's go home."

They jumped.

Home Sweet
Home

Present Day (For Amanda)

Dale was immensely relieved to at least have some semblance of an idea as to where he was in the world. Jumping into different timelines where there were different versions of himself was just plain scary. He didn't want to have to worry about meeting himself — who knew which one would vanish?

No, being home, with Amanda, made him feel better. It was her, wasn't it? Well, that was all he wanted. Never mind the fact that pretty soon the world would be empty once more — not that he'd experienced it personally before as he'd set it all strait, which was confusing as hell — but for now maybe he could just relax and pretend things were normal.

He knew it was wishful thinking and it didn't take long for his unease to manifest itself in the most worrying of ways.

Ding-dong. Ding-dong.

"I'll get it," said Amanda.

"Don't," croaked Dale, throat going dry, palms beginning to sweat.

"Why not?" she was already headed out the living room towards the front door.

"Because I have a bad feeling about it, that's why."

"Don't be silly, it's probably just the postman." She was gone.

On a Saturday, at this time? Yeah right.

Dale could hear voices but couldn't make out what was being said. Finally, Amanda came back into the living room where he was sat nervously on the sofa.

"Who was it?"

Amanda stepped aside and said, "It was the Detective Inspector. He wants to have a word."

"Thank you. How are you today sir?"

Dale stood, almost knocking over his coffee on Amanda's precious Ercol table. "Um, I'm fine. You?" he said, giving Amanda the daggers, who just shrugged her shoulders in apology — what was she supposed to do? But there was something else, an uneasiness in her eyes even though she was trying to hide it. It wasn't surprising, this was no stranger, even if Dale didn't recall meeting him.

"Good, good. Would you be Mr. Ando?"

Dale shifted uncomfortably from foot to foot, the old familiar stress reaction to those in authority surfacing — this time it was a reaction he couldn't be accused of over-dramatizing. Here he was, the man that was involved in bringing about the ruination of everything. In his living room! "I would. What can I do for you Detective Cray?"

The Detective paused just as he was about to speak. "How did you know my name? We haven't met, and your wife didn't give my name to you."

"She's not my wife, she's my partner. And, um, I guess I must recognize you from the TV or something. You know, when they interview you after you take down some drug lord or something."

Christ, I'm rambling like a loon.

Cray shook it off, moving onto other things. "Hmm, I don't know about that, but may I have a word sir? With both of you?"

"What's this about Detective?" said Amanda, moving into the room from where she'd been standing in the doorway.

"I'm afraid we are going to have to ask you to evacuate. We've had a bomb scare and we need to take all necessary precautions."

"Is that right?" said Dale.

Cray looked confused. "Yes sir, that is right. We had an anonymous tip-off and we need to be sure it is safe for you and the other residents."

"And just where is this bomb, may I ask?"

"We were informed that it is in your back garden, buried against your boundary with the fields to the east. Now, there is no need for alarm, but if you could gather up—"

"Won't be a minute Inspector, or is it Detective? I just need a word with my wife. Um, my partner." Dale grabbed Amanda and pulled her into the kitchen, shutting the door before Cray had a chance to object.

"What are you doing Dale?" whispered Amanda.

"Don't you get it? It's him." Dale wiped his hands on his jeans, smearing them dark.

"Of course it's him. He introduced himself, and I've met him before."

"I know, and he was younger, wasn't he? Look, this is the future him, the one Tellan has been talking about. He's trying to set it all in motion so that a younger him gets to have a Hexad and the whole sorry string of events happens over again, at least in whatever way it did happen now I didn't open the tin. He must be trying to force events to get back in alignment with how they happened for him in the past."

"How would he know that things didn't go according to how they did before though? It either all happened or it didn't. And how do you remember him? I thought you didn't recall any of what happened?"

Dale didn't get the chance to reply, and he didn't know how he knew Cray, or felt like he did, but he had a picture of the man in his head for some reason, and he was younger than this man.

"Because I already did it," said Cray from the doorway.

Dale felt like his palms were pouring water onto the tiles; he felt sick with himself for the reaction to authority, even when this was clearly far from normal police business.

Amanda turned sharply at the interjection. "What? Already did what?"

Cray leaned casually against the door jamb, eyes focused on Amanda and Dale like he knew they were thinking of running, but wouldn't. "I already got the Hexads and I'm still here, so I am sure that one way or another I shall get them again. The only question is whether or not you are going to make it easy or difficult for me?"

"Easy."

"Difficult." Amanda and Dale spoke at the same time, eliciting nothing but a wry smile from Cray.

Cray watched them as silence tugged at Dale like a tide threatening to pull him under. What was Cray up to?

"It's a pity, I was hoping that neither of you would remember me from whatever future you have clearly already experienced. I was honestly hoping this would be easy and you would never have met me up until now, but that doesn't appear to be the case at all, does it Dale?" Cray turned his full attention on him, clearly expecting an explanation.

"You were a good man, when we met you. Well, sort of anyway. Mostly," said Amanda, speaking for Dale.

"I'm a good guy now, too, although I did have to arrange a little accident for me earlier today so I could be here. I was a little worried about that, paradoxes and all that, but everything seems to be working out fine."

"You did that too, when we met you before," said Amanda.

"Hmm. And you Dale, what do you remember?"

"Nothing, absolutely nothing. I woke up and the world went mad on me, that's it."

"But you know me." It wasn't a question.

"Yes, no. I don't know."

"No matter. Since this isn't going to go how I had planned, I guess it will have to go like this."

"Like this? Oh." Dale stared at the gun. It felt surreal, like it was a toy. Dale couldn't avert his eyes from the small weapon in Cray's hand pointing directly at them both, and all he could think of was that he thought it would look bigger. It seemed so innocuous, the dull gray metal and the dark barrel, almost like if Cray pulled the trigger it would just shoot a jet of water and then the fun would begin.

"Something amusing you Dale?" asked Cray, raising his arm and pointing the gun directly at Dale's head.

What is wrong with me? A madman with a gun that will ruin the world and I'm thinking about when I was a kid playing water pistol fights with my mates.

"Eh? Oh, sorry. No. Well, go and get them then, that's what you are here for, we won't stop you."

"I don't think so, do you? Move, to the door." Cray motioned for them to lead the way, tapping his foot impatiently while he waited for Dale and Amanda to put on footwear that was normally banned from anywhere apart from the kitchen. Cray had clearly not been told to take his shoes off by Amanda — it just wasn't the kind of thing you did to a man that had ruined countless versions of your world, your life.

"What's the point of this?" asked Dale, hopping on one foot trying to do up his boot.

"Of what?" Cray motioned them out the door with the gun.

"Of going through this charade? Why bother digging them up? You must already have the Hexads if you are here, and have already got rid of the version of you that would have found them."

"Because this is how I discover them, so this is how it has to happen. Time's funny like that Dale: some things simply cannot be changed or you risk ripping the world in two."

"And you know what happens if you do this? That reality won't stand for it, that everyone disappears?"

"It doesn't matter, there are countless timelines to explore, and there is always the past. I can spend forever jumping back to before things close down. I survive, that's the main thing."

"Wow, nice guy aren't you?" muttered Dale.

"Just move," said Cray impatiently.

They made their way out into the garden. The robin came in to land on a low fence that bisected the garden and formed a backdrop for clematis in full glorious flower. It watched to see if there were going to be any tasty morsels uncovered — its favorite occupation as far as Dale could tell.

As Cray moved them up to the large flower-packed border that ran parallel to the fields bordering them on one side, Amanda almost tripped and held out a hand to steady herself on Dale.

Before Dale knew what was happening he found himself staring not at his own lawn but at a man dressed in full armor with a huge sword raised, ready to chop their heads off.

"Bugger," said Amanda.

Could be Worse

7 Years Future

Dale jumped back, pulling Amanda with him, realizing he wasn't in the middle of some kind of archaic battle but was in a large room full of antique furnishings stood on a very lush blood-red rug before he backed them up and they toppled over the back of a brown chesterfield sofa. The smell of ancient leather sank deep into his nostrils before dust fought for supremacy and won.

Dale sneezed loudly then managed to right himself while Amanda was already adjusting a Hexad he didn't even know she had with her.

"Be back in a moment," said Amanda, and flickered before Dale had a chance to react. "Here." Amanda handed Dale his new leather satchel, stuffed full of Hexads; Amanda had her own canvas bag, also bulging with the now all-too-familiar shape.

"What the...? How...? Why...?"

Amanda smiled mischievously and just said, "I jumped back and got our stuff while he was still leading us up the garden."

"Good idea." Dale marveled at the courageousness of Amanda. She really was a great woman.

"Look, I don't know how good Cray is at tracking but let's not stay here too long. I can't believe what he's like now, so different to how he was before." Amanda paced nervously around the room, inspecting the rather eclectic furnishings.

Dale tried not to get too uncomfortable as he noticed a giant moose head on the wall that really seemed to be staring at him accusingly. He sneezed again at the movement of a heavy drape as he pulled it aside to stare out at a beautiful open view of the English countryside.

"And what was he like before? I thought that he was the one at the heart of the problem in the end? Didn't he become like a mad tyrant or something?"

"A little, but—"

"A little bit of a mad tyrant! What—"

"As I was saying," Amanda shut Dale up with a stern look. "But he wasn't evil, not like this version of him seems. He was different, nice underneath it. He just got carried away. But this man? This Cray just seems like he doesn't care at all about anyone else but himself."

"Well, we need to stop him, and we need to stop Hexads ever being anything more than an idea in some fool's head. Where are we by the way?"

Amanda nodded, agreeing with Dale, but she looked confused, unsure of herself, her usual inner confidence dwindling. Dale waited, but she said nothing, just carried on inspecting the room as if the collection of items from bygone eras held some kind of an answer in their rusted metal or the dull fur of a huge stuffed bear looming out of the shadows.

"Amanda?"

"Oh, sorry, I was miles away. I just want to rest Dale, for it all to be over. To go home."

Dale moved over to Amanda, crossing the large room, footsteps silent as they went from thick carpet to threadbare rug to carpet again. "Hey, it's all right, we'll sort it. It's us, we're a team." Dale hugged her tight, feeling her body relax into his, her head resting on his shoulder where he caught her familiar scent. He often tried to pinpoint what it was, but could never really, truly say what the origin was. It wasn't just the smell of her shampoo, her perfume or whatever creams she used on her face, it was more than that. All he could truly come up with was that it was the essence of her, the sweet, subtle scent of a woman he knew better than he felt he even knew himself.

Except it's not her, not really. It's an older her, a different her. I love her though, more than anything. And it is her, it is.

Amanda pulled away, eyes slightly red but a smile was returning to her face. "Thanks, I needed that. So much. Right, let's get on with this, no time to waste."

"First, where are we?"

"Oh, sorry, I forgot. We're at that stately home we said we were going to visit, just seven years in the future. I guess they really did close it down like they said they were going to. Look at all this stuff, it's crazy."

"Why here?"

"It was the first place I thought of, and also, I remembered that they had weapons. We might need some, right?"

"Well, yes," said Dale dubiously, looking around the room unenthusiastically.

"Not in here silly, we just need to find the weapons room. I didn't know where it was so thought jumping to this room was safer. Just in case we landed on top of something decidedly pointy," added Amanda.

"Fair enough. Come on, let's find the room."

As they wandered around the huge rooms that made up the house, the spaces making Dale feel uncomfortable, as if he was unwelcome, disturbing the dust and the artifacts of centuries gone by, he wondered why Cray had bothered to even go to the house and try to get them out. Maybe he was just trying to ensure that things stayed as close as they could to what had happened to him in the past, but how did he even know that his actions were called for? Maybe he didn't, or maybe he did. Maybe all of a sudden other timelines were repopulated after he'd been traveling through empty worlds?

Or maybe it was simply that he knew events in his past hadn't been playing out as they should as soon as Dale refused to dig up the tin and call the police himself, so Cray had to intervene to ensure that he got his hands on the metal trunk full of Hexads? That made sense. Cray eliminated himself as what had happened to him wasn't going to happen to the past him any longer?

Here we go again, thinking about the impossible; screwing with your own head Dale.

It was no use, and he knew it, so he tried to keep his promise to himself and simply forget about the impossibility of the whole damn thing. Stick to the basics, that was best. Stick to what he could just about understand, and that was that they had to stop Hexads ever being invented in the first place, then all the rest would be just as it should be. Right?

"Here we are," said Amanda, staring into yet another expansive room, all vaulted ceilings and large Edwardian windows. The smell of steel, old carpet and the lingering hint of waxed furniture were threatening to send Dale into a sneezing fit at any second.

"Wow. They certainly were a little haphazard with their collections, weren't they?"

"Before the owner handed the place over to The National Trust, as he couldn't afford to run it any longer, he'd spent all his money continuing to collect just about anything he took a fancy to. It had been the same for generations. Each owner was kind of eccentric and they simply collected things. Not much of a system to it as far as I remember reading." Amanda hefted a sword that thudded dully into a thick hide of what looked like a stuffed boar that had been in serious need of a haircut before it met a rather unfortunate end. "Damn that's heavy. Don't think I will be using anything like this."

"Be careful, a lot of this stuff might fall apart in your hands, or have a nasty surprise." Dale wandered around the room, checking out the various antiques. Some of the most prized possessions were under glass, but the room was clearly far from ready to receive visitors. It seemed that after the home had been closed, and The National Trust stopped spending money on an attraction that had never succeeded from day one, the room was being used more as a storage area for items that would eventually all be sold off to try to help to maintain the actual structure rather than it's contents.

So swords were piled against walls, crossbows of all description were laid out carefully on the floor ready to be repaired or sold as is, and there were even a number of shields, not to mention a large area dedicated to more recent weaponry and other assorted paraphernalia from the Second World War.

Dale was attracted to a lot of it — it was amazing to see the changes over the centuries when it came to weapons from different countries, although most of it was definitely British in origin.

He could just picture the latest owner of such a strange collection: all tweed jacket, receding chin and clipped upper-class accent, lamenting the fall of the British Empire and doing what he could to make sure at least some of that bygone era and what it produced still had a home.

Now all it did was gather dust, waiting in the shadows to be sold off to the highest bidder, put on display to impress their friends and acquaintances, all functionality forgotten — just another way to show off wealth.

Dale and Amanda wandered around the room, picking up clubs, strange looking curved machetes and all manner of short-handled steel blades from the colonial past. Dale thought he recognized some things from their travels to places like the Philippines and India: older versions of everyday knives and functional equipment they had seen away from the tourist traps they loved to explore given the opportunity.

Eventually he settled on what he was sure was a parang chanting. The weight felt right and the smooth-as-glass dark wooden handle felt amazingly reassuring. The chopper was about fifty centimeters long on the blade, was convex on the cutting side, concave on the back, sweeping forward to a curved point. This was an Indonesian, or maybe Bornean chopper used like a traditional machete as well as making a very versatile weapon. Dale cut through the air in long arcs, getting a real feel for the simple yet deadly tool, feeling perfect balance in terms of the weight of the handle and the center of gravity that lay close to the blade's tip.

There was even a wooden sheath with leather straps, although he was sure the straps would have been a later addition. It was old, but it was sharp. Very sharp. As he slid the strap over his shoulder he reached behind his back to check how easy it would be to get it in a hurry, then adjusted it a little tighter so it rode higher up.

"Perfect." Dale easily reached a hand back and grabbed the warm wooden hilt, pulling the parang over and in front in one easy motion.

"Careful, you'll have someone's eye out with that. Pretty cool though," said Amanda, admiring the glinting steel as it reflected the daylight trying to wipe away the shadows through dirty windows.

"Nice eh? I've always wanted a parang."

"Just be careful. And how about this?" Amanda pulled out a very impressive blade from a leather scabbard at her side. It was a re-curving blade, slender and beautiful. The handle looked like it was made from bone with tiny brass decorations inlaid.

"Very nice. Does it feel all right?"

Amanda swished it through the air gracefully, then put it back in the scabbard. "Feels perfect. Mid-nineteenth century Indian short sword. Jealous?"

"Ha, a little. It is pretty stunning. How'd you know the heritage?"

"There was a label," said Amanda sheepishly, before smiling.

"You big cheat! Right, now what's next? And shouldn't we have guns really? These are cool and all, but a gun would be a lot more effective."

"Except neither of us have ever used one, we could run out of bullets, and anyway, these will be more functional as well."

"Functional for what? Smashing through the jungle or doing a bit of whittling?"

"Don't be cheeky, you know what I mean."

"Just messing honey. Now, let's get on with this."

"Okay."

They stood facing each other, each waiting for the other to lead. The silence stretched on.

"God, what are we doing?"

"I have no idea," said Dale, trying hard to think what would be the very best next step.

With nothing coming to mind, he pulled a Hexad from his satchel, feeling strangely happy to see the flashing 6, the warm blue glow welcoming him like a long lost lover. Dale fiddled with the settings, fingers working as if they had a life of their own, no conscious thought involved.

Maybe this was it, how to stop it all? Let his unconscious mind lead the way, take them where he couldn't consciously think of? It was something, at least, so he let his fingers do the work while he watched motes of dust dance in the streams of light finding their way into the room through windows where they had been rubbed almost clean in places, probably by one of the trustees, just so they could get a glimpse of the beautiful countryside on the other side of the ancient glass.

"Come on, let's go," said Dale, reaching out a hand for Amanda to take.

"Where to?" she said, taking hold of the offered hand, the contact reassuring for them both.

"I have no idea, but let's find out anyway shall we?"

Amanda shrugged. "Why not?"

"Whooooooooooooooooooooosh."

"Dale, will you please stop—"

They jumped.

Stupid Brain

Time Unknown

"Bugger." Dale scrambled to his feet, feeling rather foolish for not remembering to focus on landing on the ground. He'd freaked again, thinking he was falling to his death when really it was merely a split-second before his feet hit the floor.

Amanda was smiling at him, clearly expecting it and staying calm as she jumped. Dale noted the smile fading, turning to astonishment, as she took in their surroundings. Dale stood next to her, looking around at where his unconscious mind had decided was the best place to jump to. "Stupid brain, shouldn't have trusted it," muttered Dale.

"Huh?"

"Nothing, ignore me. I think I will from now on."

"Where are we Dale? This place is incredible."

"I have no idea, but it sure is rather bonkers."

They stood, they stared, and they stared some more. Dale felt like he could spend a lifetime just looking at the strange, mind-bending vista spread out before them. It made a mockery of everything that he knew about gravity, about how reality worked. About everything.

They were stood in what at first impressions would be nothing more than a simple field, all lush green grass and soft, clearly fertile soil beneath. It was only when you looked around you that everything became skewed, warped and incomprehensible until your brain readjusted to put what your eyes were seeing into some kind of order.

The only way Dale could describe it to himself was if you had a world in miniature that instead of wrapping around the surface of a globe was wrapped around a cylinder. Then, just to laugh in the face of physics, instead of wrapping it around the outer surface, you took all that you understood and played God by wrapping it around the inner surface instead.

Staring mutely at the strange views, Dale and a clearly confused Amanda, who was standing with her mouth open, brain trying to come to terms with what she saw just like Dale, traced the curve of the landscape, following it up until he was looking directly above where he stood, looking at fields as if he were high up in the sky looking down on them. He was sure he could see rooftops, even a hint of smoke trailing away from the tops of chimneys, meandering down towards him far, far below. Or above, not that there really was a top or a bottom to such a strange landscape as far as he could tell.

Dale turned to face the opposite direction, similar scenes presenting themselves. Halfway up the cylinder, tube, or whatever it was, not even sure if the words actually meant different things really, there appeared to be, quite bizarrely, a small village, complete with what Dale was sure was a cricket pitch in the middle of the twee scene. Similar traditional English country scenes presented themselves in whatever direction he looked.

Back down on the ground, for he had to think of where he stood as the ground or he had the feeling he'd suddenly fall off and end up above himself, the field they were stood in led to a small stream. On the other side, past a low hawthorn hedge, there were a few sheep, white backs gleaming like blue-tinged bone in the diffused light. He didn't even want to think about how the light worked in such a place, but guessed it must be coming from regular intervals around the whole vast interior.

There were small farmhouses scattered amongst the fields like oversized boulders, there were trees and almost blinding fields of canola, their yellow flowers like patchwork sunshine dotted around the landscape, mixing with the green of the fields, the dark brown of rich exposed soil, the blue of streams meandering between the straight lines like squiggles on a Mondrian canvas.

"How big do you think it is?" said Amanda, whispering as if she was in a library.

"Dunno. Huge. A mile long. Two? Not sure how wide, but it has to be a half mile at least, or who knows? It messes with your sense of perspective, everything is the wrong way around."

"It's incredible." Amanda, eyes wide and energized, spun in a circle, trying to take it all in again in an instant. She moved away a short distance as she spoke, bending to feel the grass, as if it was as fake as the reality they found themselves in.

"It sure is. But how is this even possible?"

"Everything is possible," said Amanda, from right behind him.

Amanda? But she's over there...

"Amanda," shouted Dale, but it was too late. She was turning, and then she was staring at the Amanda that was stood right beside him, an Amanda that was not the Amanda he had just jumped with.

Dale held his breath, waiting for the world to implode, to awake in a straitjacket in a padded cell, or at the very least for one or both of the Amandas to disappear because of the paradox.

Nothing happened. Nothing apart from his Amanda staring in total shock at yet another version of herself.

"Don't worry," said the new Amanda, "the paradoxes won't mess with things. Not here."

"And, um, where is here?" asked Dale, trying to slow his heart, stop it from leaping out of his chest and running away to hide in a dark corner somewhere.

"Why, this is home, of course. The Chamber."

"Home? You live here?"

"Yes, lots of us do." Amanda, the new one, smiled at him sweetly, a nice even tan really making her look radiant.

Dale turned to the approaching Amanda, realizing how tired she looked, and confused, which was to be expected. Heck, if he was confused and disorientated he couldn't imagine how she was feeling.

"I'm guessing it's best for us not to shake hands?" said Amanda.

"It's fine, honestly. But if it makes you feel uncomfortable..."

"You live here?" interrupted Dale, asking again, trying to get information, and to maybe occupy Amanda rather than her freak out about another her. Dale thought she had said that the other versions of her were all safely back where they were supposed to be, and that obviously wasn't really the case at all. He couldn't imagine this being where anyone had really come from and truly belonged, it was too alien in design.

Amanda smiled again, calm and totally at ease in their presence, as if they were expected. "Come, let's walk while we talk. And yes Dale, I truly do live here. Lots of Amandas do. For a while, at least."

Why don't I like the way this is heading?

They walked through the field, an Amanda on either side of Dale, making him extremely uncomfortable. Just what did this new woman know of him? How many experiences had she shared with a version of him that would make it as if they knew each other intimately? Dale thanked the powers-that-be that her scent wasn't quite right — he wasn't sure what he would do if suddenly confronted with two Amandas that both were to all intents and purposes the same woman.

Amanda tried to make sense of their situation for them both. "Amanda? Gosh, ugh, that sounds so weird, I don't normally talk to myself. Look, what's going on? How are you here? Where is here? And what the hell is this weird place anyway?"

"You don't mess about do you?" said the other Amanda. "But then neither do I so I promise to tell it to you straight. Let's go inside though, shall we? Maybe a roof over your head will allow you to relax a little. I know when I first arrived I thought my mind was going. It's a little disorienting until you get used to it, but you do. Eventually."

Amanda led the way across the open ground and very soon they were making their way between deep borders packed with flowers, reminiscent of their own garden back home — Amanda's taste obviously translating to the new environment. The house was simple, yet well built out of stone that seemed to be the main material for all the buildings Dale could see. He didn't even want to think about the logistics of building something on such a curved surface — anything of any size would give you a serious headache just trying to get things flat or straight.

As they approached the house Dale tried to see what was at either end of the cylinder he found himself in, but it was mostly just haze — they must have landed fairly close to the center of the strange world. One end was fairly bright though, a pale blue that may have been the light source, or may have been just open to whatever lay beyond. The other end was more of a dull gray, although again he couldn't be certain if it was closed-off or open.

"Dale."

"Eh? Oh, sorry, I was miles away."

"You coming in?" asked Amanda, his Amanda, as she followed the other one through the front door.

"Yeah, sure, I'm coming."

Dale stepped out of insanity and into what was nothing more than a nicely decorated home with all the trademark touches he'd come to expect of Amanda.

That just made it even weirder — it was like stepping into an alternate home, just one with no sign of him having ever been a part of it.

A Nice Cuppa

Time Unknown

"Take a seat," said Amanda genially, as she moved over to the counter top and switched on the kettle.

Dale and Amanda sat at the chairs around the compact kitchen table — the room was clean and well laid out but the kitchen was still a little cramped.

"Sorry, but all I have is instant. But then, I know neither of you mind that, it's what you usually have anyway, isn't it?"

"You know us only too well," said Dale, not really amused by such a comment, more concerned about stopping himself slipping into insanity.

"I can't stand this." Amanda stood and stared at their host, eyes wide and frightened. "What on earth is going on? And Dale," Amanda turned to him, scabbard banging against the side of her chair before she shifted it in annoyance, "where did you jump us to? You must know where you were going."

"I didn't, honest." Dale held up his hands, protesting his innocence. "I let my fingers do the decision making. I figured maybe my subconscious would send us to where the Hexads were being made so we could stop it all and that would be the end of it. Stupid brain, never should have trusted it."

Amanda turned at Dale's words, shock registering on her face. "You made the jump? Not Amanda? Interesting." She turned back to the counter, then remembered something and went over to the fridge for the milk.

Dale didn't like it. Having the same woman in front of you twice, both knowing everything about you, was simply too eerie.

As Dale listened to the teaspoon clattering in the mug while Amanda stirred his coffee he stared out of the window, a nice view over the kitchen sink — at least it would be if the artist's perspective on the world wasn't so skewed. Seeing just a slice of the strange world allowed him to get it a little more organized in his head, although it still defied all logic he could accept as a physical reality. But then, Hexads broke all the rules so why should anything surprise him now?

The window framed a view up what he had to think of as the side of the tube, where there were small parcels of land sectioned off by neat hedges or drystone walls. Everything was idyllic, orderly, clearly well-maintained, and the land was productive: a mixture of pasture land for small herds of animals and arable land for crops. Dale got the impression that the whole inverse world was self sufficient to a high degree.

It was the actual way the view played with your mind that took a while to come to terms with, although now Dale could look at just a small section it seemed to be making more sense. He focused on a green strip of land laid to grass that seemed to run right up the side of the cylinder, stopping almost above his head, although he couldn't see that far from inside. At first, as his eyes followed the land, perspective worked normally: lines began to converge the further away they got, but then it got freaky. Dale had to get up and peer out the window with his nose almost touching, craning to see the lines move away from a vanishing point and actually spread wider apart, defying both logic and gravity as he knew it.

"Sorry, I'm just trying to make sense of this place," said Dale, suddenly realizing what he'd done. He returned to his seat, doing terribly rudimentary math that he could remember, and trying to dig up information locked in his mind on vanishing points and how it would apply to a cylinder if you were inside it.

"That's okay, it takes a while before you get used to it, but you will." Amanda placed two mugs on the table, moving coasters from the center and putting them in front of three of the four chairs. She then returned with her own coffee a moment later.

Dale became lost deep in thought again, accepting the landscape, but unable to comprehend how everything didn't just slide to the bottom. *Because there isn't one, obviously.* That was the only sensible answer, one he knew immediately but couldn't quite come to terms with. There was no bottom, the same as there wasn't on the earth. This was just inverted but the same rules of physics still applied. All that really remained to be answered was how was it possible for gravity to work normally in such a place?

Dale sipped his coffee absentmindedly, then looked up. Both Amandas were staring at him, as if waiting for him to do something.

"Oh, sorry, I was miles away. Was I being rude? I didn't mean to be. This is just a lot to take in you know?" Dale pointed out the window, as if neither Amanda was aware of their environment.

"I understand," said the new Amanda. "You should have seen me when I first arrived. I was a wreck for weeks."

"And when was that?" asked Amanda. "Just how long have you been here? More importantly, what is this place and how on earth are you even here? How are we able to both be here? Dale, I want to go, I don't like this. I don't like it one little bit."

"It's okay honey, it's okay." Dale reached out and grabbed Amanda's hand, trying to give her reassurance he sorely felt in need of himself. "Look, um,

Amanda," Dale turned to the new Amanda, "can you please tell us what is going on?"

"Of course. I'm sorry, I forget that this takes some getting used to. But trust me, after a while you'll love it."

"We won't be staying here long," said Amanda. "Wherever 'here' actually is."

"Here, our home, is all there is for us now."

"Us? Who's us?" asked Dale cautiously.

"Why, all the Amandas of course. I thought you knew, I thought that was why you were here. Although we don't normally get many Dales, not for long anyway." Sadness tugged at the corners of her mouth before she put on a smile, definitely just for them, Dale was sure.

"Ugh, stop it, stop it, stop it!" Amanda put her head in her hands, hair tumbling onto the spotless table, almost falling into the untouched coffee.

"Can you please tell us what the hell is happening here? Now," said Dale.

Dale and Amanda listened while Amanda explained — he wished they hadn't asked.

~~~

Amanda put fresh coffee down in front of them, but Dale was feeling claustrophobic in the cramped kitchen, and both Amandas readily agreed to go back outside. Even the strange landscape was better than being cooped up inside as far as Dale was concerned.

The air outside was fresh and there was a subtle fragrance coming from the multitudinous flowers in bloom. There were even bees, Dale noted with interest. Now that he came to think of it there was also a gentle breeze, carrying the scent of freshly mowed grass, fertilizer and other smells familiar to the countryside, all mixed in with smoke from fires warming the interiors of the stone cottages.

What kind of systems could possibly be in place to allow for a breeze, let alone light, heat and most disturbing of all: gravity?

Dale fiddled with the Hexad he'd used, watching the 5 blink in a way that was becoming all too familiar.

Maybe he should just set it, grab his Amanda and jump?

The new Amanda must have picked up on his musings. "It won't work, not here."

"What do you mean it won't work? It's a Hexad."

"I know what it is, we all do. How do you think we all got here? It won't work."

Dale stared at the device, then at his Amanda, who walked over to him, grabbed his hand and nodded. Dale pressed down on the dome, thinking it was better to leave and have the world make sense than have his curiosity satisfied.

Nothing happened, as deep down he knew it wouldn't. "Okay, first things first. How are you here, and what's all this talk of 'we' anyway?"

New Amanda gestured to a rudimentary picnic bench and they all sat, placing mugs on the silver wood.

"You don't get it, do you? You aren't supposed to be here, at least I don't think you are. By 'we' I am talking about all the other Amandas, the ones that have been misplaced through the effects of the Hexads, or the ones that are supposed to be here, we have never really been sure. But there are a lot of us, hundreds. Some have been here longer than they can remember, some just a few weeks, one even came in today, and I'm guessing that is because of you?" She stared at Amanda expectantly.

"I don't understand," said Amanda.

"Let me explain. The Hexads inevitably lead to paradoxes, and when that happens usually one Amanda disappears, right? Well, this is where we come when we disappear from the real world. We come here, and then we have to decide if we want to stay or not. It's nice really, once you get used to it, but nobody ever came here by choice before, not like you two have, and a Dale has never been the one to make the jump, not ever."

"But how? I don't get it," said Dale. "Amanda told me that all the problems that arose from the Hexads had been solved, that everything had returned to normal, as if they had never been, all apart from in our own world, in our own time."

"Dale, you are being somewhat naive, if you don't mind me saying so. You too Amanda. I don't know what has been going on for you two, we don't get news in here, but don't you get it? There is no stopping the Hexad, it is a constant. Always has been, always will be. Whatever trifling problems you have been experiencing means nothing, not on the scale of things. The only truth is that it is all tied up to us, the Amandas, and whatever any of us have ever tried to do, and trust me there are no end to the stories of weird futures and jumping around the universes, crazy adventures and others where they simply woke up one morning, got shouted at by a Dale before catching a glimpse of another Amanda and disappearing from their reality to find themselves here, it never ends, the Hexad finds a way to return, to insinuate itself into our lives, and on and on it goes.

"You two are responsible for the Amanda that arrived today, I'm sure, so I guess you have your own problems right about now, probably all tied up with Detective Inspector Cray, The Caretaker, maybe even Laffer and Hector." Amanda waved away Dale and Amanda before they could interrupt. "But trust me when I tell you that you aren't the first, and you definitely won't be the last."

"But we are," said Dale. "Amanda here, and a version of me, set everything right in all possible realities. Ours is the only one left that still has Hexads now, and that's only because she jumped back to find me. Right Amanda?"

"Right. Every other reality was normal. Futures were full of people, there were no Hexads. It was normal."

"That may be, but we are the misplaced, and if what you say is true then we wouldn't be here, would we? We are the ones displaced by the actions of time travel, but we are also the ones that ensure the Hexad continues to exist, that we continue to exist."

"What does that mean?" Dale knew they weren't being told the whole story.

"Later. First I want you to understand that this is our home. We live here, best we can."

"Why? Why don't you leave?"

"Because we can't. Don't you think we haven't tried? Don't you think that countless women, all almost identical, want to leave this place and get their lives back? Many have gone insane, taken their own lives, or are recluses, refusing to ever talk to another Amanda, but some of us just get on with things, accept our lives now, and make the most of it. We can't leave."

"So this whole place is just full of versions of you that somehow got caught up in the effects of other Dales and Amandas traveling around in time?" asked Dale.

"Yes, sort of. It goes deeper than that, way deeper. Some were directly involved, trying to break the cycle, trying to put things right, let the future be normal, free of the crazy things people do when time travel becomes a reality, but others have no knowledge of being involved in anything of the sort, they just suddenly appeared here and don't know why. Although they were still clearly somehow caught up in it, maybe simply touched by another Amanda while they slept, one that couldn't live without a version of you Dale, and risked blinking out of existence rather than being alone."

Dale leaned back, almost toppling over before he remembered he was on a bench not a chair. "Bloody hell, this is insane."

"I know."

The questions continued for a while, but Dale didn't feel like they were getting any closer to the truth of the matter, aware that things were being kept from them, half-truths being told, Amanda probably assuming it was for their own good.

By the time Amanda had finished answering their questions, sharing her story and experiences so far, and they had time to then ask more questions they felt were important, the light had begun to fade, almost like they were in the real world, not some kind of... Well, that was one question that still remained.

"Okay, one last question please," said Dale.

"Fine, but last one. I'm exhausted," said the new Amanda.

"Where are we?"

"Why, isn't it obvious? We're in the Hexad, the original."

A Strange
Interlude

Time Unknown

Dale felt fear grip his guts like a rat was inside gnawing away at nerves, bringing them to life only to destroy them eagerly. He felt the certainty of the words echo around his mind, words he knew were the truth the minute he had stared at the far ends of the cylinder but refused to admit to himself.

Of course they were in a Hexad, the blunt gray end and the other a blue dome, it was obvious. They were in what could only be described as a giant Hexad, or maybe the first? A huge Hexad that somehow gave rise to the others?

"But... but, what do you mean? How... how do you know?" Amanda looked like she was about ready to collapse — it was easy to forget that she had been out of her normal life for a long time. Dale was feeling bad enough, who knew how mixed up Amanda was.

"Can we carry on with this tomorrow please?" The new Amanda got up from the bench and gathered the empty mugs, leaving Dale and Amanda alone.

The light was fading fast, almost as if the transition from day to night wasn't really a concern. Dale noted tiny pricks of light high above, light bouncing off the upside down ground as it spilled out of windows as people settled down for the evening.

"What do we do now Dale? What is this place?"

"It's hell, but we aren't staying." Dale was resolute: no way was his Amanda going to be some kind of prisoner like countless others, if what they had been told was true.

~~~

They were put up for the night in a comfortable spare room, told that they would be allocated a home of their own the following day.

Dale knew he wouldn't sleep as he cuddled in to Amanda under thick covers in the musty smelling room. He'd lie there, keep her company, just enjoy the closeness and try not to think — although he knew his thoughts would be going a mile a minute all night.

The next thing he knew there was pale blue light spilling in through an open window, the sound of a cockerel telling the rest of the inverse world it was awake and they better be as well.

The second of many surprises of the day wasn't long in coming.

He dressed and padded down the stairs, wondering where Amanda was, hoping that she was okay and that nothing terrible had happened. He couldn't believe he'd slept through the fake night so soundly, but the effects of jumping through time were evident in the ache of his bones and the feeling that his brain was somehow different: rewired to cope with the madness.

He felt tired, a deep lassitude that almost made him crawl back under the covers and sleep away the nightmare until he was back home and it was just going to be a normal day mowing the lawn and dozing on the sofa.

As he made his way into the kitchen he heard laughter. It was disconcerting hearing the woman you love laughing twice. Two Amandas getting on well, which shouldn't come as a surprise really. After all, they were near enough the exact same person — just not quite.

"Haha, I never really thought about that. I'm amazed it hasn't happened already," he heard his Amanda saying.

"Amazed what hasn't happened?" Dale walked over to Amanda and gave her a kiss on the head, stunned her hair looked so radiant. He put his hand to his own, realizing it was sticking up like a scarecrow's as it did every morning. He tried to pat it down, knowing it was useless — he needed a shower. "Um, morning Amanda. Wow, that sounds weird."

"Morning Dale," said the new Amanda brightly. "I was just telling Amanda here about the silly things some of us have done, the ones of us that were actually involved in jumping, having Hexads. Although," she said, turning to Amanda, "some of it was quite serious. You have to be careful."

"I will, definitely. Oh, well, if we ever get out of here."

"You won't."

Silence descended, the atmosphere darkened.

"Gee, something I said?" Dale looked around the kitchen, checking if there was any coffee.

"Help yourself," said his host, gesturing at the kettle.

"Anyone else?" asked Dale, as he filled up the kettle from the tap, glancing out the window at the weird landscape that was unchanged from the day before.

Both wanted a refill so Dale busied himself gathering mugs and making the coffee. It almost felt normal, until he turned to look at two almost identical women sat around the table.

"So, what were we talking about?"

"Oh, I was just telling about some of the things that have happened to some of the girls. The ones that had Hexads."

"What, being chased by giants, meeting The Caretaker, losing your timeline? That kind of thing?"

"Wow, I forgot how grumpy you were without your morning coffee," said new Amanda.

"Yeah, well."

"No, I was telling Amanda how some people landed in rather unfortunate situations. It's a dangerous business jumping, you can end up anywhere."

Ah, this could be interesting. I wonder how much she knows?

"I thought it was all down to setting the destination by thinking about where you want to be?" said Dale, leaning forward curiously.

"Well, yes, but it's a lot more complicated than that, a lot more. Many of the girls have ended up with near misses, almost jumping and dying, or in the middle of something."

"In the middle of something?"

"Yes. Say you set the time for however far into the future you want, then you picture where you want to be and you jump, right?"

Dale and Amanda both nodded, happy to be given any information they could get.

"Okay, so you want to jump forward maybe a day in your kitchen, just as an example. So you set it up, picture landing on the tiles that were a great investment, and you jump, probably with Dale making that stupid sound of his."

"Ha, it's so annoying isn't it?" Amanda ruffled his hair affectionately.

"Hey, it's cool. It has to be dramatic," protested Dale.

"Anyway," continued their host, "the problem is that you don't know that if you hadn't jumped then you decided to mop the floor the next day and you moved the table out into the middle of the room, then bam! The next thing you know you are stuck there in the middle of the room, stood clean through the center of the table. Game over. Or worse, the you that didn't jump is there with you, watching as you materialize right through the table, and then you both disappear. Or one of you dies and the other has to try to come to terms with seeing themselves dead and stuck through a table."

"Bloody hell, I hadn't even thought about stuff like that. We've been lucky."

"I've thought about it," said Amanda. "It's why I'm careful where I jump to and make sure I know it will be safe."

"Ugh. And when I jump I usually end up a little above the floor. It could just as easily be under it."

"Exactly. Imagine jumping only to find your feet stuck in the carpet. Well, it wouldn't last long, you'd topple over pretty quickly, your feet chopped off."

Dale felt sick. He'd never even considered such possibilities, thinking it was more or less a given that there was some kind of a system that looked after you when doing such impossible things."

"I think I'm going to be more careful from now on," said Dale.

"I told you, you can't leave. Amanda anyway. You, well, I'm sorry Dale but you shouldn't be here, you won't be for long."

This morning is not getting better with coffee.

"What do you mean?" Dale asked reluctantly.

"I mean that there have been others, only a couple mind you," said new Amanda hurriedly, "and they, well, they sort of just slowly disappear."

"What, like whoosh and they were never here?"

"No, more like they fade away slowly until they are nothing but a ghost." New Amanda looked around nervously. "Like they might still be here, we just can't see them."

Dale jumped to his feet. "That's it, we're getting out of here Amanda. I'm not staying in this place, no damn way."

"And how are you going to leave? You can't, nobody ever does Dale. Nobody." New Amanda began to cry; Dale walked outside, he couldn't deal with it.

~~~

"Sorry," said the new Amanda. "It's been so long since I spoke to you; I miss you so much Dale."

"It's okay, come here." Dale hugged Amanda tight, but it felt wrong, strange, bringing back the terrible feeling of betrayal after his Amanda came back and the woman he'd woken up with only the day before, if he forgot about timelines and how long it had really been, had disappeared, and now the poor thing was here somewhere.

Amanda came out of the house and nodded at Dale as he slowly let new Amanda go.

"Do you know how this all works?" asked Dale. "How the whole timeline thing and the different versions of you, me, everyone, really works?"

Host Amanda brightened, clearly pleased to talk rather than dwell on the life she was living. "Sort of. You want me to tell you?"

"God yes!" said Amanda.

Dale nodded his head.

~~~

"So it just goes on and on? Timeline after timeline, for ever and ever?" Dale's head was spinning out of control, and he was just now realizing that he felt somehow lighter, as if he'd suddenly lost weight or he'd become that much stronger. He hadn't noticed it before in his state of confusion, but moving was easier, things felt imperceptibly lighter, like... That was it, gravity was slightly different, a little less than he was used to. Dale returned to the conversation, trying to digest what they'd been told.

"Not infinite, well, I suppose not, but as close to it as it not mattering. Look, for time travel to be possible it means that the past and the future have already happened, right? We know the past has, as we lived it, but the future? That's hard to come to terms with. But if we can jump into the future then it's also already happened. So every time you jump you create an alternate reality, and the more jumps that happen the more alternate realities, or parallel universes there have to be. There's no other way it could be possible otherwise."

"And in each new universe there are then almost parallel timelines where different futures happen, right?" Dale thought he was finally getting somewhere with understanding it.

"Exactly. And the chances of you ever, and I mean ever, jumping back to your right timeline are just about impossible. Things will always be slightly different, as the minute you've done one jump you create countless universes, timelines and on and on it goes. Most will be so similar you would never notice the difference, but they are not the same one, and in some cases they are incredibly divergent."

Amanda interjected. "So that's why when I jumped trying to find Dale I saw him looking so different? Me and another him had set everything back to being right, without Hexads, but they were still alternate realities that then existed. Just without time travel?"

"I don't know about all of that, about them all being set right forever, but yes, they were each just distinct futures spreading out in countless ways from when each of the timelines was created." Amanda paused to think. "It's complicated, but as far as we, all the Amandas, can tell, then the possibility of you jumping creates some kind of series of possible futures where pretty much anything can happen. It sort of has to, to allow it to be possible."

"I don't get it," stated Dale.

"Okay. So, I have a Hexad, I'm sat at home and I decide that my first jump will be a week away, so I jump forward a week to the same place in my living room. So that's one future that had to happen, one where I didn't jump and just carried on with the rest of my week. But there is the new future now, where I did jump, so it's different. But what about everything in-between? What if I'd decided to jump a day later, an hour, a minute, a second? That would see the need for other futures to have happened too. And it just gets worse, spreading out forever. That's why the timelines were in such a mess for you Amanda. I guess if you had a whole generation jumping back and forth then it makes sense that reality couldn't cope, so it just got rid of the problem: people, and closed everything down to one reality."

"Then it started up all over again once we set it back to a future that never had Hexads. Everything in all of them that could have been possible is possible again, even though at the moment they are functioning with people."

"Maybe. But with you having been in your world then all those futures may have already happened again, as this is how it started for you."

"But not for you," said Dale. "So that wasn't the reality for everyone's futures?"

"No, I told you, it's endless. As long as there are Hexads then there are us here and there will always be problems out in the timelines."

"So we need to get rid of them all, then we will all just go home and not remember any of it as we will never have done it. End of story. We just need to be sure to get them all." Dale felt pleased with himself. That was the solution, just as they'd agreed ever since Amanda came into his life and warped his perception of reality.

"No, you can't."

"Why not?" Dale was startled by new Amanda's ferocity — he'd never seen her as angry or scared. Not that this was her, he had to remind himself, looking at his Amanda, trying not to sink into insanity at the perverted situation.

"Because you can't. This is our home and it's all we have. If you did manage all that, which you won't, then we will all disappear."

"And go back to where you are supposed to be. Home."

"No Dale, you still don't get it, do you? Amanda, whoever the first one actually was or is, would be it. All of us that are now alive because of what happened would cease to be. There would be only one. There would be one Amanda, one Dale, one universe and no more. If there never was a Hexad, no time travel, then there would be no need for timelines, universes or parallel universes, whatever you want to call them. The chance of jumping to the future would never exist, so there would be no need for anything but the past and the present. We would have never existed. Ever."

"I hadn't thought of it like that," muttered Dale.

"Well you should, you too Amanda. You might well be the last one out in any of the worlds now. Who knows what has happened since you jumped back into Dale's life? You said that you jumped through timelines looking for your Dale and this one is as close to yours as possible but it's still not him, not one hundred percent. But that's besides the point anyway. All those other places only existed because they had to, for you to jump into. If you eliminate the need for them to exist then you kill us all, you kill endless universes full of us, full of billions of people each."

And set reality back to how it should be. Without the chance of lumps of flesh landing on your table, without going around killing versions of the woman you love. Without the risk of waking next to a woman you don't believe is your real Amanda.

Dale said nothing, but cursed the life he now had where he thought of the love of his life as one of many Amandas, rather than just Amanda, the one and only.

Host Amanda went into the kitchen, leaving them alone in their strange inverted world with a lot to think about.

A Walk

Time Unknown

Amanda was shocked, Dale too, but there was no escaping the fact that she would feel the words of their host much deeper than he would. Although Dale understood what she had said, and it really did make perfect sense, a lot more than anything had since it had all begun, he still couldn't help thinking of it all as little more than an abstract concept. It wasn't real, not really visceral and genuine, it was more like a thought experiment than a reality where billions of lives were at stake across more worlds than he wanted to even consider.

And did it really matter? It was a very hard question to answer. Of course people's lives mattered, and he wasn't about to go around exterminating them, but at the end of the day all they had planned to do was to set the world back to how it should be, how it was, how it had always been up until time travel madness interrupted the flow of reality.

But what of Amanda? She wasn't truly, exactly, the one that he should be with, was she? So if they somehow managed, and it seemed increasingly unlikely, to eradicate even the slightest hint of a Hexad, then would she no longer exist either? She'd just pop out of existence and Dale would be with the true version of her that should be the most important thing in his life. And all the others would cease to have ever been.

Trying to think of it from his own point of view didn't help much — would he sacrifice all the other versions of himself that were now in existence, having lived lives just like his? If he answered honestly then the answer was yes, he would do that, to get his normal life back. Even if it meant losing the memories of what had been happening he would do it, as it was what was right, wasn't it? But then, he hadn't been going around having conversations with alternate versions of himself had he? Maybe he would have a different perspective and his answer would be different if he had.

"Let's go for a walk." Dale turned to a still stunned Amanda, who nodded mutely and put her arm through his.

Once they were away from the house, walking beside a stream that seemed to be obeying all the laws of gravity even as it climbed up the curving bank of a heavy-scented, picturesque meadow, meandering up and overhead where it grew wider, meeting small tributaries and ending in a sparkling lake, Dale stopped Amanda and turned her to him. "Did that make sense to you? Because it did to me. Not much does, but that did." Dale focused on her, trying to read what might be left unspoken — he needn't have worried, it all came gushing out as if the lake above their heads finally realized it was upside down.

"Dale, what are we going to do? I don't want to die. I know who I am and I remember it all. But I'd swap everything in a heartbeat if it meant things could just go back to how they were, to being normal. But then it wouldn't be with you, it would be with a different you, the one I had the other crazy experiences with right up until I left and you carried on without me. Well, not you, him, the other you. Ugh, it's all horrible, so convoluted. But yes, I'd do it. I'd stop all this, stop it all just to go back to normal. I'm sorry, does that make me horrid?"

"Hush, hush. No, not at all. Look, think of me as him, your Dale. I am, aren't I?"

"Yes, yes you are. You feel like him, act the same. You're him."

"And you are you, my Amanda. That's all that counts. Look, are you sure, as I don't want us to get into anything if you are not going to want to really do it? This is serious, like mega-serious. Forget this weird place, we'll get out of here—"

"How do you know?"

"Because I'm going to do something none of the Amandas have clearly thought of, but more importantly are you really sure that you will be happy if you and me stop all this and all these weird timelines cease to exist? No time travel, no nothing, just us, all those lives will be gone, never were."

"I know, it's horrible, but it isn't murder is it? I mean, if they'd never been real then we can't kill them, can we?"

"Amanda, look, they do exist, you have to accept that. What you have to decide is if you want to undo that, undo your own memories, mine too. We will be different people then, not the people we are now."

"Like amnesia, missing a few days, or months, years, whatever. I don't care, I just want to be me again."

"Look, this is what I'm saying. It won't be you, and it won't be me. Which Amanda are you?" Dale was serious, and she clearly knew it. Fear was there in her eyes, a deep-seated, primal fear, the fear of death, of extinction, of having never been.

"What do you mean? I'm me."

"Yes, but which you?"

Amanda looked terrified, like the question could send her mind unraveling, the answer too difficult. "Well, um, I'm the Amanda that laughed at you for wanting to dig up the tin, the one that ran from Laffer, the one that waited ten years to dig up the Hexads and all that went with that. I'm the one that then got lost, taken by The Caretaker, and then jumped back after you'd set things right with the other Amanda that helped you."

"So you are the real Amanda, the original?"

"Yes, I think so."

"You think so? You are or you aren't."

Amanda nodded. "I am. I'm her."

"But I'm not him. Not that Dale. Not quite."

"Oh Dale, I'm sorry, I don't want you to die. You can't."

"Look, it's fine. It doesn't make any difference, that's what I'm saying. Don't you see? If we do this, set things truly right, then both of us here now won't remember any of this anyway. It will never have happened. We'll wake up that morning after drinking too much and my guess is we'll not even remember the conversation about the stupid bloody tin. So whether that is this you and me, or any other version of us, it doesn't matter, it will all be the same. We won't know any different. The point is that can you take the responsibility for all other versions of yourself and me? Let alone everyone else in the universes? We may have come to terms with it, but you heard host Amanda, she —"

"Host Amanda?"

"Well, I have to call her something. If I call all Amandas Amanda it gets too weird. As I was saying, you heard host Amanda, she wants to be her, be the her she is now, with her memories, living here in this weird inverse world, whatever it really is, with all the other Amandas. Look around, look at this place."

Amanda slowly turned and looked at their environment. There were Amandas coming out of cottages, some tending gardens, most just standing staring at them, curiosity mixed with all manner of emotions ranging from mistrust to happiness to outright fear. "They're all me."

"Exactly. They are different people now, aren't they? Will you make the choice for them, take it all away?"

"We have to, we have to Dale. They don't understand, not living here like this. Think of that horrible production line, where we were brain-dead, being used. Think of all the people that were brought into existence then gone, even in the one true world, all because people played God and jumped through time. If I hadn't come back then everything would be all right and none of it would have happened, so that's what needs to be done. It's what must be done." Amanda paused. "But that's not true, none of it. Above all else I just want to go home. Be normal."

"Then that's what we'll do. As long as you're sure? You make the decision, then we can't turn back. We find out how to really end all this and then we don't stop until we succeed. Okay?"

"Okay," murmured Amanda.

"Okay? You have to be sure Amanda, this is serious."

"I'm sure. I'm positive."
"Good. Now, let's go for that walk shall we?"

Skewed Perspectives

Time Unknown

Dale had seriously underestimated the size of the cylinder, the whole inside-out thing had skewed his sense of size and perspective to a higher degree than he'd anticipated. It took them almost an hour to walk to the gray end of the structure, although in part that was because they made slow progress, having to stop to talk to the few Amandas they encountered, most simply staring at them with varying levels of welcome, others with outright hostility.

More than any other factor that slowed them down was the sheer scale of the environment, and the more they walked the more Dale was sure that gravity was slightly off — plants and trees seemed to grow that little bit taller than normal, the stems and trunks a little more slender. Even the bees seemed to be making their cumbersome, scientifically impossible flight a little more elegantly.

Most of the interior was composed of single dwellings in large gardens, or a few tiny, quintessentially English villages composed of a handful of homes at most. There was even a tiny church, but most of the landscape was composed of small parcels of farmland. Dale couldn't help wondering how rain worked here, if it did at all, until he noticed the cleverly constructed irrigation channels that criss-crossed back and forth across a patch of land close to them, deeper gullies running around its perimeter to feed into the system that would ensure the crops stayed well-watered.

So the place had its limitations, it wasn't an exact replica of the world in miniature, just inside out. The water probably all came from outside the structure and was piped into the rivers and streams to ensure that the water levels, and thus the humidity and atmosphere, stayed relatively constant.

Probably all to do with making the place rotate more easily, mused Dale, trying and failing to even begin to understand how such a system could ever be put into place.

Amanda was quiet, her face set determinedly, even though Dale knew that it was tearing her apart inside. The question of whether their decision was morally right or not still weighed heavily on both of them, but what alternative was there? To allow the rest of civilization to run rampant for a while before the Universe fought back and eradicated humanity from the planet? But if they succeeded their actions would have the inevitable consequence of destroying countless alternate universes — they would cease to exist, would never have existed, just as the alternative versions of themselves would never have been.

And what of them? Him and Amanda right here? They would be gone too, wouldn't they? Dale knew he would, for he was an alternate version of himself, and even for Amanda, who truly was the one that this all started with, she may as well be a different person too, for everything that had happened because of the Hexads would cease to have been a past that existed, so who would she be? Not the woman staring resolutely ahead beside him, probably trying her best not to think about any of the dark thoughts crowding Dale's mind.

They wandered through the madness, Dale trying not to follow the curve of the landscape too closely as it simply made him too disorientated. He noticed the same thing with Amanda: if she began staring up the curved sides, then eventually looking up at what he could only think of as the ceiling for his own sanity, then just like him she began to wobble a bit, the oddness of it overwhelming. You simply could not get accustomed very quickly to seeing buildings, animals, and tiny moving dots that were people, all hanging upside down and not feel certain that they were going to come crashing down onto you at any second.

The science behind the world may have been staggering but Dale couldn't even begin to understand why any of it existed in the first place. What real purpose did it serve? And how had he brought himself and Amanda here?

He'd set the dials on his Hexad carefully, making them neutral, a setting he had barely considered having only had very limited experience with the devices. Then he'd simply done what Amanda had said and thought really hard about where it was he'd wanted to be. There had been no time in mind, no specific location that he had past experience of, he mostly focused on wanting to be where the Hexad was first invented and just as importantly he focused on landing with feet firmly on the ground, which he'd almost got right this time. With host Amanda warning them about the dangers of jumping into the path of other objects, or jumping where there were no longer the things you remembered, he made a mental note to think doubly hard about the exact location he wanted to jump to in the future — if there happened to be one.

Despite it all, he was feeling confident. Dale was certain that the plan he had in mind to escape the tortuous tunnel would be successful, he merely wanted to wait a while so he could better understand what it was they were up against.

Cray was going to be behind it, he simply knew it. From the limited knowledge he now had then it seemed that Cray was involved in all possible futures involving the Hexad, and the people Amanda had dealt with in her earlier saving of the world were probably no longer in the picture as Dale had changed that future by refusing to follow the path that he should have gone down — new futures had opened up, unpredictable and extremely dangerous ones.

What an insane mess. If I'd thought any of this was going to happen I'd have stayed in bed and kept my mouth shut about the other Amanda smelling a little different.

Who was he kidding? Of course he wouldn't. Despite the madness, despite the danger and the fear, Dale had to admit, to himself at least, that this was one hell of a wild ride he was on. It was just a pity that if they managed to succeed then he wouldn't remember any of it and he wouldn't even exist any longer.

It was a sobering thought, but he knew what he had to do, try to do, at least.

Ignoring the dizzying sight of multiple Amandas in all possible configurations from barely out of her teens to well past middle age, from beautiful slender figures to versions where she had clearly taken up eating pies as her new religion, the effect understandably setting Amanda on edge, they finally made it near to the end of the cylinder.

The closer they got the patchier the ground became, morphing from lush grass to gorse, to finally little more than compact bare earth. Dale got the distinct feeling that if he dug down a little bit then he would uncover the material the place was made of, but he had other things to occupy his thoughts. He wanted to understand the environment before he tried to leave it — it was important, saving the world important, so he didn't want to rush things.

What he couldn't shake off was the nagging feeling at the back of his mind that Cray was going to pop along at any moment and simply eradicate them, or that something catastrophic would occur and the whole artifice would simply conform to the laws of gravity and normalcy and crumple in on itself, crushing them into tiny balls of flesh.

What he did know for certain was that there were a lot of questions remaining to ask host Amanda, or any other Amandas willing to talk to them for that matter, before he wanted to jump from where he was right now. One thing he realized he'd forgotten to ask was what they actually called this place. Did they really call it the Hexad? As in for real? Did she mean it was an actual time machine itself? No, that would be daft, wouldn't it?

~~~

Standing just a few feet away from the sheer wall that constituted the sealed end of the cylinder really put the size of the interior into perspective. Dale had to reevaluate his initial guesstimate concerning size quite dramatically as it must have been well over half a mile in diameter, and probably at least a couple of miles long — you could fit a lot of Amandas into such a space.

"It's pretty impressive, isn't it?" said Amanda, craning her neck to look up the full length of the sheer wall they were facing.

"It's mind-boggling."

"Kind of reminds me of a manhole cover, like it's just a giant lid that's keeping everyone locked inside."

"Haha. You know, you're right, it is like that." Dale stared at the surface, a dull gray, clearly made of metal; he was sure he could spot very subtle welding spots, just places that were a little lighter in color, a pattern where steel or something similar had gone through an epic fabrication process. But what kind of factory could make something on such a scale? Never mind the rest of the whole crazy place.

Thud, thud, thud.

Wrapping his knuckles on the surface, Dale was surprised at how dense it felt. There was no echo, just a dull thud, his knocking sucked up by the dense material. It was warm too, the same temperature as every surface he'd touched. He had a bizarre image flash into his mind of some giant in overalls on the other side dropping a monstrous manhole cover, sealing off his invention of a world in miniature, peering in at them through tiny holes in the cylinder, amused by the antics of the tiny Amandas and the Dale that should not have been there, and if what host Amanda had told him was true, would not be there for much longer.

How long have I got before I start to simply fade away as this isn't somewhere I belong? Is it like the way the Universe reacted to too much time travel? Will I just go pop and I'm gone? Or haunt the place forever as a literal ghost in the machine?

Dale shuddered at the thought, urgency rearing its head, telling him it was time to get the answers he wanted before they left. Soon, they had to do it soon. Amid all the strangeness he'd half-forgotten the warning about him not being welcome: an intruder in a hell made just for the countless versions of a single woman that were lost in time and space, this their only refuge.

But he refused to believe it. There was more at play here, and he intended to find out what was really going on, what secrets were being kept from them.

"You okay?" asked Amanda, noting Dale shuddering.

"Yeah, fine, just getting freaked out by this place. Let's go find host Amanda again; I have a few questions. Then I think we should check out the other end before we get out of here."

"Can't we just skip straight to the getting the hell out of here bit?" said Amanda, smiling weakly, trying to stay lighthearted when both of them knew they felt anything but confident in their current situation.

"Soon, I promise. But if we are going to beat this madness we need to know what it is we are facing. Was there any hint of any of this when you, you know, began your jumping last time?"

Amanda didn't need time to think. "No, absolutely not. I think I'd remember something like this."

"Yeah, I think you would too."

More Questions

Time Unknown

"Go on then, ask away. You haven't got a list or anything, have you?" asked host Amanda suspiciously.

"What!? No, of course not," said Amanda, averting her eyes. Unsurprisingly she was finding it rather hard to have a conversation with what was, to all intents and purposes, herself.

Dale knew he couldn't do it, he'd freak out big time.

On the way back they had tried to get into conversation with some of the other Amandas, but most were either tight-lipped, ignored them completely, or, in a few cases, spoke only to Dale and were rather forward about inviting him, and him only, into their homes.

Dale had joked with Amanda about her being rather horny and pushy but she hadn't taken it kindly at all — Dale never had been very good at judging her emotions, and proved the point once more with his rather misplaced attempt at humor. Still, a man had to try.

In the end they had given up trying to get on good terms with any of the women, although it was clear that it rankled Amanda no end that she was so unhelpful. After all, this was her, shouldn't the others be going out of their way to be helpful, considerate?

There was a definite vibe in the air though, and as they walked they discussed it, coming to the conclusion that the others had simply been here too long and had become somewhat institutionalized, maybe more than that: resentful that this was the Amanda that had started it all, skewed time and created universes, and now wanted to change it back, make as if their lives were worthless.

Did they know all that? Could they?

Then it became clear: of course they did, they were her. Amanda told Dale that they would all pretty much know what she had in her heart as they would, if not now, then at some point in time, have felt the same way.

In the end it didn't matter, their host was at home and as they settled down once more on the picnic bench, the wood warm from an invisible sun, the day clear and bright as Dale suspected it always was, their host said with a resigned sigh that she would answer their questions as best she could, just so Amanda would feel more at home, as it was, after all, where she would be spending the rest of her days.

Dale saw her visibly gulp at such a thought, knowing that she wouldn't appreciate living such an alien life one little bit, realizing that this was probably where the resentment lay with the others: they hated it, and always would. Not that this one seemed like that — she was surprisingly chipper after their words earlier in the day.

"Okay, first question," said Dale, all business-like. "What do you call this place?"

"We call it The Chamber, both capitalized."

"Why?"

"Duh." Amanda swept her eyes around the circumference, indicating what was more than obvious.

"Fair enough."

"How long have you been here and how did you get here?"

"I've been here for about three years I think, although that isn't exact," she said hurriedly. "It's hard to keep track really, every day is the same. I got here because in my timeline I was trying to escape Laffer with a Dale remarkably like you, when another jumped from somewhere and landed right beside me. I vanished and ended up where I am now."

"Do you know who the other Amanda was?"

"Yes, and before you ask, no, we don't talk, we don't get on at all."

"Not surprising," said Amanda. "Silly bitch."

"Amanda! That's you you're talking about. Jeez."

Host Amanda just nodded, as if confirming she could be a little hard to get on with at times. The other her, obviously, not either of the two at the bench.

"How do you get to be here? I mean, why not just vanish entirely, like you'd expect from the paradox?"

"Because this is how the Hexads run. Um, I mean, this is just how it is, how it all works. We are all so much a part of this craziness that as this is where it all started this is where we come to if we find ourselves in an impossible situation involving time travel."

Dale knew she was going to tell them more but caught herself and was lying, but he didn't pursue it, he had other questions he wanted answers to.

"Who runs the place, this place?"

"We have no idea, not really. We've heard Cray's voice, over some kind of hidden speaker system, but he's never actually said he's the one that runs it all, although we assume he is."

"But assuming isn't the same as knowing, right?" said Amanda.

"Exactly."

"All right, the really important one. You said that this is a Hexad, the original Hexad, do you really believe that? You think this is an actual Hexad? What makes you think that?" Dale was really keen to hear the answer to his question, it would lead to a lot more questions for him to ponder, sure, but if it really was, well, the mind boggled at what that could mean. Such a huge place jumping through time, it didn't bear thinking about.

She shifted uncomfortably on the bench, an all-too-familiar twitch at her right temple, visible as her hair was brushed back, telling Dale that there was no way she was going to tell the whole truth. Amanda seemed oblivious to the coming deception, but then she probably didn't know the subtle signs she made when she was lying or trying to be evasive.

"Just look at this place, isn't it obvious? The Chamber is just like the shape of a Hexad. Long ago some of the girls actually measured it and it conforms exactly to the dimensions of the Hexads, the portable ones. Blunt end, blue curved dome on the other, what else could it be?"

"A prison?" offered Dale.

"That too, but it's better than being dead."

That's it, they are living here as they don't like the alternative, but there's more. She's nowhere near to telling us the truth.

"But that doesn't mean anything, it doesn't mean it's a Hexad. How do you know?"

Host Amanda got up, looking cross, folding her arms. "I think that's enough now, if you're going to question my answers then what's the point?"

Amanda stood too, staring her in the eyes for the first time. "I understand how you feel, I really do, me more than anyone. But we're just trying to figure things out. Look, you said that Dale is going to just disappear from this place, that he doesn't belong, we need to find a way to get him out."

"I'm sorry, but no, that's all I have to say." Host Amanda turned to Dale. "I'm sorry Dale, but we've seen it happen before. You don't belong here, you have a day or two at most and then you will be gone. It's why most of the girls won't even look at you, let alone talk to you. It's too hard for us. We love you."

"I love you too Amanda."

He got a dirty look for that comment from his Amanda, but he just shrugged. What else could he say? It was true after all, wasn't it?

Their host, placated somewhat, and clearly surprised by his words, relaxed a little and said, "Look, I'm sorry, I know this is hard for you both, it's hard for everyone that comes here, but I can't say more than I already have, not yet. Not until..."

"Until I'm gone, right?" confirmed Dale.

She just nodded before walking back into the house, leaving Dale and Amanda alone with the flowers and the bees in the upside-down world that still threatened to fall from the sky onto their heads.

Amanda turned to him, looking as cross as the other her had just done.

"What?"

"Nothing." She shifted her arms to her hips, a sure sign he was in trouble.

"Aw, come on, you know what I meant."

"Do I? Do I indeed?"

"Honey, what can I do to make it up to you?"

"You can help me save the world," said Amanda, smiling, her eyes sparkling with mirth.

"Eh, what? You were joking?"

"Of course I was, I know I'm gorgeous. Got you!"

"Very bloody funny." Dale couldn't help chuckling, he really did love this woman.

To the Dome!

Time Unknown

Amanda was as keen as Dale to explore the other end of The Chamber, although he had the sneaking suspicion that she would do anything to get away from company that was in effect herself. It must be almost impossible to hold yourself in check when you see another you acting in ways that you find disagreeable, so they set off at a decent pace, slowing the further they got away from their temporary accommodation.

As they walked they talked, Dale asking Amanda if she noticed how evasive their host had been when it came to The Chamber and how she knew it was a Hexad, let alone that she'd said something about this was how Hexads ran when he asked her how come they didn't just disappear from reality when they became involved in what would be seen as a paradox.

Amanda had no answers, neither did Dale, but the more they talked the more they got the idea into their heads that somehow the women in The Chamber were directly involved in keeping everything turning, in making the strange reality they found themselves in continue to function.

It was confusing as hell. What were they involved in and why wouldn't they say?

"Maybe they are just scared. Maybe they are being threatened?" offered Amanda, trying to make excuses for her doppelgängers, clearly thinking she owed them the benefit of the doubt.

"I think it goes deeper than that Amanda, a lot deeper. She was certain that this is a Hexad and she was also certain that all the versions of you in here are the ones that are making Hexads possible. I think that's why they are so evasive of me, and you too. They are totally freaked out that we are going to somehow discover what's going on and stop it, eliminate them all."

"Wait a minute," said Amanda, stopping in her tracks, "are you saying that they are going along with whatever is happening so they can carry on living even though they know it means that whole worlds full of people are disappearing left, right and center because of it?"

"Yes, that's exactly what I am saying." Dale stared at her defiantly, daring her to disagree.

"I suppose you could be right," said Amanda quietly, mulling it over. "After all, that's what we are trying to do, isn't it? Let the real us go home, eliminate countless whole worlds that have sprung up because of the Hexad."

"Exactly. It's the same. Look, I don't blame them, it's human nature isn't it? Especially when you can't really accept multiple worlds as anything but a generality. It's too esoteric, too out there to let you think of it as a concrete reality. It's more like a lesson in abstract thinking than something you can convince yourself is truly happening."

"I suppose you're right. So what does this mean?"

"It means that I think if we aren't very careful then we are going to have hundreds of very angry versions of you coming after us and trying to kill us so we don't mess with their weird lives."

"I wouldn't. I would never do that."

"You would, I would, they definitely would. What, you wouldn't sacrifice one version of you so that you could survive? So that all the other women could too?"

"Well, now that you put it like that," said Amanda grimly.

"There you are then. You already did it, didn't you? A version of you, one that you made disappear and is now in here somewhere I might add, has already been in that terrible production line room you talked about and then jumped into countless timelines and killed countless versions of you. They were you, they were people and you killed them."

"For the greater good!" protested Amanda.

"Yes, I know. I'm just saying there is a lot that people will do when their backs are against the wall and they can't see any alternative. It's just the way it is. I'm not casting blame, that's for sure. All of this has really opened up my eyes to who I am too. It's a scary way to think."

"Let's walk, if we are going to have hordes of angry, but beautiful women," added Amanda, smiling, "after us, then let's do what we have to do and get the hell out of here quick smart."

"I'm working on it." Dale took her arm and linked it through his; she stuffed her hand into his pocket while Dale tried to match her brisk and businesslike pace.

They headed for the domed end of The Chamber, for them a convex dome that became more and more intimidating the closer they got to it — it was certainly more interesting than the blank wall they had encountered at the other end of their hopefully very temporary new home.

~~~

"Well, it's impressive, for sure, but it doesn't really help, does it?" said Amanda, leaning forward, trying to peer more closely at the strange end to the world.

"No," said Dale dejectedly. "Not one bit."

The blue was an almost exact match of the domes of their Hexads, and there was little doubt that this was the light source for The Chamber. What Dale assumed was exactly halfway up the dome there was a tight beam of light that came through a seemingly solid surface, then ran down almost the whole length of the center. He tried to remember if it hit the far end wall but was sure he hadn't noticed it. This was probably how the interior was lit, maybe heated as well, although it was impossible to find out as it was so far above them.

As at the other end, the ground turned from lush greenery to arid, bare earth the closer they got, until all they were faced with was the curve of the dome going meters deeper than they could touch.

Dale knelt and touched it at the base — it was warm, but not unduly so. As he lifted his hand he marveled at the fact that the light shone almost through his hand, like when you hold a torch light up close and your skin becomes translucent.

All of it meant nothing to him. Absolutely nothing.

"Come on, let's go. This is getting us nowhere. Nothing in here is explaining what this is, so it's time to leave."

"Just like that?" asked Amanda dubiously.

"Just like that." Dale looked around the area closest to the dome, noticing quite a large number of Amandas walking up the side of the curving interior toward another unremarkable stone building about halfway up the side. What were they up to? Was it worth a peek, or would it put them in unnecessary danger? Squinting, Dale thought he could just about make out one woman stepping inside at a time, then emerging again a few minutes later. They seemed subdued, nervous, but formed an orderly line, waiting their turn.

"Come, on, let's go check that out." He pointed up what he felt should best be described as a hill, and with Amanda looking rather confused he took her hand and led her toward the building, looking to see if there were any Amandas close to them — the ones that were at the building seemed to be it for now, he couldn't see any others going in the same direction, so they took to the border of one of the many fields and approached as cautiously as they could in such an exposed and convoluted environment.

Dale had a bad feeling about it, a very bad feeling. If he had a Spidey-Sense it would be tingling like mad, he was sure.

Amanda kept glancing at him nervously as they made their way up the steeply curving hillside, land that swept up and over like a tidal wave waiting to crush them. She was furtively looking left then right, clearly worried that they were going to get into serious trouble for going somewhere maybe they weren't supposed to.

Dale knew that she was also feeling that whatever was happening was important, otherwise why look so tense? He also wondered if she was nervous as she knew that the other women would react badly if they were caught, which, in a way, meant she herself knew that she wouldn't take kindly to such snooping.

As they followed the tracks between the sectioned land, keeping low and trying to move beneath the cover of the hedgerows and small copses of trees that were dotted about in a facsimile of naturalness, although not quite pulling it off, Dale realized this was the first time they had walked anywhere they hadn't thought of as the ground. He wasn't surprised to find that it felt just like they were walking on the level below — he could see where they'd been, the land curving down if he looked back, and it was the first time he truly appreciated the fact that there was no right way up, no up and down or main heart to The Chamber: it didn't matter where you stood, up was always up, down was always down.

It was creepy as hell.

"I don't like this Dale, it feels too strange. Look, you can see where we were, it's like we have suction boots or something and are climbing up the sides of a tube like some kind of insect."

"I know, I don't like it either. But look," Dale pointed to the building that was now getting close, "the line has almost gone, only a couple more to go. We should be fine to go take a peek once the last Amanda goes inside."

"If you're sure?"

"Kind of."

"Not very convincing, but okay. Let's just be quiet, and then I really want to get out of here. If you think we can?" Amanda looked hopefully at Dale, face full of misgivings but trying to give him the benefit of the doubt.

"Trust me, okay?"

"Okay Dale."

They waited until the last Amanda had stepped through the door into an interior they couldn't see, and watched as a handful of women walked back down the path they had all walked up, before it split in various directions and they took the route that would lead them to their homes. All the women were subdued, heads down almost as if they were ashamed. There was no conversation, no laughing or even crying. Nothing. Just silence.

Dale noticed that most of them wore loose blouses, some with buttons still undone almost down to the navel, nothing on underneath, others were wearing simple t-shirts. As they made their way down — he had to stop thinking of it as down, there was no down — the various paths he could see that a number of them kept rubbing at their backs, trying to remove an invisible irritation.

He didn't need to see, not now. He knew what was going on, understood what host Amanda had meant when she'd talked about knowing for sure this was a Hexad, that she knew how things ran.

"Dale? Dale, are you okay?"

"We should go, now."

"What? What do you mean? What's going on?"

"You don't want to know, trust me, you really don't."

Amanda stared into his eyes, searching for an answer he didn't want to give. There was a glimmer of understanding, a recognition of the look he was giving her maybe? Or maybe she'd just pieced it all together herself.

"Come on, we're going to take a look," said Amanda, tugging at Dale's arm.

"I don't think we should," said Dale. "It won't help."

"I need to know. I need to see for myself. Are you coming or not?" Amanda let go of his arm, waiting for him to answer. When he said nothing she began striding across open ground toward the cottage.

"Amanda!" whispered Dale.

It was no use, she was resolute, so swearing under his breath and checking they hadn't been seen, Dale ran after her.

He caught up with her right at the front door, a terrible look of shock, incomprehension and disbelief on her face, all mixed up in sadness and despair at what she herself could be driven to if the circumstances were right.

Dale didn't need to look inside the room, but he did anyway.

He really wished he hadn't.

Into the Abyss

Time Unknown

In complete contrast to the rough-hewn exterior, the inside of the cottage was stark, clinical, and bewildering with its white open space taking up the whole interior right up into the rafters.

The floor was perfectly laid white tiles that gleamed, the walls the same, even the joists. All around the room were banks of equipment, huge monolithic things with no clear indication of what they were there to accomplish, blank-faced, and as black as night.

Death sentries.

Strange lights flashed on and off on some of the machines, the only sound a gentle whirring. It paled in comparison to the main attraction though: a huge contraption in the center of the room that reminded Dale of a robotic milking machine he'd seen a few years ago. Actually, hadn't Amanda said that was what the machines reminded them of when she'd been in the room full of Amandas hanging from the ceiling like so much dead meat?

This was worse, surely?

This was voluntary.

The massive machine loomed over the standing figure of an Amanda, it's jointed arms moving effortlessly, enveloping her like a cold and uncaring lover. Naked from the waist up, the Amanda stood inside the contraption with arms hanging limp by her sides, face almost turned away from them but he could see the set of her jaw, the clenched teeth against what she obviously knew was to come.

One part of the huge robotic machine moved again, an arm extending from one side. Dale focused on nothing but mechanical movement and muffled whirring. It turned and a small hatch opened, a tiny single-jointed arm pushing out, holding some kind of vial. The large arm clamped down on the vial with a fast rotation at a joint, then retreated with a slight suction noise like a foot being pulled from mud as the arm pulled back — it would have been a comical sound if the scene wasn't so terrifying.

It now had a large needle at the end of the arm, attached by some kind of rubber locking device to a tube that ran down the length of the arm before trailing like a dead snake into the main part of the machine.

Dale and Amanda watched in horror as the arm twisted, moving slowly closer to the exposed lower spine of the woman in the machine. Suddenly there was a red beam of light, a laser probably, that pinpointed a spot low on the back of the now shaking Amanda that clearly knew what was coming.

With the reading of the woman's vitals obviously recorded, a metal clamp came out of the machine and wrapped tight around her midsection, locking her firmly in place. Dale got the impression that even if she collapsed she would be completely immobile until the machine finished its work.

The needle advanced, slowly puncturing her skin, going deeper and deeper. She let out a loud gasp and her hair shook, almost gently like it was nothing more than a cool breeze playing across her head.

Amanda next to him gasped and the woman, locked tight in the machine, turned her head. Her eyes went wide when she recognized them, clearly expecting it to be one of the women that made The Chamber their home.

She kept on staring, eyes alive with distress, but also defiance, as if she was asking who were they to judge the things she did?

The machine beeped; Dale saw the plunger on the needle pull back. Another beep, this one much deeper in pitch, and then it was over. The needle retracted, a few drops of precious fluid could be seen in the tube, before another liquid from within the robotic arm must have mixed with it, carrying it away.

The clamps came off the woman, the entombment retreated, the machine unfolded then became still, silent. It loomed high above the puny looking woman, and she staggered a little, but as soon as she was certain she was free of the machine, and rapidly buttoning up her blouse she screamed "Help," at the top of her lungs. Dale knew that they had to run.

"You fucking traitor bitch," shouted Amanda back at the woman, using language Dale had hardly ever heard her use in their many years together. If Amanda swore then you knew she was angry. Really, really angry.

"Come on, we gotta go. Now!" Dale grabbed Amanda and they ran from the scene of voluntary prostitution — it was the only way Dale could think of it now — scores of Amandas lining up like cattle to let themselves be milked of their cerebrospinal fluid, to allow the existence of functioning Hexads to continue, all so they could ensure that their lives didn't disappear in the blink of an eye.

"Help me," came the scream of the released Amanda behind them, shouting shrilly from the doorway, pointing at them as if there could be any mistake as to who she was accusing.

They ran away from the building, down land that made Dale, and Amanda too judging by the way she kept almost falling over, feel dizzy and disorientated. He could see the ground curving below and in front of them, as if he was running down a hill, but his body was telling him he was on the flat, so his posture was all wrong — he was trying to run like he was going downhill, holding himself back, leaning away from the steep slope, but in reality he was, for all intents and purposes, moving across flat ground.

The subtly subdued gravity didn't help — you noticed it a lot more when moving fast, and Dale knew that one of them was going to go crashing to the ground at any second if they tried to keep up such a pace.

"They know, they know," came the voice of the woman behind them, which to Dale sounded contradictory as surely they would have to tell Amanda sooner or later if she was to be a part of their terrible trade-off. Thoughts whirled as they ran, Dale holding onto Amanda tightly, slowing her down so she didn't fall.

What were they doing? How could they be a part of such a terrible giving of themselves? This was nothing more than an alternate version of the huge warehouse Amanda had told him of, the only difference being this time it was voluntary.

Why would they do it? Was it simply that they valued their lives more than those of the worlds they were allowing to be emptied by the continuing existence of Hexads?

It was a terrible price to pay, but maybe he would do the same in their shoes? Just what lengths would you go to when it came to ensuring your own survival?

No matter, he wasn't going to play any part in it — they were getting out of The Chamber, and now seemed like as good a time as any. They'd got the information they wanted, understood enough of what was going on to have made their minds up about whether or not they wanted to continue trying to put things right. Now there was no question: the rest of the universes were worth more than these pitiful, subjected women and—

Ooooof.

Dale hit the ground hard, dragged over by Amanda who was still trying to run away as fast as possible.

"Bugger," moaned Amanda, getting to her knees, looking down the sloping landscape in horror.

Dale grabbed her a little sharply and yanked her to her feet, caring less about manners than about the horde of Amandas descending on them from all directions.

"I don't think you are very happy about what we just did," said Dale.

Amanda stared at him crossly. "Seriously? You're trying to crack a joke at a time like this?"

Dale shrugged. "Gotta stay positive babe. Come on, to the Batmobile."

Amanda just stared at him, before Dale pulled her along and they started running again. The Amandas were closing and none of them looked in the least bit happy. They weren't running though — after all, what was the point? Dale realized this as the women took their time slowly closing in on them from all sides. Why run when there is nowhere to go?

"Okay, here goes nothing," said Dale. He crossed his fingers, said a little prayer, and thought harder than he'd ever thought before in his life. Dale scanned the area quickly; he saw their salvation and turned Amanda in the right direction before starting to run again. He punched the air and said, "Yes!"

"What? What did you do? What's happening?"

"There, in front of us."

Amanda shifted her gaze from focusing on her feet, trying to keep her balance better by not looking at the landscape. Dale pointed.

He'd done it.

"It's a hatch. A hatch!"

"Yup." Dale smiled. "I told you I had a plan. Can't believe it worked though, but goes to show that we were destined to get out of here. Come on, run, run fast. Keep looking at your feet, make sure they keep moving, and leave the rest up to me. You know what honey? You are one crazy lady."

Amanda took a moment to register what he meant, then said, "Those deranged bitches are not me, I am absolutely not like that."

"Language," admonished Dale.

"Sorry, but, well, this is a little stressful Dale, in case you hadn't noticed. We're being chased by hordes of me!"

"I know, almost there. Look up now and get ready to leave this hellhole."

Dale could see the opening in front of them, it couldn't be more than a hundred meter sprint now. All they had to do was keep on their feet and get in the damn hole. He held his breath as he picked up speed, letting it out once he realized he was starving his body of much needed oxygen. Also realizing he was extremely out of shape — too much booze, not enough exercise.

The dark patch on the ground was about two meters square, easily large enough to get through, the open hatch revealing the murky interior where he really hoped they could make their escape.

Amanda began to slow but Dale dragged her along, pulling at her arm until she increased her speed.

They were there, at the hole. Dale could make out a steep staircase leading down where the light was a subdued blue of the Hexad. "Go." He held on to Amanda's hand as she knelt then put her foot on a step, letting go as she clambered down, glancing to the right as she did so, her head now level with the ground.

"Hurry up Dale," she said, before she disappeared.

"I'm right behind you." Dale dropped on all fours, quickly inspected the hatch as he climbed in, and pressed a simple button before turning and beginning his descent. The hatch lifted up on pneumatics with a hiss and Dale turned and jumped down a couple of steps, crouching low as it slammed shut behind him, almost hitting him on the head.

The sound of the women above disappeared, replaced with the voice of what Dale knew was a version of himself going "Whooooooooooooooooooosh," then jumping before Dale could set eyes on him. He made a mental note to be sure to make that task a priority as soon as he was able.

"Where did that come from?" said Amanda breathlessly, bending over, hands on her thighs trying to force air into her lungs.

"I opened it," said Dale. "Told you I had a plan."

"You opened it? How?"

"You gave me the idea, all that talk about saying you would do things in the future so that they happened when you wanted. Well, I promised that in the future, after we escaped The Chamber, I would jump back to here at this time and open up the hatch. So that's what I did." Dale smiled smugly, he couldn't help himself. It was a damn good plan.

"You know what?"

"What?"

"Sometimes I like paradoxes." Amanda smiled, then moved to Dale and gave him a huge hug. "Dale, those women, those, ugh, women that were me, what do you think they would have done if they'd caught us?"

Dale held onto Amanda's arms and drew her back so they were looking at each other. "Honestly? I don't know. But they weren't you, okay?"

Amanda just nodded, clearly unconvinced.

"They weren't, honey, not any longer. Look, some of them were probably in here for years and years. I don't know how long it would take before anyone caved and began to do what they were doing, but who are we to judge? Maybe it's part of the rules: give up the spinal fluid or, you know..." Dale made a slicing action across his throat.

"Dale!"

"What? Look, I don't know what was going on there, what was driving them to do such a thing. Maybe they would just blink out of existence if they didn't do it, didn't stay a part of the system so that all the other universes could be available to jump into. I just don't know. And right now I don't care. I just want us to get out of here."

Amanda looked around the small room they found themselves in; Dale followed her gaze to find that the space was rather nondescript: there was the staircase, the closed hatch, blue lights dotted around the ceiling and not a lot else.

"Good idea, let's go." Dale made to move off toward a corridor to their right, but Amanda stopped him.

"Dale, where is here? Shouldn't we jump?"

"Jump? I don't think so, not yet. Not until we find out what the hell that place was. We're on the outside now and I want to find out what it is and where it is."

Amanda was beginning to panic, Dale too, even though he was trying to hide it, but he could see that his leg was shaking like he was trying to get a ferret out of his pants.

"What if there's an alarm? Someone might come."

"I expect they will, so let's be ready. First, can you come here?" Dale had moved back to the stairs while talking so Amanda followed him over. "Look, wait here for a minute. No, a second." Dale pulled a Hexad out of his bag, set the dials, grabbed hold of Amanda and pushed the dome. They jumped.

They were back exactly where they had been standing, and Dale released Amanda and ran up the stairs. He pushed the black button and the hatch began to lift.

"Okay, over here now."

They moved over to where Dale had heard himself a few moments ago and they both waited silently as they heard the sounds of countless Amandas shouting and screaming from within The Chamber. While they waited Dale set the Hexad again, staring at the 5. As they saw Amanda's feet come down the stairs Dale nodded to the Amanda beside him, and she held on as he went, "Whooooooooooooooooooooosh," and they jumped once more.

All there is is Time

Time Unknown

Dale stared at the 4 on the Hexad then put it back in his satchel, buckling it safely.

They were just a few meters down the corridor now, but all was quiet.

"What did you do?" asked Amanda.

"I jumped us to here but ten minutes in the past, just so we don't bump into ourselves coming down the stairs or doing the jump to open the hatch. Damn this stuff is confusing. Now there are three of us right here."

"Yeah, and how many new worlds did we just create with those jumps?"

"I don't even want to think about it, but it doesn't matter. Right?"

"Right," said Amanda, nodding vigorously, hair shining weirdly in the blue light. "Now we put an end to this, all of it. For good."

"So let's go find out what this 'Chamber' really is."

They made their way down the corridor, all metal struts and thick coils of cables running along the walls, somehow just as Dale expected to find the working parts of a man-made world where gravity made no sense. Actually, now Dale thought about it, he wondered if they were even on the floor at all. They clearly must still be spinning at the same speed as The Chamber for gravity to still be working, so at some point they were going to come to a place where they'd have to step off and come back to earth, the real earth, where it wrapped around the globe, not some convoluted aberration of what reality was meant to be.

Dale tried not to think about how he'd even jumped with the Hexad, he didn't know when they were, and it seemed to be showing the neutral setting, so he'd just acted like it meant nothing, made his settings and prayed — everything else was so messed up, so why not that too? It had worked, but he really wished he knew when they were.

They walked.

And walked, and walked.

They didn't talk; couldn't. The claustrophobic atmosphere got worse the more they walked — a seemingly endless corridor of blue light, ducts and cables, their feet echoing dully on the bare-metal floor. Dale was sure they had been going for miles, but the truth was he had no idea. Surely it had to end soon, had to run out once they'd walked the length of The Chamber? Or maybe it kept on running and running, leading them away? Could that be the answer?

Eventually there was a door up ahead, a red, innocuous fire exit door that they'd both seen countless times in countless buildings. It even had the sign above it and the push down bar halfway up the plain surface.

Or halfway down, thought Dale, smiling wryly to himself.

"What you smiling at?" asked Amanda, staring at him quizzically.

"Nothing. Fancy doing the honors?" Dale pointed at the bar.

"Ugh, no way. Be my guest."

Dale reached out for the bar, then pulled his hand back. "What if it just opens up into blank space? What if we're in a ship out a trillion miles into the Galaxy and we open the door and get sucked into a vacuum?"

"Dale, don't be daft, there aren't spaceships like this in our lifetime... Oh."

"Right? We could be anywhere, any time, in anything."

"Well, I doubt they'd have a simple red exit door if it meant we'd get sucked into space, would they?"

"I guess there's only one way to find out then."

Dale pressed down on the bar, sucked in his breath and closed his eyes.

~~~

"Shut the door, shut the door," shouted Amanda, almost hysterical.

Dale peeked and really wished he hadn't. It was impossible to get any kind of bearing or take in what was on the other side, apart from that it was a large open space and there were a lot of lights and machinery, maybe. Dale really couldn't begin to understand it in their current situation.

He didn't know how fast they were spinning but it was pretty fast, and judging by the bright blue light that was all around them then they were at the dome end of The Chamber.

Dale shut the door.

"Bloody hell, that made my head hurt more than a double paradox," panted Dale, trying to let gravity do what it did without him thinking about it.

"We're going really fast Dale. I never really thought about it in there but it must be quite fast for the gravity to work. How are we going to get out of here?"

"Same way we got in I guess. Jump."

"To where? We don't know where we are so we can't just jump to the ground around this damn thing."

"I couldn't, but you could. Come on Amanda, you're great at getting the jumps right, think you can do it?"

Amanda thought for a minute, gnawing at the corner of her lip, absentmindedly brushing her hair away from her eyes — it was a mess from the rotation when they'd opened the door. "Maybe, but we'll have to open the door again and somehow try to get some bearings, see where the floor is at least."

"That's the spirit. Look, maybe if you lie down then it won't be so disorientating? Think that would help?" Dale had no idea if it would but somehow it sounded right, like it might work.

Amanda stared at him dubiously, but obviously didn't have a better idea so just nodded. She got down on all fours, head facing the door and then said, "Do it."

Dale opened the door and immediately felt the strong wind, an effect of the spin, and Amanda began moaning as she pushed forward little by little before lying prone. Dale looked out again, trying to make sense of something, anything, but all he felt was dizzy. It was like being on the worst fairground ride ever. He'd never been able to ride anything that went fast, even swings left him green and feeling extremely sick — this was like his idea of a really bad day out magnified a thousand-fold.

He tried to just focus on looking at what was down for him, and things began to slowly fall into a little bit of order. They were clearly in some huge space, and there were a series of long girders, criss-crossed by struts maybe, that were running away from the dome, but he found it really hard to make out much at all, and was sure of even less.

"Close it," croaked Amanda from the floor, her words almost lost to the void and the wind. She crawled back gingerly and moved to the side; Dale battled against the pressure difference but eventually slammed the door shut.

Time to Leave

Time Unknown

Amanda crawled back further away from the door, letting out faint moaning sounds, like the disorientation was a physical pain.

"Are you okay? Did you see anything?" asked Dale.

"Give me a moment, that's made me really dizzy. I feel sick." Amanda sat up slowly, then stood.

"Whoa, careful!" Dale grabbed her just before she fell over. Her face was ashen and she looked like she was going to throw up any second.

"Ugh, my head's still spinning." Amanda slumped to the floor, sitting with her legs out straight, head bent, hair tumbling in all directions. "I'll be fine, it just takes a little getting used to."

Dale didn't want to hurry Amanda but at the same time he knew that just hanging around like this wasn't a good idea — they had to be ready to jump at a moment's notice. Who knew what kind of alarm bells they'd set off opening the door? If they hadn't been watched the whole time they were inside The Chamber anyway.

Glancing around nervously, Dale searched for hidden cameras now that the thought was in his mind.

"Okay, I'm fine now."

"Good. What did you see?"

"It was hard to really focus, we're moving pretty fast you know? But I could see the ground. It's quite a way away but at least the room this mad thing is in makes some sense. Come on, let's jump." Amanda pulled out a Hexad and set the dials. She grabbed Dale and with a nod to each other, and no sound from Dale, Amanda put her hand on the Hexad's flashing dome. Dale placed his over hers; together they pressed down.

~~~

Dale hadn't even thought such cavernous rooms were possible, but then, he'd never been so rich that money and numbers became little more than abstract concepts. Cray had obviously spent a handsome sum on The Chamber, but even that probably paled in comparison to what had been used to build the facility that housed it. It was like a mad scientist's idea of heaven.

They had jumped onto the floor, a real floor, where things made sense — there were walls, a ceiling, and gravity felt normal. The space, what Dale could only think of as a cave really, was so large however that it was hard to come to terms with — such proportions were as alien as The Chamber itself.

He had guessed roughly correctly about its size: at least a mile and a half long, half a mile in diameter, and it took up but a small portion of the space as a whole — it must have been miles long, well over a mile high. Seeing The Chamber from the outside made you appreciate just what a miracle of engineering it was. The scale was staggering, a man-made object that was bigger than anything ever built in the history of humanity, in his history anyway.

They stared at it open-mouthed, both trying to understand it better, to let it give up its secrets. They were standing about a third of the way down its length on a bare rock floor that was perfectly smooth, polished so it shone in the strange blue light that emanated from the dome of The Chamber. Dale could make out the shape, the simple cylinder, blunt at one end, curved at the other, just like a Hexad, but there the similarity ended. There were numerous ducts, groups of cables thicker than a human torso, and what he assumed were passageways for maintenance, like the one they had walked through, running its entire length, making the thing as a whole far less elegant from the outside than it was inside.

What was most fascinating was the way the unnatural environment actually functioned. On the inside Dale couldn't have imagined how it actually rotated to create the artificial gravity, and had seriously wondered whether they were out in space, hurtling toward unknown stars, the gravity created by some kind of thruster system, not that he knew the first thing about how such an effect could be created or even if it was possible, but he'd never imagined the whole thing was set up inside one large room of its own. Room seemed such a petty word, more like gigantic mind-bending futuristic uber-cavern.

Jutting out from the far end of the cavern were giant poles, impossibly thick, jet black and shining like they were covered in oil. They ran directly to either end of The Chamber, connected with numerous clamps each as large as a soccer pitch. The clamps themselves were connected by a series of concentric rings, originating at the thick poles but then running in series down at least a third of The Chamber at either end. The poles were spinning flawlessly, turning The Chamber, the clamps branching off to provide further structural support. It was hard to see exactly what was going on as the whole thing was simply too vast to understand, and Dale wondered how far the poles ran through the bedrock to be able to provide such immense support, he didn't even dwell on what was actually fueling them, it would be something gigantic and immensely powerful that was for sure.

It was overwhelming and dizzying in both complexity and the sheer audacity of such an endeavor.

Thinking about it was like trying to unravel the secrets of time travel itself — a dead-end that simply left Dale scratching at his head in puzzlement and wonder that such an epic project had ever been dreamed of, let alone undertaken.

And why?

Above all else that one question remained unanswered: why had this been done? What purpose did it serve? Or was it the simple manifestation of madness, power and greed of one man? Did Cray really build such a thing?

Why? Why? Why?

"Can you get us back here if we need to return?" Dale turned to Amanda but she was lost in the madness all around her. He put an arm to her shoulder. "Amanda?"

She turned and took a few seconds to focus back to a sight as normal as Dale's face. "Huh?"

"I said can you jump us back here if we need to return?"

"Yes, not that I'd want to. Why?"

"Because I think we should go. This place is insane, and creepy as hell. And I get the feeling we are very much unwanted here. I'm amazed that nobody has come and..." Dale saw movement out of the corner of his eye and turned to see a figure in the distance walking slowly toward them. "Time to go." Dale nodded in the direction of the figure; Amanda turned to look.

"Right, where to?"

"Home?"

"Home," agreed Amanda, fiddling with the Hexad still in her hand. Dale stared at the flashing five before Amanda grabbed his arm.

~~~

1 Day Future

Dale blinked at the change to the light, then found himself staring at the familiar sight of the apple tree in his garden, masses of flowers in full bloom in the borders, the fragrance seeming almost too normal after the alien environment they'd spent the last day in. A robin landed on a branch, eager to see what the new arrivals were up to, seemingly unperturbed by the sudden appearance of two rather disheveled looking humans in his garden.

A squirrel ran for the cover of the conifer hedge, startled out of its plans to steal the seed that was taunting it from a feeder hanging from the tree, now dangerously low as it hadn't been filled for some time.

"I think I'll feed the birds. Oh and it's tomorrow. Um, I mean we jumped to one day into the future — for you. Ugh, I keep forgetting I'm ten years older than you now," said Amanda, before she went to gather up the feeders and wandered over to the shed where the bird seed was stored in plastic bins to stop the mice overrunning the shed and making it a permanent home.

"Um, okay." *Guess she wants to feel normal. Why a day in the future? And is it one day in the future if we've spent longer than that in other timelines? We have, haven't we? Ugh!* Dale just stood there, feeling the sun on his face, a gentle breeze stirring his hair, the familiar sound of neighbors mowing their lawns in the distance welcoming him back to suburbia, to normality. *So it's just another Sunday?*

Dale left Amanda to her chores and wandered towards the house, feeling completely bizarre digging the keys out of his bag and unlocking the entrance to the kitchen that led out onto the side garden where they normally sat and drank coffee. Such a simple thing felt weird, like he didn't do 'normal' anymore.

"Coffee?"

"Yes please," shouted Amanda, as she finished hanging the feeders on the tree.

Dale could see the squirrel sat on the fence behind the hedge, and smiled as the robin landed and began to sift through the seed, discarding what it didn't want onto the lawn, greedily eating the sunflower seeds it prized most. Dale smiled and wandered into the kitchen.

"Shit, I forgot." Dale was staring at a festering lump of meat on the kitchen table, dark pus and thick slime oozing onto the tiles. There were tiny tracks of viscera all around the lumps that had dribbled off the table, probably from a mouse that had feasted on the stinking bounty, decomposing rapidly in the warm summer heat.

Welcome home Dale, welcome back to the madness.

Welcome Home

1 Day Future

Dale did what any sensible time traveler would do: he ignored the stinking mound, sidestepped the goop on the tiles, opened the fridge, got the milk out, took the cap off and sniffed cautiously. "Not too funky."

Once the coffee was made he took it outside where the air was slightly less foul.

Amanda was sat staring into the distance, lost in her thoughts.

"Don't go into the kitchen, it's a mess. Messier than yesterday." She stared at him, eyebrows raised in question. "You don't want to know, trust me."

"Okay," said Amanda wearily.

"Did that all really just happen? How the hell are we supposed to sort this mess out?" Dale didn't know where to start, what to think, what to do next. Life was too surreal to make any kind of sense any longer.

"We stick to the plan," said Amanda, jaw set firmly. "We stop all this, stop everything that has happened just because I used a Hexad and jumped back to find you Dale. I can't believe it, I can't believe that everything had been put right by another me and another you and then I ruined it all by just wanting to come home. It's not fair, it's just not fair." Amanda was in tears — flowing freely like they had been building and building until she had the time to vent the sadness of every Amanda that had ever been, every version of her that had lived then died at the hand of another her, or wiped from existence when she terminated countless parallel universes when she stopped the production of Hexads from ever happening.

Now it was all back — one jump to find the man she loved and she'd opened up all of it again, setting in motion a chain of events that had created countless alternate universes where madness reigned and Amandas willingly gave up their bodies to insanity just so they could survive.

The floodgates were open: Amanda looked like she could cry tears for centuries.

"I know honey, I know. We will, we'll stick to the plan and we'll sort this mess out. Then it will be just you and me again, peaceful, hanging out in the garden, trying to stop that damn squirrel nicking all the bird seed. Look, there it is again the cheeky bugger, the feeder's half empty already."

Amanda wiped her tears and turned to watch the squirrel hanging upside down from the branch the feeder was suspended on, tipping it sideways so seed spilled onto the lawn.

"You can't beat a squirrel, they're like Tom Cruise from Mission Impossible. Doodle-ooh, doodle-ooh, da da." Amanda hummed the theme tune as they smiled and watched the squirrel in action.

Dale sipped his coffee: maybe the milk had been off after all. He wondered if he was even in his own timeline, and if another version of him and Amanda had just this minute left and gone to the pub, not wanting to deal with the pulp in the kitchen, or maybe they were in their right world, and everything was just normal, for now. He very much doubted it but you had to have hope. What else was left? Dale thought for a minute, then remembered it was Sunday, so maybe this was their home, their time.

"Is this home Amanda? Our home, our world?"

"Dale, I don't know. I simply don't know anymore. I'm sorry."

"Hush, it's okay, it's not your fault. You can't be blamed for wanting to find this gorgeous hunk of a man. Nobody could blame you for that." Dale smiled, then flexed a bicep.

"True, how could I resist?" Amanda grinned then said what they were both thinking: "Let's go somewhere else, somewhere away from here, just until we know it's home again."

"Good idea, let me just put the mugs away, don't want to leave things any different to how they were when we arrived. Just in case..." Dale left the rest unsaid, he didn't really know what the just in case was, but if he'd learned one thing it was not to mess with timelines that may not be your own.

With the mugs rinsed and put back in the cupboard Dale went back outside. Amanda was ready, she held the Hexad out so Dale grabbed her by the hand, did the appropriate "Whoosh," and they vanished.

The squirrel dropped to the ground to feed on its prize; the robin landed on the table, cocking its head and checking if there was anything worth eating.

~~~

Cray scowled at the squirrel as he appeared next to the apple tree, before it did a double-take and scampered into the hedge. He walked down to the house and cupped his hands to the kitchen window, peering inside. He noted the mass of flesh, noticed the condensation on the spout of the kettle and muttered something about being too late before adjusting his Hexad and disappearing.

An Interlude

Present Day

Dale and Amanda had been talking for hours, but it didn't really get them anywhere. However much they discussed The Chamber, and the vast space it was housed in, they kept just coming back to the same question: why?

Why build it? Why were Amandas inside it when they could have been contained in a less adventurous prison, and why was it called a Hexad, or The Hexad as the Amanda had called it?

They needed answers, but the only person that could provide them was Cray, or maybe The Caretaker, both of whom they couldn't simply go and ask.

They were on their own, they had to figure it out for themselves, or not — they were both past the point of caring, all they wanted was for it to be over.

They talked and talked, the normalcy of the people enjoying their vacation on the beach they had jumped to making their recent adventures more surreal by the minute — nothing but a bad dream they had surely awoken from.

But they hadn't, one look inside their bags was enough proof that their life was far from normal, Amanda's much stranger than Dale's. After all, she'd been caught up in the madness for over ten years now, and just when she thought she had finally put it all behind her it simply got worse. Nothing could have prepared her for the consequences of her actions and now she was faced with having to deal with countless universes, all devoid of people in the end, that popped into existence when she began to mess with time, leading to such far-reaching consequences that all came back to her simply wanting a life of her own once more.

She told Dale all of this and more, explaining as best she could the feelings roiling inside of her, waiting to spill over into madness. More, there was a deep sense of shame and guilt about putting her own needs first, but Dale would have none of it — she had done nothing wrong, she wasn't responsible for the actions of others.

First it had been Hector and his mad giant Laffer ruining the future for everyone, now it was an incarnation of Cray, an evil Cray in one of endless worlds, each of them now playing out in who knew how many different ways? She could hardly be the one responsible for that — it was the universes, not them. Nothing more. Who could say they had already fought the Universe and won? She could, and that was certainly no mean feat.

"And now you will do it again. Well, we will. Together, as always."

"Always," said Amanda, wriggling her toes in the sand, smiling at Dale as he tried to get grains out of his mouth.

"How does sand find its way everywhere like this?" muttered Dale, poking his tongue out and rubbing it with a finger. "What?" Dale asked as Amanda stifled a laugh.

"My hero."

"Yeah, well, it's annoying."

"Come on, let's go eat, that fish still smells amazing. A drink would be nice too."

"Now you're talking." Dale jumped to his feet then began hopping around from one foot to another. "Hot hot hot."

"Put something on your feet you idiot," laughed Amanda.

"Then my socks will be full of sand," complained Dale.

"Oh, the things you have to worry about. Come on, you're buying."

They walked up the beach, at least Amanda did, Dale hopped about like he had serious issues.

He guessed that he did. He really did.

Back to the...

Present Day

As Dale leaned back in his chair, sipping on a cold beer and letting his meal digest, he couldn't help wondering what it had been like to have saved the world once before with an Amanda. The woman opposite him had said that he wasn't exactly the Dale she had known, but that he was as close as it was possible to be without actually being him, so Dale assumed that whatever adventure he and Amanda had been on then he, the one thinking these thoughts, had been on one very similar indeed.

It felt strange to think of yourself as not the right you, just as the Amanda he'd woken up with just a few days ago wasn't the right Amanda, even though they'd pretty much saved the Universe together, or a couple so close to them that it didn't matter.

What did get very confusing was that once they'd stopped the proliferation of Hexads then all the universes were supposed to have collapsed in on themselves, gone as if they'd never been, so how exactly had he been alive to be aware of anything? The mere fact that Amanda jumped into countless universes to find him was how — just by doing it she brought the almost parallel worlds into existence. But it was still an impossible concept to come to terms with: that he had never existed until Amanda showed up with her Hexad and everything began to go into free-fall.

How could entire universes just pop into existence fully-formed like that? Full of pasts and futures just waiting to be messed with so easily? And as soon as they succeeded? Rather, if they succeeded? Then all but one Dale and Amanda would cease to exist, with no memory of what had happened as it would never have happened if they put an end to Hexads for good.

So did it really matter which version of them it was? He supposed not. After all, if they succeeded then they wouldn't remember anyway, as there would be nothing to remember. And yet... Amanda remembered, didn't she? Remembered the fractured timelines, the madness. Maybe that was the problem: if she'd never remembered then everything would have been fine. No Hexads, no countless versions of everything and everyone stretching off into infinity, making a mockery of all that he'd believed to be true and absolute his whole life.

Madness. It was sheer madness.

Enough thinking, we've got to deal with this, deal with it once and for all.

"Let's do this thing."

"Let's get on with it."

"Haha, snap," said Dale.

"I guess it's time then?" said Amanda.

"Afraid so. You ready?"

"Wait, I just need to pay. Um, Dale, don't suppose you have any Bahamian dollars?"

"Oops, no. Well, I suppose jumping without paying isn't going to hurt, just this once. After all, if we sort this mess out this universe won't exist in all likelihood anyway."

"Dale!" admonished Amanda. "That's not the point. These men work hard to feed us, it's not right to not pay. We have to."

"Fine. Wait here." Dale pulled a Hexad out of his satchel, flickered and then pulled out three bills from his jeans.

"Happy?"

"Yes, thank you Dale."

"Never thought I'd use time travel just to make a visit to the Bureau De Change," muttered Dale, pushing his chair back and standing.

"It's all about standards Dale. First it's running out without paying for food, then before you know it it's the death of civilization as we know it."

Yeah, it's exactly the same, thought Dale, knowing better than to say it out loud.

"Let's walk down the beach, just, you know, in case it's the last time we ever get to do something like that."

Amanda smiled and they walked onto the cooling sand arm in arm, two content vacationers walking off their evening meal.

~ ~ ~

They made their way along the shoreline, saying nothing, just enjoying the atmosphere of the isolated beach. The only sounds were the waves lapping languidly and the shouting of the staff at the open-air restaurant.

Dale looked longingly at the beach, wondering if he'd ever see one again, smiling at the man in a rather uncomfortable looking suit as he walked close to the water, skipping out of the way as the tide threatened to get his shoes wet.

Wait. Shoes? Suit? It took moments to register, and Dale slowly followed the figure up to his head. He fumbled with his buckle then pulled out a Hexad, a 4 flashing. "Time to go honey, we have company."

Amanda looked where Dale pointed and grabbed hold of him moments before they jumped, leaving Cray striding towards empty air. He really didn't look very happy, then he was practically livid as the waves washed over his tan shoes.

~~~

2016 Years Future

"I thought something felt different," said Dale, slipping the parang back into the sheath as Amanda did the same with her short sword. They'd jumped away, ending up at home once more, but then Amanda immediately jumped them back to the beach to where they'd hidden their blades as it wasn't really the done thing to sunbathe with dangerous weapons and they certainly didn't need the hassle of standing out like a pair of outlaws. Amanda smiled at him and then said, "Ready?" and with a nod they jumped again.

"Watch it," shouted a man in a white jumpsuit as Dale stepped aside before getting run over by the electric buggy with a huge trailer towed behind.

"Sorry," said Dale, staring at Amanda, questioning where she'd taken them to; when as well. Amanda just stared past him so Dale turned and mouthed a silent, "Oh."

The Chamber was open all along one side, like a window on the mysterious world running its entire length, thousands of people milling about inside, vehicles of all description moving like insects on an oversized hollowed-out tree trunk. All around them was chaos. People of all description in all manner of clothes and performing all manner of duties were working frantically, sauntering around open-mouthed, or running like their lives depended on it.

It was like a circus with little in the way of order as far as Dale could see, but there would be offices full of countless bureaucrats to run such an epic undertaking, Dale had no doubt about that.

"Come on, move over here," said Amanda, grabbing Dale and dragging him away from the open space they had materialized into.

She led them to a huge wall of crates and containers, towering over them, stacked higher than Dale thought was safe. It was like a maze in amongst them, the walkways large enough for machinery to enter, but it was quiet — they made their way deeper into the steel labyrinth.

The sounds of industry became muffled, yet still towering above everything was the sight of The Chamber, open for all to see, the interior bare metal, conduits, ducts and things Dale had no name for snaking across the huge sheets of metal that constituted the bare-bones of the world-to-be.

More Madness

2016 Years Future

Seeing the partial Chamber made Dale feel sick — exposed as it was, the sense of scale became more acute. Being able to put it into perspective with the chaos that surrounded it brought home quite how vast it was. All Dale could think of was that it was like mankind building some kind of Ark, ready to traverse the cosmos, sending humanity on a mission into the void.

The huge thing towered above the stacks of containers, dominating everything wherever you looked. Dale watched tiny ants that were people and huge trucks with tires as large as houses, looking like little more than tiny toy vehicles — it was too much to cope with, he had to look away, he couldn't take in the scale, the work involved.

How long had it been going on? Something of this magnitude would take forever.

Come to think if it, when were they now? He'd simply put his trust in Amanda, knowing she was much better at gauging these things than he was.

"When is this Amanda?"

"It's a few thousand years into our future; I just guessed really. We're a little too late, don't you think? Should we jump back further?"

"I'm not sure. If we're going to stop this then I suppose that it wouldn't hurt to watch for a while, see who's in charge, what the setup is here. It might help."

"Okay, but we aren't going to be able to just wander around, not for long anyway. Sooner or later somebody will ask questions."

"How about up there?" Dale pointed up.

"The Chamber? Are you mad?"

"No, on top of the stack. I never want to go inside that thing again. Ever."

Amanda visibly calmed. She obviously had the same misgivings about the inside-out world-in-construction as he did. "Good idea. We can watch what goes on hopefully without being seen. And if we are it will take a while for anyone to get us down. Let's do it."

Dale held on, something that was becoming all too familiar. They jumped.

~~~

The height made next to no difference when it came to The Chamber — it still dominated the vast space, but it gave them a bird's-eye view of what was happening — it really was pandemonium. It appeared chaotic, but there was order underneath the chaos, that much was clear. Supervisors wandered around what appeared to be their sections, directing workers. Vehicles of all description were constantly moving, bringing materials and labor, and even as they watched, the open gash in The Chamber was slowly closing up as massive machines moved even larger sheets into position while various crews worked frantically to seal the interior.

As they lay on the top of the stack of containers, Dale took in the scenes on the ground, noticing a huge mountain of what appeared to simply be soil being added to by scores of massive dump trucks, the pile spreading out, a man-made mountain soon to be inside The Chamber. Dale wondered how you could spread soil over the surface, he supposed it would have to wait until it was rotating.

Other activities were lost in a haze, the space so vast that it seemed to actually have its own micro-climate. Dale was sure that there were actual clouds high above, which would be a real concern he would have thought, with so much machinery and electronic equipment involved. The issue was soon explained though when far up in the sky something changed and massive vents roared into life, a deafening sound piercing the background noise as the cloud was sucked away. Even so far below he could feel a wash of fresh, dry air brush his face, a collective sigh echoing around the cavern as the humidity drained away and arid air took its place.

They watched for over an hour, whispering to each other about the sights they saw, trying to make sense of it, trying to find a way for the knowledge to help them in destroying the thing, halting Hexad productivity and Hexad existence once and for all. How were they to do it? Where to begin? What would guarantee they succeeded?

"We need to find out what this has to do with our Hexads," said Amanda. "Obviously this is the root cause of all our troubles. Somehow this is what everything leads back to. It's like Hector and how he produced Hexads, only very different. But the same thing applies: this is to get the spinal fluid from all those versions of me, and somehow it then produces the machines. It's got to be a part of it."

"Maybe not at first though," mused Dale. "For all we know they are building this for an entirely different purpose and then just hit on the whole Hexad thing."

"I don't think so, look." Amanda pointed down not far from where they were hiding. It was Cray, stood amongst a group of men in all manner of bizarre outfits, Cray, as always, in his enduring plain suit. They watched in silence as the sycophants laughed at whatever was being said, nodded sagely at words of wisdom, and smiled plastically at the end of the meeting. Just as they were about to disperse a noise came thundering out of the air.

Bing-bong, came the beginning of what was sure to be an announcement, as if they were in a supermarket and the special offers were about to be read out. The air filled with a beautiful female voice, but what she had to say was far from beautiful.

"Ladies and gentleman, please note that progress is lagging behind by at least seventeen hours now. It is in your best interests to ensure that we meet our work quota and that The Chamber is completed exactly on time. Remember, this is your future we are creating here. The prize of a free Hexad for all involved is a promise Mr. Cray wishes to keep, but please do note that your contracts expressly state that this is conditional on work being carried out as efficiently as possible and that there is absolutely no delay concerning the deadline. Thank you."

Bing-bong.

Dale turned to Amanda, eyebrow raised. There was no doubt now what was going on. The room exploded into an increased hive of activity, noise levels rising as workers and supervisors shouted orders and picked up the pace.

So this was how Hexads became common to the masses — once The Chamber was complete countless thousands would be given one, and Dale was sure that many millions more would be sold, if they hadn't already been, to furnish such a massive undertaking.

"Of course," said Dale, to himself as much as to Amanda.

"What?"

"It's obvious. Cray could simply keep jumping about once he came to the future and showed them what he possessed. He could have jumped back countless times, got his hands on numerous Hexads, or whatever, even steal a few, the ones in the trunk anyways, and he could sell them each for the price of a country.

"He will already be rich beyond imagination, that's why this is possible, and once it's done he's clearly going to go into mass production, give thousands away and probably sell millions upon millions making him ruler of the whole bloody world."

"He'll probably own the world," said Amanda. "It makes sense Dale, he's made a fortune and now is going all-out to ensure that he can never be stopped and that he can get what he needs from Amandas as and when he wants."

"But why this? Why something so..."

"Big?"

"Yeah, big. There's more to this Amanda, a lot more. Let's do a little exploring."

"I don't think so, I think you should stay right here."

Dale and Amanda jumped at the voice. It was Cray, even though they could see him down below.

They turned, and there he was: same suit, same hair; but older, and a lot angrier.

Dale didn't even try to reach for his weapon as it wasn't much use anyway, not when you had a gun pointed directly at you and the love of your life.

Dale sighed. "Fancy giving us a minute to think about what to do next?"

Cray shook his head, motioning with the gun for them to get to their feet. "No funny business, I'm really not in the mood. If you think I'm going to let you two just run around like this then you are sorely mistaken. You should have left well enough alone; it's not your business."

"Not our business?" spat Amanda. "Not our business when you are keeping those women in that abomination of a thing and ruining everything?"

"Like I said, I won't let you interfere. Now, we have to go. I can't very well have me down there getting involved in this, now can I? Never mind, I didn't, so I won't. Hold hands," ordered Cray.

Dale and Amanda held on to each other tightly as Cray stepped close, gun in one hand, Hexad in the other. He took hold of Amanda by the hair, pulling her head back, and pointed the gun square in her face before turning to Dale and saying, "Press the dome down. Now."

Dale pressed it. They jumped.

Secrets Revealed

Time Unknown

Dale was expecting to jump to some dingy basement where Cray would tie them up and maybe torture them while laughing manically, telling them of his plans for world domination in every possible timeline, at every possible point in history, so it came as quite a surprise to find himself in the same vast space they'd just been in, except now it was devoid of the mass of people, the machines, the noise, and The Chamber. He could tell by the look on Amanda's face that she was as shocked as he was.

Cray still had the gun however, and it was still pointed at them both.

"You know, you two are really rather slippery. I've been chasing you for some time now, and it's beginning to get a little bit tiresome."

"You could always just stop," said Dale.

Cray stared at him like he was about to smack him across the head with the gun, and Dale noticed a twitch of the arm. He flinched as he waited for a blow that never came. Cray seemed to get himself back under control and swept his free hand around the enormous room. "You see this? This is the beginning of it all, the start of what I know you have seen. Have you any idea the kind of organization it took to get this kind of a space ready for what I did? No, of course you don't, you don't know anything. This is the largest undertaking of its kind in the history of any world, let alone what comes next. And you, you two idiots, you want to ruin it all, put an end to a great future that changes the entire course of history forever."

"And gets everyone in all the universes killed," said Amanda, surprisingly calm and composed.

"No, it doesn't. I don't know what it is that you think happens, but it isn't the end, not really. I've seen it all, seen what happens when I bring Hexads to the masses, seen the mess that it causes at first, the closing down of timelines, the disappearance of humanity, but that's not the end of it all. I've seen the future, the far future, and it is once again populated with people, just different. My family. And yours." Cray pointed at Amanda, who shook her head, not understanding.

"Well, maybe not you exactly Amanda, but as we know there are plenty of yous out there, jumping about in time, creating universes, disrupting everything and killing yourself in a million different ways, but plenty of you end up in The Chamber, where it all begins. You try to destroy yourself but all it means is that more of you are drawn into that beautiful world, and there you make your choice. You accept your new life, or you don't, it's as simple as that."

"You built it on purpose, to get Amandas to live inside. Why?" Dale had to know, he simply had to.

"Dale, this isn't the movies where I tell you all my secrets right before you escape."

"Why not? Why not tell us how Amandas jump there rather than just disappearing because of a paradox? Why not tell us how it works, what it's really for? What difference does it make if all you're going to do is kill us?"

"My dear boy, how simplistic your view of the world is. Why on earth would I tell you all that? You might want explanations but I'm afraid you won't be getting them from me. What I build here is the most important piece of science and human experimentation ever performed, that ever will be performed. It is the single most important place on the planet, housing the greatest gift humanity will ever know, and you would like for me to spell it all out for you, tell you of my accomplishment, just like that?"

"Um, well, yes please." Dale knew he was playing a dangerous game, but he refused to bow down and act like the nervous child he actually felt — he would stand up and be a man, even if his palms were sweating and he feared Cray was going to do terrible things to Amanda before his eyes.

"Sorry, no dice. Oh, and about that killing thing, what kind of a man do you take me for? I'm not going to kill you, I can't."

"Well, that's... good," said Dale.

"Hmm, maybe. I'm not about to risk all that I do, all that I have done should I say, by killing you two. Amanda, it is you that started all this, although if I'm honest I'm not exactly sure why or how, but no matter, you must survive so that all that has happened will happen again, and you were to spend your time with company you are sure to like: other Amandas. But after your rather splendid escape, which I must congratulate you on, I'm afraid there is going to have to be a change of plan."

Dale didn't like the sound of it one bit, and he also wondered just what it was that Cray actually knew. This Cray would have lived a life where there was a different version of Dale and Amanda, a world where he'd found the trunk full of Hexads after the rather daft attempt to follow what they thought they were supposed to do and call the bomb squad in. After that he would have got his first Hexad and that would have been the beginning of the future Cray lived.

But what did he know now? He knew enough to jump back and to try to set events right, but most of it would have been with him acting blind to the change in events caused by Amanda returning. It was too confusing to understand, with worlds disappearing and then being recreated in an instant, just because Amanda jumped. It was all part of the same thing, all wrapped up tight in a mystery it would never be possible to solve.

"Before you do whatever it is you're going to do," said Dale, trying to buy some time, just on the off chance something happened that could save them, "have you really considered the consequences?"

"Dale, I know where you are heading, and it won't work," said Cray, almost, but not quite, smiling.

"Hold on, I haven't finished yet."

"Fine," sighed Cray. "Continue."

"Are you really sure that doing anything but letting us go is the right course of action?"

"Ha."

"No, wait. Look, you are here, right, so are we, and so is The Chamber and countless Hexads in the future. Right?" Cray just nodded; Dale continued. "So, that means you win, doesn't it? It means that we don't get to save the world and stop you from doing this madness."

"Not yet, no. But you stopped different ways of Hexads being in existence, so you could do it again."

"That's my point, we can't because we are here. If we do what we want to in the future then this conversation won't be happening, will it? No, it won't because it won't have ever happened."

"Dale, do you take me for a fool?"

"No, I'm being serious. We've seen it, been inside your Chamber, seen the Amandas, all of it, so there is a future where you do all that. That's the one you've already lived, right?" Cray just nodded, maybe Dale was actually convincing him? "So, if you leave well enough alone, leave us alone, then that future comes to pass, already has. But if you kill us, or do anything else with us, then how do you know that what you do won't change everything and you will fail?" Dale smiled, sure his words had an effect on Cray, maybe saving them from whatever he had in mind for them.

"Dale, Dale, Dale, good try my friend, but I am no newcomer to this. I understand the sheer impossibility of ever coming to terms with how time travel works. I gave up even trying a long time ago. Sure, I have lived a blessed life so far, constructing The Chamber, collecting the Amandas, all of it, so yes, all of that has already happened, and I know it could be changed, but it hasn't, has it? No, so whatever I do to you now will have absolutely no bearing on those events."

"It will, and you know why?"

"Please, enlighten me," said Cray, actually smiling at Dale's vain attempt to win their freedom.

"Because it already has. You doing this, jumping back to get the Hexads, it's led to this, so this is how it plays out now. We will win."

"No, you won't. And you don't get it do you? It may be me who invents the Hexad, but only because I knew of their existence because of you two. So there you go, what do you have to say to that?"

"What I say to that is where's your gun Cray?"

Cray took a moment to register what Dale was saying, knowing that he still had his gun in his hand.

Dale smiled wide, nodding his head at the gun now held by Cray's side.

Slowly, realization dawned; Cray's eyes widened. He lifted the gun up in front of his face before throwing away the plastic replica in disgust.

Dale held out a hand to Amanda who took it, almost in shock, and then Dale reached out a hand and caught the Hexad that appeared in the air a split-second later.

"It's not just you that can play God Cray. We're coming for you buddy, so you better get ready."

"I'll be ready Dale, you can count on it."

With a farewell smile, Dale pressed down the dome by pushing it at his chest and even managed a "Whooooooooooooooooooooosh," before Cray was left alone with nothing but a vision of the plastic gun sliding across the polished floor as he kicked it away in disgust at himself for being fooled so easily.

A Vast
Improvement

Present Day

"I think I'm finally getting the hang of this," smirked Dale, fiddling with his Hexad, disappearing for a split second then reappearing beside Amanda with a very real gun held carefully pointed at the floor. "Do you know how to work these things?"

"Dale, can you please warn me if you're going to jump? We need to stick together," admonished Amanda.

"Sorry, but it wasn't like I could tell you what I was going to do in front of Cray."

"That's okay, and wow, that was pretty clever."

"Yeah, gotta say I'm surprised myself; I got it all spot on. Well, obviously, I didn't even notice, did you? And Cray didn't."

"I didn't notice, no. How did you do it?"

"Simple, I just promised myself that I'd do what I just went and did then, which was jump back and take Cray's gun while he wasn't looking, and he did go a little mad by the way and nearly had me, so I jumped away and then just jumped right back to the very second I took it, just a fraction after so I didn't land on myself, and replaced it with a fake one I got from our time. Kind of amazing, right?"

"Amazing? It's totally incredible. You saved us." Amanda smiled, then looked warily at the gun. I think you should keep that pointed well away from us, and I think it works just by flipping off the... Haha, who am I kidding? I have no idea."

Dale stared at the gun, like he had after taking it to try to match it with a replica, seeing the same Heckler brand and various numbers as well as P99 at the base of the grip, if that was what it was called. Past that he had no idea how to work it apart from that you pulled the trigger and there was usually some kind of safety feature with a gun so you didn't shoot yourself. After giving it the once-over he decided that the best thing was to not use it if at all possible — he wasn't even sure if it had bullets and had no way of re-loading anyway. Dale stuffed it into his satchel nervously, praying the trigger couldn't accidentally be pulled.

"I think we need to find out how to use this thing, otherwise one of us could end up getting shot," said Dale, feeling really uncomfortable knowing it was so close.

"I think so too." Amanda shifted to his left side, just so the gun wasn't anywhere near her.

"Thanks for the vote of confidence," said Dale, not blaming her one bit.

"Let's just go somewhere quiet and have a look Online so we can at least use the thing." Dale took off his weapon, Amanda did the same, and Dale scuffed a shallow depression underneath the nearest tree and covered them up with leaves. He set his Hexad and they jumped.

~~~

"Perfect landing, I really am getting good at this."

"Took a while," said Amanda, smiling.

"I'm like fine wine, I—"

"Cost too much and usually disappoint."

"Hey, no fair."

"Just joking, you did amazing. Where are we?"

"Present day, stood in the disabled parking space outside the local cafe offering free WiFi."

"Let's go check out YouTube then."

Ten minutes later they had a rudimentary understanding of how to fire the gun, so once outside Dale jumped them back into the woods and rather nervously made the gun safe — he was lucky he hadn't shot himself, or both of them, as the gun really was as ready to kill as he feared it had been.

"Okay, done. Let's stick to the blades, guns make me very nervous."

"Me too, but it let us get away so that's something."

"Yeah, but if Cray had it in for us before then now he's going to be seriously annoyed."

"Dale, we will beat him, I know we will. I wish he'd told us though, how it all worked."

"I have an idea about that, and it might even work."

"Well, good, be a bit pointless if it didn't." Amanda smiled and gave Dale a hug, holding on like she never wanted to let go.

"Hey, what's that for?"

"Because I love you, and because you are so brave."

"Brave? Me? Not really. Well, not at all, I was terrified. I've never even had a fight in my life. You're the brave one, incredibly so. Now, let's get our blades and get on with saving the world." Dale kicked away the leaves and bent down, handing Amanda her short sword and then dusting off the parang before strapping it back on.

"Now, about my idea..."

~~~

Various Futures

They spent days watching, learning, and the more they uncovered the scarier the whole enterprise became. Dale had come up with the idea of jumping high up above The Chamber, on one of the gantries that hung down from the ceiling, there to perform maintenance on the huge ducts that ran for miles back and forth across what felt like a world in its own right.

They took their time choosing suitable equipment, consisting of high-powered digital binoculars and the like, along with assorted basics like water and food, and ensured that their stash of Hexads were there at hand in a moment's notice.

Once set, they jumped through countless futures, moving far forward in time, and back to the early evolution of The Chamber during its construction.

Many of its secrets were revealed; many sad deaths were witnessed.

What became apparent was that the strange appearance of Amandas within The Chamber came as just as much of a surprise to Cray as it did to the women themselves. With incredibly powerful audio equipment they listened in on numerous conversations going on below over the course of many years, some where it was obvious Cray had not lived normally in the intervening years, others where he seemed to have aged appropriately in the time that would have elapsed if he'd experienced all that went on in-between.

The Amandas had simply begun to appear —
Cray didn't have to go out and get them himself. There
were a few instances where this was the case: they
witnessed Amandas kicking and screaming before they
were jumped away from the ground and taken inside
by Cray, but it seemed that merely constructing the
machine with its purpose so ingrained into its very
fabric was enough for what Cray wanted to simply
happen.

The universes, and the immense pressure such a
machine put on reality, meant that the Amandas simply
appeared inside to allow the messed-up reality Cray
had created to continue. It was obvious really: the
universes that were created had no choice, this was
how things worked, how Hexads worked, and here was
the source of the universal confusion, a self-feeding
prophecy caught in a paradox of its own making, fed by
time itself, keeping the whole system functioning as
everything else slowly faded to non-existence.

They witnessed that too: the slow fading away
of people that once milled about constantly below.
Gradually the space emptied, the initial buzz of
construction replaced by regular faces there to maintain
the impossibly complex machine and take away the
most prized possession of all: Hexads.

They watched as technicians put the final pieces
together all around the domed end, saw what was
behind it, what was going on within. They watched the
immensely complicated machinery installed before the

dome was put into place, watched as vast and convoluted systems were connected via delicate robotic arms, working in miniature against the behemoth.

And they watched as groups of men worked in shifts, carefully packing finished Hexads on the ground far below. They were linked up to the production facility that worked unseen behind the blue glow of the gigantic dome, sending finished products down to the ground via a series of incomprehensible systems of gravitational forces as they were extruded like mechanical bowel movements down onto conveyor belts where each was treated with as much care as a mother taking her newborn into her arms for the first time.

Time and time again they witnessed the various stages of the great machine, Dale never able to shake the image of the mechanical milking machine seen in his younger and much more innocent days.

The more they observed, the more they learned, but it had to end, it simply had too. Both of them were completely exhausted, Dale became aware how much it had taken out of him when he turned to Amanda on the gantry beside him, just about to pass a comment about what he'd seen, and realized that she looked absolutely terrible.

Her hair had lost its luster: it was hanging limp, plastered to her head like a bad wig. Her face was drawn and the skin was dry, lips cracked. But it was her eyes that told Dale they had to stop their vigil — it was doing too much damage to them both.

Amanda's eyes were haunted, like she'd watched the death of her family over and over, which Dale supposed was not even coming close to what she was really going through. She was experiencing the death of herself repeatedly, watching her incarcerations in the machine from countless points in time, seeing her prison constructed, seeing a few women put inside before procedures changed and they were jumped inside, and witnessing body after body taken away — for some reason they were never left buried within The Chamber.

Dale found the removal of the bodies fascinating — it was the only time it seemed that Cray himself got involved with actually entering the construct. Oddly, they were never jumped out, he brought them out and was lowered to the ground via a vast platform, the unfortunate Amanda always shrouded in simple white linen, but Dale and Amanda witnessed enough of the bodies uncovered as they were moved to know that they hadn't all died peacefully. It must have been terrible to acknowledge that whatever happened to the women was caused by versions of herself, to know that you were multiplied endlessly in different universes and each one could diverge to have characteristics very different to your own. It wouldn't make it easy to stomach when you knew, deep down, that at some point they had been you.

The terrible stress showed in Amanda's eyes. They were dark and sunken, all light gone. All Dale could think of was that her usually sparkling eyes looked like they had borne witness to the end of countless worlds, which he supposed was exactly what they had been witnessing.

Amanda was staring intently at the scenes below, eyes locked on the solitary figure magnified through binoculars: Cray, now the lone gatekeeper to the destruction of humanity. They'd witnessed everything slowly eroding, sometimes seeing people fade out of existence before their very eyes, their colleagues showing the fear, waiting for their own turn to come. People stopped coming, either vanishing or trying to escape the inevitable by jumping away through time, running from something that would catch up with them whether they liked it or not.

Then it was just Cray, but mostly the space was empty. They jumped back and forth, trying to see what happened, and The Chamber endured, it always endured, although all around was emptiness.

Dale wondered how long it would go on for, how long the machine would keep functioning, and whether or not there were still Amandas inside, bodies piling up, living and dying year after year, decade after decade, none of them knowing any longer what was happening to them or why, just tales passed down from one woman to the next, everything warping the bubble they lived in, telling tales of madness from other worlds.

Would it go on indefinitely? Surely there had to be an end to it? With Hexads causing the closing down of universes to time travel, and people vanishing, then how did society continue to provide Amandas to fuel the system? And what was going on inside with nobody to run it?

But then the next jump would reveal another Cray, looking slightly different, younger or older, confused or reveling in power, workmanlike, a king or a pauper, but enduring. Dale thought he understood, realizing that Cray acted as his own recruit, aging so far then convincing other versions of himself to continue the madness, taking himself from endless timelines to the future to continue the task he had appointed himself, waiting for things to change, for society to be reborn far into the future, a line with him as the founding father, and who knew how many unfortunate Amandas.

In the end there was only one conclusion: the man had lost his mind and was waiting for something that was not worth the price paid, but he refused to go back on his decision, his creation, and was simply consumed by madness and was waiting it out, ensuring the future he had seen far ahead would come to pass, using himself as sentries to guard the powerful machine.

Dale watched Amanda absorbed in the scene below, and knew he had to get her away — she was close to being broken. This was enough; there were no answers to this any longer, nothing to be learned, to be gained by such a vigil.

"Honey, we have to go now," said Dale gently, putting a hand carefully on her shoulder, feeling the bones even though for them it had been only a few days of watching. Her body was eating itself, running fast and furious, trying to give Amanda the energy she willed herself to use so she could keep watching the terrible scenes they had witnessed over and over again. "Amanda, we have to go."

She turned to him, staring vacantly into his eyes, a zombie that wasn't with him any longer, obsessed with the terrible actions of a man just as consumed as she was.

"We can't, we have to see."

"We've seen enough love, we need to leave now, before we aren't able to stop it."

"Look Dale, look what's happening."

Dale turned to look below, lifting the binoculars as he'd now done hundreds and hundreds of times, staring down from above to watch the tiny figures brought large by the power of technology.

Shit, this is really bad timing. Not now, not now.

Dale grabbed the Hexad that was rigged to his belt, there to be used at a moment's notice, and without asking he grabbed Amanda and pushed the dome to his chest.

They jumped.

Time to
Recuperate

Present Day

"What the hell did you do that for?" shouted Amanda, absolutely furious with Dale for taking her away at such a momentous moment.

"If you look in the mirror then I'll tell you why. And look at me, really look." Dale grabbed her and then put his hands either side of her head, making her stare him in the eye, study his face. He knew he would seem a wreck, just like her. "Look at me. How do you think you compare? And how do you feel? Think about it. We need to stop, to rest."

Amanda did as he asked, her eyes taking a long time to search his face. She visibly sagged. It was as if she couldn't really focus without the binoculars, no longer used to just looking at things close up with her own eyes unimpaired.

Dale wondered just how bad he appeared — judging by her reaction he probably wasn't a pretty sight. He ran a hand through his hair, or tried to, and realized it was a mass of knots. How bad could he have got in only a few days? Clearly quite bad. It was the jumping, it had taken too much out of them. The body simply wasn't built to do such things, and Dale feared it had aged him in ways he was going to pay for later on, pay dearly for.

"Dale, you saw it, saw what was about to happen, we have to go back. I know how exhausting this is, I can feel it inside, I can see it in you and I'm sorry, but—"

"But nothing, we have to rest. You're forgetting one thing Amanda: we are in the now, in our time. We are back in the present and we have Hexads. We can jump back there whenever we want, but we need to rest first, we need to be ourselves again."

"Okay, you're right, I'm sorry. It's just..."

"I know honey, I know. Just relax." Dale could see the nervous energy bundled up; he felt the same. Amanda was like an exhausted animal that had been hunted until she was running on fast-dwindling reserves — she could do little in her current state and she seemed to be finally realizing it. Her posture was terrible: shoulders hunched, head at a slightly strange angle.

Dale had an idea and fiddled with the Hexad, a feeling so familiar he was past just hating it — he couldn't stand the damn things any longer, but what choice did he have? He took Amanda's hand as gently as he could and said, "Trust me," before they made yet another jump.

~~~

9 Hours Future

Steaming water erupted all around Amanda and Dale as they landed. Dale had the forethought to hold his breath, cursing himself for not at least warning Amanda. They surfaced simultaneously, both gasping for air, thankfully finding their feet in the relatively shallow water.

"A hot spring?" spluttered Amanda, once she realized she hadn't been jumped into anything more dangerous than a nice relaxing pool.

But there was a sparkle, Dale could see it. She was trying to be cross but couldn't, not really. How could you? Dale just smiled, then slowly, as they accepted the absurdity of their situation, they both began to laugh. It was a weird chuckle at first, as if they'd both forgotten that they had it inside of themselves to be happy, but it came, and it got louder and louder, the stress evaporating like the steam rising all around them.

Dale had taken a risk, he knew it, but he didn't have a choice, he had to get them away from the madness, the insanity that was building year after year, decade after decade. They needed space and they needed to feel normal, if for just a short while.

"You did this on purpose didn't you?" said Amanda, once she'd finished laughing. "You actually jumped us right into the middle of the water with all our clothes on."

"Well, I figured you wouldn't come if I asked, and I figured that if we had to bother with undressing then you'd find a way to argue and we'd be back going slowly mad. Okay?" Dale looked at Amanda, hair soaked from splashing into the incredibly warm water, clothes ballooning around her, looking as comical as he felt.

She nodded. "Better, much better. Thank you Dale."

"For you, anything. You know that. But look, we have to get it together. Up there, on that gantry, it suddenly hit me just what a mess we both are. We haven't slept, haven't eaten for days, just staring down at more and more craziness. We can't deal with this the way we are, we need to stop for a while, take care of ourselves."

"But Dale, how can we? You saw what was about to happen. The Chamber was... It was getting ready to jump, to time travel with all the people inside... If there are people inside. We need to stop it."

"And we will. But this is time travel Amanda, we can jump back there whenever we want. Cray isn't able to alter a timeline enough so that we won't have Hexads. He can't, or he will have never had them either, and he hasn't killed us as we are still here, so we're good. We can chill out and get our act together and then we are going to put an end to this. We need to be fighting fit, we need to be able to think clearly and act sensibly, and I do not feel like I can do that at the moment. I know damn well that you can't."

"You're right. So, where are we?"

"You can't guess?" Dale smiled, watching Amanda try to figure it out.

"Ha, got it. Iceland, right? At the hot springs we saw that program about."

"You got it baby, nailed it it one. We always said we wanted to go, and now here we are. Middle of the night, nobody around, the area locked down until the morning. It's all ours."

"Wow, amazing." Amanda squirmed about in the warm water, letting her arms play out to the sides, her clothes drifting about her like seaweed in the shallows near the shore.

Dale stood and moved out of the natural pool, saying, "I'll be back in a minute, just relax, enjoy it."

"Where are you going? You're not going to leave me, jump, are you?"

"No. If I had it my way I'd never jump again in my entire life, just stay here forever and never think about any of it again, but we don't have that luxury, although for now we do. You just wait, I'll be back in a few minutes. Trust me."

"Okay Dale, I trust you. More than anyone. You know that."

Dale nodded and made his way out of the pool of light that shone down on the steaming water, squelching as the water dripped onto the rock.

"I'll be back," said Dale, turning just before he was lost to the dark.

"Haha, very funny Dale. You sound as much like Arnie as I do."

Dale sloshed off into the dark.

~~~

"Surprise," shouted Dale, as he walked toward the steaming pool.

"Bloody hell Dale, you nearly gave me a heart attack." Amanda splashed about manically like she was anything but defenseless in the pool, but smiled once she saw it was safe.

"Oh, sorry, didn't mean to startle you. Look, I found some food. The restaurant was locked down tight but I did get into some sort of kiosk. They have weird food here though," said Dale, eyeing the tins and snacks rather dubiously.

"I could eat anything, I'm ravenous." Amanda followed the movement of Dale's armful of food greedily. "You okay?"

"It's freezing out here, kind of forgot why it's called Iceland."

"Well I'm lovely and warm, jump back in. Get your clothes off though, it'll make you feel better."

Dale didn't like the idea of stripping down naked, fearing it would be so much colder, but the wet clothes were sticking to him like he was shrouded in ice and already he could see crystals forming on them. "You think I should? It will be horrible to have to put them back on."

"Well, I have something that might make you change your mind."

"What? Oh."

Amanda dropped her hands into the water then flung a pair of pink panties at him. She stood, water cascading down her slender body, breasts glistening with steam and water droplets, her blond hair tumbling down her shoulders like liquid gold.

"Oh, wow. Definitely."

"Some things never change," laughed Amanda, as Dale dropped the food and danced about awkwardly, hopping from one foot to the other trying to pull his soaked jeans off.

"You not too tired?"

"Never too tired for an elicit rendezvous in a hot spring in Iceland, big boy."

"Well, good. Let's call it a little bit of jump therapy shall we?" Dale lowered himself into the pool and waded over to Amanda before wrapping his arms around her. He brushed the hair away from her neck and kissed the salty, warm skin. "Ah, that's better."

"Mm."

They forgot about the snacks; they forgot about everything apart from each other. For a while it was just them, the sounds of the water gurgling and the togetherness they had come so close to losing.

~~~

"Go on then, show me what you got," said Amanda, eyes sparkling like they hadn't for days, her body energized like the clock had been turned back.

"What, already? I'm not as young as I used to be you know?" said Dale, looking slightly nervous about her demands.

"No, silly," said Amanda, punching him on the arm. "The snacks. I'm starving."

"Oh, right. Yeah." Dale held onto Amanda's hand and they moved to the discarded pile of food and clothes and hauled themselves up onto the side, keeping their legs dangling in the water.

"Oh my god, oh my god, it's freezing out here. I'm getting back in." Amanda dropped down, ducking until just her head was out of the water.

"Guess I'll be serving the snacks then." Dale picked up some of the packs he'd pilfered and tried to make sense of the contents by reading labels — it didn't help. "Here." Dale passed Amanda a brightly colored packet and she studied it before shrugging her shoulders and ripping it open.

"Uh, this stinks." Amanda poked her nose back into the packet and took a cautionary sniff once more. "Definitely fishy." She pulled out a brittle piece of something dark and gave it a little lick. "Tastes okay though." Then the hunger must have kicked in and Dale watched her grab a handful and stuff it into her mouth.

Dale sank back into the water gratefully and took the packet off Amanda. "Harðfiskur. Hey, that rings a bell. I think it's dried fish, they love it here apparently. You can get it like chips, or jerky, or brittle like this stuff. Yum, not bad at all." Dale tore open packs that seemed to contain more conventional snacks as well as opening a number of bottles that had a drink that tasted somewhere between milk and cheese. The feast began.

By the time they were finished the food was mostly gone, although some things were simply too strange to do little more than tentatively sample, and both were feeling the full effects of the come-down from the last few days of constant vigilance.

"Happy?" asked Amanda.

"Happy," said Dale, nodding. "We needed this, right?"

"Definitely. I can't believe how nice this is after what we've been through. But we have to go back, don't we?"

Dale knew that they did, although he would have given almost anything to stay right where they were indefinitely. But he wouldn't give up their future, the future of everyone, just to stay happy himself. "Let's go and find some clothes, something warm, and then let's get some rest. Tomorrow is another day and we are finally going to put an end to the madness, once and for all."

"Dale, would you mind if I stayed here while you got the clothes? It's freezing out there."

"No problem. I won't be long, I have just the thing."

Dale jumped out of the pool naked and rummaged in his satchel. "See you in a minute, save me a spot. Whoooooooooooooooooooosh."

Dale was gone.

Lone Adventurer

Present Day

Dale had jumped back home, not out of any overwhelming desire to see the place again, but because it was simply practical to go home to get clothes.

As soon as he landed in the kitchen he felt really strange, like everything since Amanda had appeared and warned him about digging in the garden had been nothing but a dream. He actually checked his hand just to make sure he really had just jumped from a hot spring in Iceland, half expecting to be holding a glass of water — or maybe a half-consumed bottle of whiskey — rather then the Hexad it was gripping tightly.

Waking from a dream and stumbling about drunk or going to get some water after a heavy night would make more sense than what he'd been through, and he really doubted he would have been surprised either way. Yet he also felt relief, knowing that at least he wasn't losing his mind, just his clothes and the lives of billions, but still, it was comforting in its own way.

Shivering, and shaking his wet hair, Dale padded across the cool kitchen tiles, leaving a puddle that would have annoyed the hell out of Amanda had she been there to see it. The room was quiet, only the humming of the refrigerator and the dim blue light cast by the temperature controller stopped it being totally dark and silent. He ignored the scary mess on the table, and the mess it had made on the floor that made his own watery mess pale into insignificance.

As he opened the door out into the hallway Dale had the strangest idea: what if he just went and got Amanda now and they ditched all the Hexads, jumped with a final copy, came back home and just forgot about the whole thing? Would everything then just slot back into place as if none of it had ever happened? He sighed, knowing the answer, just grasping at anything to finally put an end to the craziness that was escalating with each passing minute.

It felt surreal, knowing what was going to happen in the future: The Chamber, the paradoxes that caused the countless Amandas to wind up in such a place, the lives they led. He knew there was more, a lot more, the way that time became so twisted it didn't even make sense to itself, so universes just shut themselves off, eliminated the problem by eradicating humanity before it had a chance to warp reality so much that nobody would ever have been born in the first place.

How many ripples had been caused by so many people having the ability to jump back and forth? It didn't even bear thinking about really. Each jump would effect the future, maybe wiping out countless people with each deed they did that hadn't been done before. Ripples lapping at the boundaries of what was once reality, twisting things, changing the future forever, creating new timelines and almost-parallel universes with each jump, each action.

Then it all ended, or would end, and there would be nothing, just one world where the madness started up all over again — his world, now already responsible for the creation of countless others just because Amanda had jumped back and the cycle played out in a different way to how she said it had before, one of any number of futures across infinite versions of him and her, sometimes locked together, sometimes never to find the right version of each other ever again.

"What a mess," muttered Dale, finding himself in the bedroom, sliding coat hangers across the rail, looking for clothes for Amanda.

"You can say that again."

Dale's heart froze as the voice whispered out of the darkness, then carried on beating once he realized it was Amanda. Dale turned and said, "Hey, how did you get here so fast? Oh, right. Duh." Dale stared at her, but something wasn't right. "Amanda?"

"How could you Dale? How could you do this to me? To us?"

This wasn't her, not his Amanda. This was the other Amanda, the one he'd woken up to in this very room not long ago and began freaking out as it was the wrong woman. Now she was back.

Amanda stared at him as if she could read his mind, eyes full of sadness, but there were no tears. "I'm sorry, I don't mean that. But she took my life Dale, that other woman, she took you from me."

"But you took my Amanda from me, didn't you? This is who you are Amanda, it's what you do. It's what anyone would do. Look, how are you here? You should be..."

"Where? Where should I be Dale?"

"Trust me, you don't want to know. You okay?" Dale sat on the bed next to her, catching the strange scent that marked her as a woman he had never known in his life, not that he could recall anyway. Did that make it all right? What if he'd just had amnesia, would that make a past with somebody meaningless?

"When I saw you and her, out in the garden, I felt it, felt the pull of something, but I don't know what happened. I just ended up here, but everything feels different. I'm scared Dale, I don't know what's going on. I'm getting flashbacks, or memories, or something, but about things I don't remember doing. Terrible memories Dale, terrible things I did, that we did, that happened to us. At least I think it was you. I've just been sitting here trying to remember what happened, but at the same time I know, I just know, that I've been involved in things that were just awful." She couldn't take it any longer and collapsed into his arms.

"Hush, it's all right. Things have just got a little strange lately." Dale soothed her, rubbing her head, having absolutely no idea what he was going to do. How was she here? How long had she been sat on the bed, lost in memories of things he had no memory of himself? Of time they had shared together, when she'd appeared in his life and his Amanda, now relaxing in a hot pool, had herself vanished and he and this woman had set the world to rights themselves. That was one hell of a past to simply dismiss. "We saved the world together Amanda, you and me. That's what you are remembering."

"Then why does it feel like it's all gone wrong?"

"Because it has. You are better off not knowing, you really are."

"Dale, can you help me? I've been... well, not sure really, like I've been jumping without meaning to. I can feel myself disappearing, leaving here, almost like I'm waiting to go to a final place. I've been flickering, that's the best way I can describe it. Popping in and out of reality, coming back, like I've been waiting for something. For you."

"I'm here now." Dale really didn't know what to do. How could he help her? "Amanda? Amanda?"

It was too late, she flickered like a faulty TV then Dale was left staring at a depression in the bed covers where she had been sat, hand in the air, the soft hair beneath his fingers now gone.

"I'm sorry Amanda, so very sorry. I hope you're safe." Dale couldn't take his eyes off the depression in the bed, hoping Amanda would return, knowing she wouldn't. He sat there in a daze, already wondering if she had been real or if it was simply an hallucination brought on by lack of sleep and the overwhelming number of bizarre things that had been happening.

Eventually he got wearily to his feet, a sudden tiredness threatening to engulf him and send him sinking into unconsciousness on the familiar, inviting bed. What he wouldn't give to just lie down and sleep, wake up and for it all to be over, for the day to be waiting for him, stretching out in front of him with promises of a pleasant relaxing morning in the garden, maybe a pint down the pub. He couldn't though, could he? No, he had things to do, momentous things, but he needed sleep. The rejuvenating effects of the hot spring had gone, leaving him naked and increasingly cold. Alone.

Dale stood shakily, not even realizing he'd sat back down, then dressed in a daze of sadness. Where had she gone to? To The Chamber, her final home? In all likelihood she had, drawn there by whatever cruel trick the Universe was playing on her, all the versions of her. Would she right now be cowering, terrified of the inside-out world populated by others just like her, only to be told of the hellish existence she would have to face if she wished to survive? And when? What time period would she have jumped to?

And it's all your own fault Amanda. What a cross to bear that must be.

Dale realized then, maybe for the first time truly understanding, just how terrible a burden this was for Amanda, knowing that by messing with reality she had brought such things to pass, inflicted such a cruel fate on herself through countless incarnations. How could she cope? It was no surprise that she had become so all-consumed with The Chamber and the events that were continually unfolding around the strange world at countless moments in time in endless almost-parallel universes.

It was time to go, time to return to her and end the nightmare once and for all.

Dale finished dressing, grabbed clothes for Amanda, then stared ruefully at the crumpled bed. He bent and straightened out the sheet, then went back to Amanda.

~~~

9 Hours Future

"Hey," said Amanda, from the steaming water. "Hey."

"You okay? You look... not sure, just more worried than usual."

"I'm fine, just tired. It really hit me once I was out of the water. Come on, I got your clothes, let's go get some rest."

Amanda stood and moved to the side, as beautiful as ever. She smiled at Dale as she took the offered towel, cocking her head quizzically as she stared into Dale's eyes. "You sure you're all right?"

"I'm fine, but I'm dead on my feet. Let's go sleep."

"And where are we going to be spending the night may I ask?"

"Haha, now that would be telling. Come on, get your clothes on or I won't be taking you anywhere but back into the water." Dale tried to maintain the facade of being upbeat, but doubted he was pulling it off.

Amanda's pink skin shone with vigor after the soaking, and Dale was pleased that she seemed to have returned to her normal self. This was what they needed: time together, just them, no insanity. Well, hardly any, but he felt it best to keep quiet about what had just happened — no point spoiling her mood, it wasn't like she could do anything about it. Not yet.

Amanda watched him carefully as she dressed, clearly unsure why Dale had lost some of the happiness he'd displayed mere moments ago for her, but she kept quiet and dressed quickly.

"Ready?"

"Ready."
They jumped.

A Little Luxury

11 Years Past

"No. Way." Amanda stared around the lavish room with total and utter admiration. Dale couldn't help thinking that it was a little over the top when all he'd done was use the Hexad — it wasn't like he was paying for it or anything. "Is this where I think it is?" asked Amanda, opening the door to the en-suite and returning with a handful of tiny packs of soap and shampoo.

"It is. Yep. It's the Burk Al Arab. Only the best for you."

"But how? How can we be in this penthouse? Surely they are booked up for ages? Have you been jumping without me knowing?"

"No, nothing like that. But I remembered that they closed the place for a night the same day we were passing through on our way to Thailand. Remember, when they had a bomb scare? So here we are, the place to ourselves. There wasn't a bomb by the way, just in case you're getting nervous."

"Cool. Look at that view! You even jumped us to daylight so we could see." Amanda continued stuffing toiletries into her bag, seemingly unable to defy the law of pilfering from hotel rooms even if they hadn't paid to stay there.

"Well, I figured we could do with a nice long rest before we... you know?"

"Oh, yes, right."

The mood changed instantly, the thin veil of happiness lifting to reveal the constant tension and sadness lurking beneath. Dale moved over to her and put his hand on hers. "You don't need to take them, it won't matter. They won't be there if we are successful, none of this will have happened."

"I know, but for now let's just pretend we are on vacation and this is what you do. You nick stuff and you make the most of it."

"Okay, you're right." Dale walked with Amanda over to the window, and stared down at the man-made island the luxury five star hotel stood on, a beacon of wealth in the emerging world-famous tourist destination of Dubai. It was stunning in its scale, yet Dale knew that it would fit into a corner of The Chamber as if it were little more than a toy.

Damn, here I go again, thinking morbid thoughts.

"Let's try the bed. I'm so tired, but I don't know if I can sleep. But just lying down in comfort would be great."

Amanda smiled and followed him through the open doors to the bedroom. Piles of feather pillows complete with welcome chocolates and even a bottle of champagne on ice greeted them. Amanda popped the cork noisily then poured them both a glass. "To us," said Amanda, clinking her glass against Dale's.

"To us."

They lay back on the pillows. Both of them were asleep within seconds.

~~~

"Dale, Dale," whispered Amanda, nudging him more forcefully in the ribs.

With a terrible sense of somebody about to jump him and stab him, or finding Cray stood over them with a gun, Dale reluctantly opened his eyes.

"What? Is everything all right?"

"Yes, but we slept late. It's gone ten already."

"So?" Amanda just stared at him, waiting for him to catch up. "Oh, right, damn. People will be coming up to the room. The guests that booked it, or the staff at least."

"Exactly." Amanda hopped out of the bed, still dressed just like Dale, and moved fast to the en-suite, almost bouncing the carpet pile was so deep.

Dale walked over to the window again, looking across the beach where sun-worshippers were already gathering, probably with bathing suits that cost more than the average person's monthly wage. Dubai always held mixed feelings for him, more so every year as additional hotels were built, each vying with the others to be the tallest, the most luxurious, the most expensive, and it wasn't just limited to the hotels either — Dubai was now synonymous with money, and much as Dale would love to be rich he could never quite feel comfortable with the levels of spending involved with such places.

Material wealth was all well and good but how could you possibly spend a year's wage on a gold tap, or buy a shirt that cost the same as homing a family for a few months? It just didn't add up, but then he guessed he was only looking at it from one side, so who was he to put the world to rights? Ha, that was a funny one, he was exactly the one to put the world right, him and Amanda — the only people that could.

"Lovely, isn't it?" said Amanda, coming up behind him, putting an arm over his shoulder, admiring the view.

"Beautiful. But it's all fake, it's not real. Well, the beach maybe, but this little island is totally man-made. Do you know it took them three years to reclaim the land from the sea, the same time it took to build the actual hotel?"

"No, I didn't, but I do now. And hey mister, stop being so grumpy. Not everything made by people is bad, we've achieved some great things."

"Yeah, and some very bad things too."

"Yes, well, let's not get morbid. Especially before breakfast. Come on, get ready. Then let's explore a little before we..."

"Before we end the madness and wake up like it never happened and get up and mow the lawn rather than jumping through time, staying in nice hotels, seeing inside-out worlds, running away from madmen and then having nice rests in hot springs? That what you mean?"

"That's exactly what I mean. If we aren't going to remember any of this then we may as well enjoy it, just for a few hours. We deserve that much, you were right Dale. I'm glad you took us away from that horrible place, we would have been dead if we'd tried anything."

"Okay, I'm going for a quick wash. Then we'll go get some breakfast."

Dale left Amanda to take in the view while he went to the bathroom.

The taps were gold. Dale wondered what would happen if you sliced a piece off and tried to leave with it in your luggage.

He eyed the soap suspiciously, having the distinct impression that even the soap cost more than he'd normally earn in a day.

He used it anyway.

It felt glorious on his skin; maybe you really did get what you paid for.

~~~

The hotel was as luxurious as Dale had pictured it, although he couldn't shake the uncomfortable feeling of not really belonging. Everything was too shiny, and there was definite emphasis on gold — it seemed to be on almost every available surface. As they wandered through the various restaurants, and took in the amazing atrium, he had to admit that it was something he could get used to if he had the money. And why not? If he'd worked for it then didn't he have the right to spend it?

It was all abstract though — he could never imagine the kind of money involved in staying in luxury and spending vast sums just to sleep somewhere for a few nights.

After eating a glorious breakfast, with Amanda gushing over her eggs like they too were made of gold, and Dale paying without batting an eyelid at the cost, knowing it wouldn't mean anything soon anyway, they left the hotel and took a short ride across the bridge to the mainland.

"We seem to make a habit of coming to beaches," said Amanda, looking at the bodies browning on the sand with obvious envy.

Dale couldn't see a single female that had an ounce of excess fat on her, the same was not to be said for the men however. "Because they're relaxing, and we definitely need to relax." Dale stared longingly at the water, wishing he had his swimming trunks with him. Now wasn't the time though — he was getting more and more jittery, wanting to get things over with, or at least try. It felt wrong now, after the rest that they so sorely needed, to not be back in the middle of the madness, trying to do something about it.

"We should go," said Amanda reluctantly, saying what he was thinking.

Dale squeezed her hand tight and said, "Yes, I suppose we should."

They turned around and headed back towards the towering hotel. All Dale could think of was that it looked like it could stand there forever, but nothing, absolutely nothing, lasted forever.

Not even time itself.

What's in the
Bag?

11 Years Past

Dale and Amanda chatted as they walked through the entrance to the hotel, deciding to just sit quietly at one of the bars, have a drink while taking in the view for the last time. Then they would put an end to the things Cray had done. There were numerous ways they could deal with him, at least in theory, but every option came to nothing but a dead-end once they actually talked it through. They'd gone over countless scenarios in the days they'd kept their vigil over The Chamber, none of them ever leading anywhere but to frustration.

Could they go back and kill him as a young child? No, as what would there be in his place? It could be something much worse. Everything stemmed from the fact that Amanda had possessed a Hexad and jumped back into reality, causing ripples that built into a tidal wave of time-hopping that gathered momentum the more widespread it became.

No, it all came down to The Chamber and what it stood for, as well as what it actually produced. They had to think of things as if only their world existed, and the future it contained — as soon as you thought about the endless others then you would go mad with indecision, never knowing if any of it would mean anything at all.

The scene they were about to witness before they left their vigil because of utter exhaustion was where everything led to, and that time, that point far, far into the future, was where they had to be. It was the crux, the end game, the result of everything that had gone before, and it was there where they could change the past, eliminate Hexads once and for all, make it so they had never been, and never would be.

"So it's settled then? We'll go there, and once it's over we'll—"

"Excuse me sir," said an immaculately dressed security officer, hardly a hint of an accent. "If you wouldn't mind?"

Dale and Amanda had been pre-occupied and hadn't noticed the security as they entered the building, but as Dale turned and saw a large walk-through metal detector where the man had pointed he went cold inside. It was not going to go well if he walked through, not for Amanda either. He looked at Amanda; she shook her head.

They'll lock us up if we go through there. What will they make of the Hexads? Oh shit, I've still got the gun too.

There was no doubt that even if he could explain away the Hexads, which he couldn't, there was no explaining having a loaded weapon in such a place. How could they have been so stupid? To have not taken into account the possibility that something bad could happen to them? They should have just kept trying to stop Cray until they dropped down dead from exhaustion.

This was idiocy on a grand scale. Dale honestly hadn't given it a second thought though, not really considering anything would happen to them in a normal situation — it was only Cray that was of concern and he hadn't been able to find them since they took the gun from him and made their jumps, or hadn't bothered as Dale's actions had shown he was a match for anything Cray came up with to try to stop them.

"Oh, sorry, you know what? I just realized we're in the wrong hotel. Excuse us." Dale grabbed Amanda by the arm and began to leave. He felt a firm hand on his shoulder and was stopped.

"I'm sorry sir," said the man in elegant English, "but I'm afraid that won't be possible. Anyone entering the building must pass security, even if they wish to leave. You understand? We had a bomb threat yesterday, so we must be cautious."

"Yes, yes, I understand, but we haven't gone in yet, not really. And we are in the wrong building." Dale was sounding desperate and he knew it.

"Just the same, please step this way." The guard motioned with his head to the two men at the metal detector and they began to walk towards them.

Dale fumbled in his satchel, hand gripping tight. He pulled out the gun, knowing as he did so that he was playing an extremely dangerous game.

"Nobody move, get down, on the floor. Now!" Dale swung the gun back and forth from the guard to the two others; people in the lobby began screaming as they saw the weapon.

"Dale, what are you doing? Are you mad?" said a shocked Amanda, staring in astonishment as he turned to look at her.

"Saving us, saving everything." Dale turned back to the guard just as he was about to lunge for the gun. "Don't make me tell you again."

The man dropped to his knees, nodding for the other guards to do likewise.

"Flat on your face," said Dale, feeling out of control and dreading what would happen if one of them went for their own weapons.

One of the two guards spoke fast in Arabic and the guard closest to Dale shouted something at him angrily before the man eventually got down onto the ground.

Alarm bells rang out angrily from inside and outside the building and people began rushing from all directions towards the exit, most unaware that it was where Dale and Amanda were causing the problem in the first place.

Things were spinning out of control fast; Dale was finding it hard to keep up.

"What should I do now?" asked Dale, trying to keep an eye on the guards.

"How should I bloody know? This was your idea. Think of something."

"How about this?" came a voice from behind. Cray's voice. It was too late, Dale crumpled to the floor as Cray hit him hard over the head with a cosh.

"Dale!" shouted Amanda, before she was grabbed by the closest security guard and her shoulders began to scream in pain as her arms were pulled up behind her back forcefully.

Cray stood there, smiling like he didn't have a care in the world. "You know, you should be more careful where you go Amanda. When you make it into the papers it does make it really rather easy to find you." He held up a newspaper for Amanda to see, the headline reading 'DUBAI — BRITS ARRESTED: Attempted armed robbery in famous Dubai Hotel.' Even as Amanda stared at the picture it began to morph, Cray suddenly appearing in the background behind the image of her standing right where she was now, with Dale unconscious on the floor. Just as Cray lowered the paper to his side she heard a click and turned to see a tourist snapping a picture.

The next thing she knew she too was on the ground, hands cuffed behind her back while all around the chatter grew louder and louder, mostly drowned out by the alarm bells and the approaching police sirens that were roaring across the bridge to arrest the British armed robbers.

Dale groaned from the floor, unable to move with the security officer's knee wedged in the small of his back as he cuffed him angrily and thanked Cray for helping to disarm the dangerous criminal that dared to disrupt the peace of such a magnificent hotel.

Cray said it was nothing, that he was glad to help, and he would wait while the police arrived in case he could be of any further assistance and to give a statement. Did they know he was an English detective inspector? He dealt with this kind of thing all the time back home.

They chatted until the manager arrived, who quickly took charge of the situation before rushing to greet the police that were heading towards the foyer.

"Dale, how are we going to get out of this one?"

Dale just moaned.

The police were ushered into the building and things went from bad to worse.

Locked Up

11 Years Past

Dale came around in the back of a van with a lot of very angry men staring at him, but that was nothing compared to the look Amanda was giving him. "What?" said Dale sorrowfully.

Amanda just stared at him like he was a complete idiot, but what choice had he had? If they'd gone through the detector then they would have been in serious trouble so he thought it best to at least try something. It just hadn't worked out quite as he'd planned. That was the understatement of the year though, and he'd definitely made a bad situation a lot worse than it could have been.

"You don't know yet as you were unconscious, but guess who whacked you over the head?" said Amanda, sitting across from him, dwarfed on either side by two very large and very intimidating policemen. They had guns too. Big ones.

"What do you mean? Who?"

"Cray."

"What!? How?"

"Because your little stunt made it into the papers, so in the future he obviously found out about it, probably by checking records automatically, and all of a sudden we would have popped up as two idiots where one of them was waving a gun about in the most well known hotel in the world. That's how."

"No more talking," said one of their escorts.

Damn, Cray's here. That's not a good sign at all. Nice going Dale, how are you going to get out of this one?

As they headed toward what Dale assumed would be some kind of decrepit police station where they'd be beaten and locked in disgusting cells for daring to disturb the peace of the mega-rich, Dale tried to think of a way out. There had to be a solution, a way that he could jump back from the future and allow him and Amanda to get away. What could he do? What could he send back to allow them to get out of the plastic handcuffs that were cutting viciously into his wrists? And what about the satchel full of Hexads and Amanda's bag too?

This was a nightmare and it wasn't as easy as just making a Hexad appear then jumping clear — he had to get all the Hexads they'd brought with them or the future would be dramatically changed and time travel would be known about now rather than in the future as it was supposed to be.

This is what you get for messing with time, it leads to way too much confusion. Ugh, I actually waved a gun around at people. What was I thinking? There was no way I could have shot anyone. I don't think so anyway.

"Dale," whispered Amanda, disturbing him from his thoughts.

"What?" said Dale, palms sweating as the fear of incarceration built, for once not just a nervous reaction to authority but a very real probability.

"I have an idea. Wait until we're at the police station and together."

"No talking," came the reminder from the man next to Amanda.

Dale nodded at her, mouthing 'Sorry,' but she looked less than impressed.

~~~

They drove through crowded streets, past a seemingly endless number of massive hotels, sparkling in the bright sunlight. Soon enough they arrived at a very modern, and very clean looking building that was definitely not how Dale pictured an Arabic police station, surprising himself that he maybe had such prejudices anyway. They were escorted less than gently up the steps before being very quickly processed.

There was no sign of their bags, or Cray for that matter, but if he was in this time then there was no doubt he would be after them now he knew exactly where they were, and where they would in all likelihood remain for many years to come unless Amanda really did have a very good plan in mind.

~~~

"Those plastic cuffs really hurt," said Dale, rubbing at his wrists, the deep red lines testament to the effectiveness of such simple restraining devices.

"We were lucky we didn't get shot on the spot," said Amanda without sympathy, rubbing at her own wrists.

"Look, I'm sorry. I panicked."

"Panicked? You went bloody mad is what you did. What were you thinking?"

"I wasn't."

"No, you weren't."

"I just had a vision of them getting the Hexads and then everything we've been working for would have been totally pointless. I didn't know what to do."

"We could have tried just running, you could have kicked the guy in the shins and we could have made a dash and jumped."

"Yeah, yeah, I know. Look, it's done, and you said it was Cray, so he's going to be getting those Hexads really soon, you can count on it. Now he knows where they are then he's going to be jumping and nabbing them, and then that will leave us stranded here, in jail."

"I know, but the only saving grace is that he obviously doesn't know about what happens in the future yet, this is the him that has been chasing us about, not a future version, so at least we have that going for us."

"But not a lot else," muttered Dale.

They'd been put into a room alone, a plain-walled, bare room with just a table and a few chairs, nothing else. Dale knew they were being listened to, or at least expected they were, but the situation called for them to talk and none of it seemed to matter when you had the worry of countless universes on your shoulders.

"Okay, this idea of yours, you going to do it? Is it safe to tell me, with them listening?"

"Oh!" Amanda put a hand to her mouth, clearly not thinking about eavesdroppers at all.

"Yeah, they are sure to be watching and listening, what do you think the mirror is for? It's about as cliched as it gets."

"Well, it won't matter if I tell you anyway, not if it works."

"So, you planning to jump us out of here then?"

"Something like that." Amanda smiled and Dale stared at her quizzically.

"What? Tell me."

"Look, we can't let this happen, any of it. Us being here will in all likelihood have changed everything in the future. This conversation for a start, not to mention the fact that what we've done could mean we spend the rest of our lives in prison, well, you anyway. But Cray will get the Hexads now, and we won't be able to stop him. But us being in the papers will change the future course of our history, so we need to undo it."

"Undo it? Okay," said Dale warily. "What did you have in mind?"

"It should begin in just a few seconds. Get ready."

"Ready? Ready for..."

Dale felt himself losing his grip on reality, felt things were out of reach, intangible and just not really real any longer. He stared at Amanda, stared at his own hands, and watched in horror as he could see right through her to the plain wall behind. He looked at his hands again, squinted at the tiled floor through nothing more than what looked like a poor projection of his own self.

What did you do Amanda?

It was Dale's last thought before he disappeared entirely, just like Amanda.

"The First Rule
of Time Travel...

11 Years 2 Hours Past

... is don't go getting yourselves in the paper," read Dale, seconds after grabbing the note that appeared in mid-air in front of him as they walked across the bridge towards the entrance to the hotel. Dale looked at Amanda, but she was just as nonplussed as he was.

"It looks like your handwriting." Dale offered the note to Amanda, who looked at it suspiciously.

They stopped and looked around, but there didn't seem to be anything out of the ordinary. Amanda carried on reading.

"Don't go to the hotel, trust me when I tell you it's a bad idea. Dale goes mental with a gun and—"

"I what!? Yeah right."

"Quiet, let me read it. Dale goes mad with a gun and then you get locked up and Cray comes and you make a real mess of things. Amanda, this is me, well, you, and you need to not go to the hotel. Be careful, if you lose the Hexads then everything is over. Finish this now, no more delays. Oh, first thing first, take out your notepad, write this note, and then be sure to do what needs to be done so you read this. You have changed your own future by doing this, and I don't know how successful it has been, but hopefully it has worked out. If you are reading this then it will have."

"What the hell is all that about?" asked Dale, as confused as Amanda.

"Sounds like you did something stupid and I saved us," said Amanda, smirking at Dale.

"So, what, you got us out of it by right now writing a note and leaving it for us? That doesn't make sense. How would we have got out of whatever trouble we were in so you could write this note?"

"Because I'm doing it right now and sending it to us a few minutes ago, so I guess whatever happened in the hotel won't happen now. Haha, can you imagine you with a gun? I bet you would drop it your hands would be so sweaty."

"I could use it if I had to," protested Dale.

Amanda rummaged in her bag, found her notebook, then very carefully copied the note word for word. When she was finished she said, "Let's walk back away from here before I jump, I don't want us from a few moment's ago seeing us standing here, it will get too confusing."

"Like it isn't already? Look, I don't get it, surely we can't stop a future that just happened to us by doing something we wouldn't have been able to do because we should be somewhere else."

"Dale, this is time travel, it's supposed to be confusing. Anyway, you did it, with the gun and Cray."

"That was different." Dale scratched at his head, feeling exposed on the bridge, the salty air carrying with it the terrible heat of the day. "Wasn't it? Come on then, I'm burning up out here. How can people live in this kind of heat?"

"They have air-con." Amanda began to walk back the way they had come, holding on to the two notes.

Dale caught up and said what was really bugging him. "Hey, why bother writing the note? You have it already, so why write it again?"

"Dale," said Amanda, exasperated, "because it has to get written in the first place, doesn't it? Jeez, you need to keep up."

Yeah, like all of this makes perfect sense.

They made it around the corner and after crouching down behind a building Amanda disappeared then re-appeared a moment later.

"Done?"

"Done. Now, let's go save the world. No more distractions this time."

"Hey, don't blame me. Whatever happened clearly hasn't happened now, so it wasn't my fault."

"Hmm." Amanda gave him one of those looks; Dale knew better than to argue.

"Are we really going to do this now? I mean, it feels sudden, almost like it isn't happening."

Amanda squirmed uncomfortably, face reddening in the intense heat. "I know what you mean. Part of me wants to believe that everything is great and we're just on holiday. Amazing what a soak in a hot spring and a good nights sleep can do to you."

"Yeah, if it wasn't for the fact we were in Iceland one minute, Dubai the next, and just caught a note that magically appeared in mid-air then I'd feel the same."

"That's not what I meant and you know it. All the other stuff, The Chamber, what we saw happening in there, what we saw happening far into the future with the place, that just doesn't seem like it could actually be true. I want to just go home Dale, I want to be bored and read the Sunday papers and laugh at you trying to devise ways to stop the squirrel eating all the bird seed." Amanda was almost in tears and Dale didn't blame her.

Heck, he felt like joining her, just sitting down on the scorching hot asphalt, putting his head in his hands and weeping until everything went back to normal. But it wouldn't, he knew it and it hit him like a bolt out of the clear blue sky. Nothing was going to be okay, not until they finished what they were caught up in whether they liked it or not.

"Right, one last jump. We have to go back to the hot springs and get our other weapons. Judging by the note I'm not to be trusted with guns, and besides I kind of feel naked without my parang now. Is that silly?"

Amanda sniffled and tried to smile. "No, I know what you mean. You get used to it, it makes you feel a little less vulnerable. Come on, you going to do the honors?"

"Sure." Dale pulled out a Hexad and set up the dials. "Ready?" Amanda nodded. Dale tried not to think about what would have happened if they'd walked into the lobby — he just couldn't get a picture of him waving a gun around like a madman out of his mind. He had to smile at that; how different a man he was to just a few days ago, when he woke up with a hangover and starting digging in the garden. What would have happened if he'd dug up the note they'd buried? It couldn't have been worse than this, surely?

~~~

1 Day 9 Hours Future

The hot springs gave a sense of comfort, like it was a regular haunt. Dale had jumped to the day after they'd been there before, same time, thinking it would be nice to have a familiar atmosphere while they collected their weapons. He went to retrieve them from where they'd been hidden, and returned to the pool a few minutes later.

"Hey, what you doing? I thought we were going to finish this?" Amanda was in the pool, hair floating about her like golden seaweed, steam rising invitingly from the water. Her clothes were folded neatly beside the water.

Amanda stood, just as she'd done the night before, water cascading down her trim body, breasts jiggling as she wiggled in the way she knew got Dale going every time. "Well, I just thought while we were here... After all, it's going to be the last time. When this is over we'll be different people, the old us, and we won't remember any of it. So, why not?"

Dale didn't need to be asked twice, he already had half his clothes off by the time she'd finished speaking. "Watch it," said Amanda, laughing. "You'll fall in with your jeans still on if you're not careful."

Dale hopped about on one foot trying to pull his remaining sock off, and after carefully unbuttoning his jeans and taking off his boxer shorts he was in the water and grabbing for Amanda before she had the chance to change her mind.

"I agree."

"With what?" laughed Amanda.

"Everything you say. Now come here."

~~~

"Ready?" asked Dale.

"Yes," said Amanda, staring wistfully at the pool, now dressed, hair still damp, ice forming in the freezing air.

"Well, okay then, let's do his thing."

"Whoooooooooooooooooooosh," said Amanda.

"Hey, that's my line—"

They jumped.

Lost Something?

2900 Years Future

Dale grabbed hold of the rail on the gantry, steadying himself after the familiar, yet always strange feeling he got following a jump. However good he and Amanda now were at ensuring they landed with feet on the ground there was always that sensation of falling. It was too risky to imagine landing perfectly on any terrain, as even the tiniest miscalculation could mean you ended up with your feet a few millimeters into the surface — not something Dale wanted to ever dwell on as it sent his heart racing every time.

The silence became almost a physical entity; Dale knew instantly that something was very wrong. The absence of sound was too strange — there was always a background noise. Always.

By the set of Amanda's shoulders there was a lot worse to come. Dale peered over the edge, down to where they had looked at The Chamber and the ever-diminishing workforce through countless time periods.

The space was empty.

It wasn't only The Chamber itself that was missing, everything was gone, there was nothing but emptiness, you'd never know anything had ever been there. Lucky for them some basic infrastructure was still intact, otherwise they'd be plummeting to the ground far below right now.

"Where's it gone?" said Dale breathlessly, nervously putting his hand through his hair, brushing it away from his neck as if it suddenly felt ticklish.

"Dale, of all the questions you have ever asked me that has to be one of the stupidest. How the hell should I know?" Amanda was leaning over the rail, searching the space below as if The Chamber could be hidden away somewhere. She moved along the metal walkway, looking left then right, willing it to be where it should be. She was getting frantic.

"Did you jump us to the right time? The one we left last time?" Amanda just stared at him, telling him in no uncertain terms that she hadn't messed up. "Well where is it then?"

"I don't know. It's gone."

"This doesn't make sense, it can't be gone. It was here before so it should still be here. Nothing has changed."

"It must have. Us jumping back, we must have changed something somehow. What other explanation is there?"

"Maybe we just need to go back a little further, it might just be that we missed it."

"Why would we? It should be here, everything should be like it was before."

"Well it isn't, so let's try."

Dale had a terrible feeling, like they were too late, like they'd ruined everything by jumping away because of exhaustion when they should have done something at the time. Now they'd missed their chance — it was as though The Chamber had never been.

Amanda looked like an animal frozen to the spot in the middle of the road as a vehicle hurtled toward her with no intention of slowing down. She fumbled with a Hexad, hands shaking, face pale and drawn like they hadn't had the chance to recuperate at all.

"It's okay Amanda, calm down. We'll sort this out, I promise."

"No Dale, it's not all right and it's all my fault. I can't bear it, it's too much. All those women, that was me in there Dale. Me!"

Dale hugged her tightly, the only thing he could do, feeling inadequate, unable to give her what she needed, but he felt Amanda slowly relax and pull herself together again. "Stay strong, we've been through enough to know that reality gets confusing. This isn't the end of it, it's just going to be different to how we thought, that's all."

"I hope you're right. I really do. Dale? Dale, what is it?"

Amanda followed his eyes, then rushed over and grabbed the binoculars from where they'd left them in the corner of the gantry. She ran back to join him, but Dale knew she didn't need them, not really, she just didn't want to believe what she was seeing. After a few seconds she lowered them.

"It's us."

"Yup, sure is."

"What are we doing down there? How are we there? What the hell is going on Dale?"

"I have absolutely no idea, but I think we need to go and find out. Oh, look, we're waving, isn't that nice?"

"Nice? Nice!?" said Amanda hysterically. "No, it's not nice. What do we think we're playing at? Why are we waving at us? Do they expect us to go down there and have a nice chat with them? We can't."

"Well, as it's us I'm guessing that it's safe to go down as we aren't very well going to make ourselves disappear, now are we?"

"I suppose not, no."

"Should we jump do you think?"

"I guess we'll have to. It'll take forever to find our way down off this thing, if there even is a way down now."

Dale made adjustments to a Hexad, noting that the one he was holding was on its last jump, the 1 flashing as if in accusation for squandering the greatest, and worst gift mankind had ever been given. Amanda held on to his arm and Dale pressed the blue dome. He also crossed his fingers, not that he didn't trust himself or anything.

~~~

"Don't come any closer, not yet," warned Amanda, and Dale's head started to get seriously messed up.

"This is too weird," said Dale quietly to Amanda, finding it next to impossible to have her talking to him from across the divide between them.

"You're telling me. Does my hair always look like that?"

"What? Yes. You should be used to it, we've met loads of you, but look at me, I look like I've been dragged through a hedge backwards. Why is my hair sticking out like that?"

"You always look like that," said Amanda.

"What!? Really?"

"We can hear you, you know?" said Dale, from at least fifty meters away.

"What? Oh, sorry, this is just a little bit weird."

"I know," said the Dale.

"Sorry about this, but we had to come," said the Amanda.

"Um, okay. Why?" said Amanda.

"Because when we were you we had this exact same meeting, so we had to jump to be sure that it happened as it did."

"Oh bloody hell, do we have to go through all these mind-melts all the time? You jumped here to talk to us, because when you were us you had this exact same conversation?" said Dale, sure his brain was right now oozing out of his ears.

"Yes, exactly. We didn't want to risk it so here we are."

"And what if you didn't jump, what then?" asked Amanda.

The Dale and the Amanda stared at each other, and then the Dale said, "We really were that stupid, weren't we? Bloody hell."

"Hey!" said Dale. "We can hear you too."

"I know, but it's what we said when we were you. Well, what the Dale and the Amanda said when we were you. Damn, now I'm doing it. And damn, this is what the Dale said when I was where you are."

The Dale was obviously just as confused as Dale was, but he supposed it was understandable — after all, the Dale was saying exactly what another Dale would have said to him when... "Ugh, okay, enough of this, what the bloody hell is going on?"

"This is what's going on, and we're sorry, but it has to be done." The Dale held the Amanda's hand and they began walking toward Dale and Amanda.

What are they doing? Don't they know they are going to create a paradox if they get much closer? We'll just disappear and... Oh no.

"So you get it then?" said the Dale. "You know what has to happen?"

Dale nodded his head, trying not to freak out.

"What? What has to happen?" said Amanda, looking as worried as he felt.

"We're creating a paradox. That us is doing this to us, just as they had it done to them. And on and on it goes."

"I don't understand," said Amanda. "Stand back, you're coming too close," she warned, as the Dale and the Amanda walked towards them.

"Sorry Amanda, but it has to happen this way. You understand?" said the Amanda.

"No, I don't understand. What are you doing?" Amanda began taking steps backwards, but Dale held onto her arm with a tight grip. "Dale, let go of me. What are you doing?"

"We have to go back."

"Back? Back where?"

"Inside," said the Amanda. "You have to go back inside."

"The Chamber you mean? No, I'm not going back in there, I can't. It's too awful."

"I'm sorry," said the Amanda, and she and the Dale rushed toward them, Dale holding her in place as they got closer.

"Dale, let me go. Let me go!"

"I'm sorry, but if they think it's for the best then we have to trust them."

"No, I can't."

It was too late, the Dale and the Amanda were just a few feet away now.

Dale and Amanda disappeared.

Inside Out, Again

Time Unknown

"No, it can't be," cried Amanda, letting her head fall forward, hair covering her eyes so she didn't have to look.

"We obviously had no choice Amanda. We wouldn't have done this to ourselves just to be mean. But stay quiet, let's not draw attention to ourselves." Dale was glad of the cover provided by the canopy. At least jumping into a forest meant the upside-down world of The Chamber was somewhat less dizzying, although the glimpses he got of fields and farmhouses in miniature far above his head were still doing funny things to his insides.

Dale knew it was coming as soon as the Dale and Amanda began walking towards them in the huge empty space. The one thing he hadn't expected was to end up in The Chamber — if he was honest with himself he'd kind of expected to just disappear, even though there was another Dale saying that was what happened to him, so clearly he'd managed to survive. Knowing and believing weren't the same thing however, so he'd just accepted that he had to trust himself and let them do what they felt they had to. Anyway, it was him and Amanda, so they'd already been through it and survived, right?

That was the problem: nothing was guaranteed. Just because they were here now didn't mean something couldn't go horribly wrong.

"We're going to die in here. We're going to get attacked by those horrid Amandas that gave themselves to that disgusting machine and we're going to die."

"I don't think so. If we're still in the right time, which I think we are, then remember what it was like when The Chamber was still where it was supposed to be? Cray was alone outside it, there were no more Hexads being produced, and we came back so we could stop it actually being used as one giant time machine. That was the plan, right? To jump up to the gantry like before, and then stop him from doing who knows what with it. Something's changed, sure, as it wasn't there, but we, the other we, obviously found out where it was and then came back to make sure we do too."

"No Dale, they didn't do that did they? They just jumped because when they were us that's what happened. Who knows what happened to them before they came and did this to us."

"Amanda, you're not thinking straight. I know you're scared, but the only logical explanation is that we are doing exactly what they did, so everything is going to be fine in the end. It's kind of encouraging."

"Dale, don't be absurd. This is time travel, nothing happens how it should. For all we know that was a version of us that would do anything to avoid this, so they jumped back and made us come here instead. Anyway, I thought this was a place where the lost Amandas came, not Dales." Amanda suddenly realized something, her hand going to her mouth in shock. "Oh."

"Yeah, exactly." Dale didn't want to think about it, but he knew what would happen now he was inside.

"Oh no, Dale! And you let this happen? You're going to just fade away, disappear into nothingness. We have to get out of here. Now."

"Look, I trust myself, and I trust you, okay? If we made ourselves come here then we sure as hell make it back out. We just need to find out what's going on first. Oh." Dale grabbed the thin book that thumped to the earth, brushing the dirt off it. On the cover it said, 'Stuff You Need to Know in a Hurry,' and that was all.

"Well, I guess we've been through all this a few times if we manage to write a damn book about it," said Amanda, peering over Dale's shoulder and reading the title.

"Guess so. Shall we?" Dale indicated a spot under a tree and they both moved onto the soft moss and sat down. Dale opened the first page. Judging by the thickness there weren't going to be many of them, and the handwriting was large — Dale's usual style in other words.

"You really do need more practice writing," observed Amanda, trying to decipher his almost illegible script.

"It's not my fault. I never use a pen anymore, it's always the keyboard."

They read the thin book. It didn't make them feel any more comfortable; it made them feel a whole lot worse.

~~~

"Well, looks like we are really in for it. Wish we could have been a little more specific. This is just background stuff, not actually telling us anything much at all."

"We're not exactly very helpful are we?" said Amanda, leaning back against the tree, dappled fake sunlight highlighting her hair.

"At least we know why The Chamber wasn't where it was supposed to be," said Dale, putting the book aside.

"It's something."

"A lot of it's conjecture though. Anyway, I don't really get our own explanation if I'm honest."

"I do, I think. Everything that we've done, all the jumping, all the reversing of things we've done that we then changed by sending notes and who knows what else, it just warped the future for us a little, well, a lot, so The Chamber still exists, and still functions just like it has all along, but Cray changed the location of where it was housed. I bet us watching had something to do with it. He may have found out and simply decided to build it somewhere else, or maybe whatever it was that happened in Dubai still had consequences that led to it being relocated."

"Well that's what we say in the book, isn't it? But it doesn't actually explain any of it. Nothing."

"I don't think it matters, the exact same things will have happened..." Amanda paused for a moment, thinking. "No, wait, that's the point, isn't it? We don't know what's happened as things have changed. For all we know we followed it to the new location at some point, did something, but once the future got changed then we wouldn't remember that. We only remember what's happened, not what's been changed because of something we did."

Dale looked at the book again, wondering why it didn't tell them more. "And the last bit?"

"I agree with it. It said to get a move on and that we have two days at the most to put an end to this, or I'll be stuck here, and you'll be..."

"Gone. For good."

"Let's get busy then shall we?"

"You sure?"

"What choice do we have?"

She's a brave woman. This must be terrifying, knowing what she's going to see, who she's going to meet once we get out into the open.

Dale wondered if there would be any memory of them being here before and what happened. If the timeline was the same then they would all be long dead by now, that happened thousands of years in the past, well, the future he supposed, not that any of it mattered any more. All that mattered was stopping Cray from using The Chamber as a giant time machine, if that happened then the repercussions would be devastating.

They'd talked about it endlessly while they kept their vile vigil on the gantry, arguing over if it really was a time machine and what would happen if it actually made a jump, and where it might jump to. The conclusion was simple: it would end everything, permanently.

Cray seemed unconcerned by his actions, he'd said that it didn't matter to him that Hexads ruined things, that people ended up gone, as he could spend lifetimes jumping back to before the events occurred, but clearly some future version of him had decided to finally make use of what he'd built and perform the largest jump of all, complete with everything inside the chamber, plus everything that made it function, Dale assumed.

Such a massive shift through reality would do damage that would reverberate through time and universes in ways Dale and Amanda didn't even want to imagine, but there was no doubt that it would put a strain on everything, destroying an incredible number of lives.

It wasn't just that though — the fact the thing existed meant it had to be destroyed. There was no way they could live knowing that there was no future for anybody, and that an endless procession of Amandas became warped inside the machine, endlessly looping back on themselves, paradoxes building up, all so that Hexad production continued until the time in the future they had witnessed where it seemed it was just Cray alone with his machine, all other people gone.

The strange thing was that maybe the Cray they had been meeting didn't even know about that yet. After all, what they witnessed had been a future version of him — he was much older and definitely a lot more insane than the version they had the misfortune to encounter.

"Right, come on then, let's get to it." Dale jumped to his feet. He was tired of thinking; it was time to act. Time to do something. He just wasn't sure what, but hiding under a tree definitely wasn't the answer.

Same but
Different

Time Unknown

The tiny forest they had jumped to, although Dale didn't really see it as jumping as they hadn't physically used a Hexad, was cool and quiet, the thick carpet of decaying leaves and moss emphasizing the slight difference in gravity, making Dale feel like he was a man on the moon and could bounce around with giant leaps if he so wished. But soon enough they were at the edge, looking at The Chamber in all its topsy-turvy glory.

Except it didn't seem quite the same as it had before — there was something about it that was intangible yet definitely changed. The air was a lot warmer for one, and the humidity level was high. In the forest Dale had assumed it was due to the dense canopy and the trapping of moisture between the trees, but it was the same out in the open.

They had moved from the tree-line into a green open field, but it wasn't a healthy color, it was as if the grass was clinging to life under less than ideal conditions. As they stood mute, taking in the inverse world that spread out in all directions, self-contained and nothing but a giant coffin, it became apparent that the rest of The Chamber was in a similar condition.

The once almost gaudy patchwork of arable land was stained brown where it should have been shining with healthy crops, and everything just seemed listless, less animated, almost like the entire landscape was slowing down for autumn, or in semi-hibernation.

Something was wrong. Very wrong.

Amanda stood nervously beside him, reaching out a hand absentmindedly, taking his and squeezing tight, eyes locked firmly on the curving landscape. Dale couldn't think of it as up and down any longer, it was all just the same really — if you walked around it you would feel like you were walking on the same flat ground, even though you could end up above where you once stood, the top of your head viewed by anyone that was now in your place.

"Something's not right, can you feel it?" asked Amanda, squeezing his hand tighter, wiping her forehead where beads of sweat were forming due to the high moisture content of the air.

"Definitely. It's hot too, and the light is different." Saying the words made Dale very aware of the fact that the light was far from normal: it too was duller, as if the artificial sunshine was unable to shine properly and give out enough energy to sustain the artificial environment.

Suddenly Dale's stomach did a somersault, guts churning in panic and dread, before it subsided. He'd had a moment of sheer terror, thinking that if the interior wasn't being maintained properly then what would happen if the gravity was suddenly cut off, or it sped up or slowed down? What would happen then? Would they be flung into the center, trapped by weightlessness, or could they be crushed to death, flattened like a pancake if the pull became too great for the human body to withstand?

No, that at least felt just as it had before, but Dale really didn't feel like hanging about to see what would happen — he couldn't, this place wasn't for him. If he didn't leave soon then he'd just fade away into non-existence, as if he'd never been. For whatever reason, the whole Hexad mystery and everything that came after was tied up with Amanda, and the rifts in time that were the result meant that pure logic simply didn't apply anymore. They ran because of her, everything was because of her, and he may have played a large part in her life, be a part of the madness, but he knew he was nowhere near as important to the continuation of the universes trying to correct themselves as she herself was.

"Let's walk, try to find out what's going on here."

"Okay," said Amanda reluctantly. "Do you think they'll remember us from before? Remember what happened?"

"I doubt it. If we are in the same time as the one we were in on the outside, although to be honest I'm really not sure, then there will have been countless generations of Amandas since then. We won't even be a memory. And besides, this time will be different. We know what to expect, we just need to figure out what to actually do. Are you okay? Can you handle this?" Dale turned to look at her, and there was no doubt that she was a bundle of nerves, but that was to be expected. The question was would she be able to cope knowing what the women were doing, that some of them wouldn't take kindly to their interference, understanding it could mean the end of their existence if they meddled in the way things were?

"I'm okay. We don't have a choice, we have to do this."

"Right, let's go then. How about over there?" Dale pointed to the closest building: a stone cottage of quite generous proportions, although the haze of the atmosphere made it hard to make out much detail, the air thick almost like they were looking through a dirty window.

Amanda nodded in agreement; they began to walk.

The air was alive with a dull thrumming in the background. The noise of the machinery, Dale supposed, although he didn't recall being aware of it before, but that didn't mean it wasn't there. Then it hit him: he could hear it as there were no other sounds.

Where was the singing of the birds, the humming of the bees, the distant chatter of women? A constant noise that was here once, now making itself felt by its absence. It wasn't right, the ecosystem was broken somehow, everything was changed but for what reason Dale couldn't fathom yet. There would be answers soon enough though, answers or death, for him at least. Maybe both of them.

They carried on walking.

~~~

The cottage was quiet. No Amanda came out to greet them, nobody shouted at them, tried to attack or stared at them with cold, unwelcoming eyes. All that remained was the humming of The Chamber and an unkempt garden. Plants had grown large and wild, once neat borders were thick with weeds, previously neatly cut lawns spilling over onto once well-maintained paths.

Fruit trees were gnarled and sickly, raised vegetable beds full of nothing but a few self-seeding salad plants that had been faring well left unsupervised and without control.

As they walked up the garden Dale realized what else was different about The Chamber: there was no smoke coming from any of the chimneys, no signs of life at all for that matter.

The place was dead.

What the hell was going on?

"Dale, do you think we're too late? Could something have happened and we've arrived only to fail before we even try?"

"I don't know, I'm not sure what to think. Part of me feels relieved if it really is true there aren't any Amandas locked in this terrible place, but I don't know what that actually means. It could be good, it could be very, very bad."

"I don't get this, something's way off here," said Amanda, shifting uncomfortably from foot to foot, rubbing her arms as if she'd suddenly gone cold.

"We came to put things right, to stop what Cray does, and people or no people in here, he's still ruined the future for everyone, so that hasn't changed. If it had then we wouldn't be standing here, we'd know nothing of any of it as we'd have never done any of it. It would be wiped from our minds and we'd be back where we should be before we ever took our first jump, so whatever is going on it doesn't change anything." Dale was resolute, determined to see things through. The lack of life was certainly disconcerting, and didn't bode well, but they still had their job to do, no matter what.

"Let's go look inside, maybe we can find a clue." Amanda walked reluctantly up the little path and pushed open the simple wooden door to the cottage. Dale followed behind, knowing it would be fruitless.

Standing in the middle of a low-ceilinged living room it was apparent that the home had been unoccupied for some time. There was an air of decay to the dark, cramped space — much smaller than Dale had imagined from the outside. Dust clung desperately to the furniture in layers, making strange swirling patterns probably due to the slightly abnormal gravity. When Dale put a hand to the bright scatter cushions he could feel the dampness and a musty smell stung his nostrils.

The kitchen was the same; they didn't need to look any further. The house was strange, like many different Amandas had occupied it and each had their own quirks. Pieces of furniture were painted with bright designs, while more recent occupants had clearly disliked the tainting of the wood and had tried to make it original again. There was even an unfinished project on the kitchen table, a small footstool that was partially sanded back to bare wood.

Dale had seen enough and hurried outside for some stale, but still much fresher air.

Would it be the same everywhere? Were there no women left inside any longer?

They began to explore, heading towards the dome where they knew they had to be if they were to have any chance of stopping Cray from using The Chamber as one monstrous time machine.

There were strange sights as they made their way: random holes dug in the ground, revealing dirty metal far below, as if an attempt had been made to find a way out, to no avail. If you didn't know where to dig then you wouldn't stand a chance, and that was far from the only sign of discontent. They passed a few fire-damaged buildings, definitely a bad idea in a sealed environment, but from all appearances the flames had been doused well before the buildings themselves crumbled, it was more that the interiors were blackened, everything covered in soot, but not completely destroyed.

Other signs of neglect were more horrific. They came to what Dale knew was a graveyard, a surprise as they had witnessed countless bodies through numerous timelines being taken from The Chamber. At some point all that must have changed and now row after row of neat mounds dotted a field where stunted daisies clung to life, maybe giving their last energy to flower in the hopes of pollination that would never happen. But many of the holes were so shallow that Dale could see limbs poking out of the soil as it settled back down, skin shining dull blue in the sickly light like fading neon tubes.

"What do you think this means?" asked Amanda, staring at the desperate makeshift wooden markers, the insanity of the name Amanda scratched roughly into each and every one of them.

"That Cray gave up caring, or couldn't cope any longer. That things got bad in here, very bad I would imagine. It's humid in here, but if the systems for providing water to the crops didn't work then that wouldn't be enough to allow them to survive. There aren't any animals anymore so I assume they died, maybe that's what... Oh, sorry."

Amanda was on her knees, bent over a particularly rough marker, Amanda scrawled on it in nothing but pen, gone over and over until it was thick, the faded ink almost impossible to read, the grave still dark where grass had failed to grow over the infertile soil. Dale crouched and dug a hand into the dirt, finding it dry and brittle, the clumps falling apart in his hand like sand. There were no worms, so what other important creatures of the earth were missing? Such considerations would be of vital importance if an enclosed ecosystem had any chance of succeeding.

Would that mean that the bodies of the women would mostly still be there, not really rotting, not being eaten by the bugs and the worms, forever entombed in their strange world, never even truly returning to the earth and finding a final peace?

Dale shuddered and got to his feet. "Come on, I know this is going to be bad but we need to go to that machine." Amanda looked aghast, eyes dark, the skin underneath as blue as the ailing light emanating from the dome. "You can wait outside, but I need to check. I'm sorry."

That Funny
Feeling

Time Unknown

Dale whispered for Amanda to stay back, although it was clear she was reluctant to be alone, if even for a few minutes. But it wasn't the sight of the innocuous stone building housing the terrible machine that had stopped the pair of them in their tracks, it was the sight of the back of an old woman, squatting down wearing a faded Paul Simon t-shirt that hung off her gaunt frame like it was draped over a wooden pole, which gave them both pause. They could only see the back of her head — her skull was visible between the long wispy strands of sick-white brittle hair.

"Wait here," said Dale again, Amanda tugging at his sleeve as he went to leave. "What?"

"Just be careful, and be kind. Whatever has happened, she is an old woman. And me." Amanda stared deep into his eyes, making sure he understood. Dale nodded.

The woman didn't turn as he approached, just carried on squatting there, seemingly unaware of his presence. As Dale got close the terrible state of her body became more apparent — there really was little left of her but flesh and bone. Was she the last? Were there more like her? Time to get some answers.

"Hello, I'm Dale."

The woman turned her head to the side as Dale walked around her to be in front, following him with dead eyes; uncomprehending eyes. She looked away from him, dismissing him as if he wasn't even there, and continued with what she was doing. She was digging. Digging in the dead soil with a stick that was as twisted as her own arthritic hands. The stick was all sharp frayed edges where she was clutching it like a prized possession and her hands were bleeding as a result — it was clear she neither cared or felt it any longer.

It was Amanda, as he'd never seen her before, as he never wanted his Amanda to see herself — she was broken, an empty shell. More dead than alive.

Dale crouched down in front of the woman, watching as she tried to dig out the soil with the stick, but she was so weak that she barely scraped the surface, more like a child with a crayon trailing it along paper before really understanding how to draw. "Can you hear me?"

The old Amanda looked up at him, almost as if she recognized the voice finally, and said, "Worms. There should be worms." Her voice was little more than a whisper, dry and raspy, like she had a mouthful of the dead soil.

"There should be. Where did they go?"

"Old, old worms, all die. Everything die."

"What happened here?" asked Dale quietly, mesmerized as the woman continued her futile digging, never stopping for an instant.

"Worms, there should be worms. Worms, worms, worms."

Dale tried again to talk to her but she was lost, no longer of the world, gone to her own place, maybe to escape whatever it was that had happened.

Knowing he would get no answers, and worried he would upset her if he pushed too hard, Dale moved away and left her to it. There was nothing to be gained from disturbing her, nothing good anyway.

Signaling to Amanda, Dale continued to walk away from the old woman, and a relieved Amanda joined him, never once trying to go talk to her herself. She knew it would be too much to take, so kept well away.

"Was it me?" Amanda asked.

Dale nodded. "She's gone though, lost to herself. Let's leave her be." Dale couldn't say more, he didn't have it in him. It felt like the joy, the life and the thankfulness, was being sucked out of him like that foul machine did in the room he had yet to enter. He felt like just giving up, waiting for it to all be over. Would he ever laugh again? Would he and Amanda ever be together? Be normal? It didn't feel like it. Not now, not ever.

"I don't think we're going to find much in here," said Dale. "I think we need to go back outside, soon. This place is doing things to me, strange things, and I get the feeling it's just going to get a lot worse."

"You feel it too? I thought it was just me, not coping very well, but it's like all the joy is being eaten up and replaced with nothing, like this place is sucking my soul, leaving me all empty and dead. Just like this." Amanda kicked at the dirt, dust flying up a little bit higher than it was really supposed to.

"Yeah, one more stop then we get out."

"How?"

"Just like last time, hopefully."

They walked in silence towards the building, Amanda getting slower the closer they got, until she stopped altogether when they were a few paces from the partially open door, light, clear and bright, spilling out onto the barren earth.

Dale squeezed her hand and said, "It's all right, wait here."

He opened the door wide enough to squeeze inside; he closed it behind him.

~~~

The stark interior was almost blinding, bringing home just how wrong the light was outside the room. As he got accustomed to the change, his pupils constricting in reaction to the light, he took in the familiar surroundings of probably the worst place he had been in his entire life.

"It's not working, it's supposed to work."

Dale spun at the voice, Amanda's voice. "I thought you were going to wait...?" It wasn't her, it was a Chamber Amanda, clearly institutionalized to a high degree. She paid little attention to Dale, simply stood by the machine, waiting for it to take her, carry out its terrible operation. The Amanda turned to look at him again, before seeming to come to a decision.

"You're here to fix it," she stated with conviction. "Yes, yes. You've come to fix it, to fix everything. You'll make it okay, you will, won't you?"

"I don't think anyone can do that, not now." Dale almost broke. He could feel it inside himself, feel the will to forge on waning, his ability to not get caught up in the pity and the disgust for what had happened to these women almost leaving him. The shame that he knew could be his if he let it, that every person had a breaking point, however strong they believed themselves to be — given enough stress anyone could break, lose their mind, lose their dignity. Lose their very souls.

"You've got to, you must!" shrieked the Amanda, banging her fists into the machine. "It's how things are, what's meant to happen. We give of ourselves so The Chamber endures. This is all there is for Amanda, and we must give of ourselves to receive. There is no other way."

"Where are the others?"

"All gone now, just me and the old crone left. Nobody comes, nothing happens. I come every day, like a good girl, like the Mothers said I should, but then they got old, and they died. Everyone died. I come, I wait. It doesn't work, it's supposed to work." She banged on the machine again, fresh blood shining bright against faded brown smudges where she must have repeated her pleas for years.

Dale left her to her madness, his heart breaking as he closed the door on his way out, the sound of battered flesh smacking against the machine his only farewell.

He walked slowly to where Amanda was standing, leg shaking with an unnoticed nervous tic as she stared at the curving landscape, her back to the scene of so much distress.

"It's not working."

"Anything else in there? Any clues?"

"No, nothing. Come on, let's get to the dome, see if there is anything there before we try to get out of this place, make this bloody obscenity disappear like it's never been."

Neither of them spoke as they made their way across the empty landscape, feeling sicker as they got closer to the dome. Dale wondered if it was some kind of radiation leak or something — would they be riddled with fast-growing cancers and tumors, live out stunted lives in a hospital ward even if they did escape with their lives?

We've got to get out of here, this place is doing funny things to my head.

Judging by the grim set to Amanda's face she was faring a lot worse — Dale knew he'd made the right decision not telling of the Amanda in the room, it could be the last straw.

They kept moving, skirting empty homes and dying vegetation, hope almost lost, but not quite.

~~~

"Look," said Amanda, pointing ahead at the dome, now no more than a minute away.

Dale lifted his head from staring at his feet and looked where she was pointing, turning to shield his eyes against the blue. It was a figure, no doubt about it, and male, so not an Amanda then. Could it be one of him, a Dale? He really hoped not, as, quite frankly, he was the last person he wanted to meet at the moment.

Almost the last.

It was Cray.

Familiar Faces

Time Unknown

"What should we do?" asked Amanda in a whisper.

"I think we should go have a little chat. There's no point trying to hide in here, is there?"

"But he could kill us, do anything."

"I don't think so, not in here."

"How can you be so sure?"

"I'm not. Come on." The only thing giving Dale even a semblance of confidence was the fact that they themselves had made them come into The Chamber, meaning they'd survived, left somehow and managed to jump to do it. Plus the book; it gave him hope.

He was terrified.

"Ah, Dale. Amanda. Oh, 'the' Dale and Amanda, what a nice surprise."

"You mean you weren't expecting us?" said Dale. "I very much doubt that."

"I wasn't, but he was," said Cray, staring in disgust mixed with disappointment at a much older version of himself lying dead and mangled on the ground, blue light highlighting the lumps on his face, distorting his features.

"You beat yourself to death then? How very insane of you."

"It's not madness," spat Cray, "it's justice. This idiot of an old man was in no way me. No way. I hunted high and low for you two, but in the end I couldn't catch you, but I knew you'd be watching, somehow. So I moved The Chamber, started it all over again some place new."

"We know," said Dale. "We told ourselves."

Cray looked at him, nonplussed for a moment until he understood, then waved it away as unimportant. "I found you'd been watching so changed things, but then I had to be sure to see it through to the end. To make certain The Chamber endured, did what it was designed to do when the time came, so I checked. It all fell apart, everything got worse, just terrible. This wasn't what I wanted at all."

"What did you do Cray? What have you done?"

Cray stood, unapologetic yet the burden of failure hung heavy, that was clear. "It wasn't me, it was this idiot." Cray kicked the dead Cray, pure hatred dominating his features. "This idiot, this last Cray to ensure what was done came to pass, he ruined it. There have been many, I am sure you know from your spying, countless versions of me I have taken from various times, some willing to carry the burden, others nothing but cowards, as I couldn't live forever through the time it would take for The Chamber to be ready, but I wanted to watch it develop, become what it was meant to be, but this one, this last guardian of all my work, he has let it degenerate into this. The fool." Cray kicked the body again, then sagged as if the fight had left him.

"Where are the Amandas, Cray? What happened to them all?"

"They're all gone, all used up. None left now."

"What do you mean," shrieked Amanda, "all used up? You bastard, you treated them like cattle. You abused them, you locked them up and you took everything away from them."

"And what would you do? You would see to it that they never existed, that none but you ever even had the chance to live," shouted Cray. "At least I wanted to give them life. The Hexad created life in countless universes and that is down to me. Me! I created worlds, I created infinite people to live their lives in infinite ways and you dare to accuse me of anything? You, both of you, would see to it that none of it ever happened."

"Because you took people from those worlds Cray, the time travel closed the universes down, the people eradicated to restore the balance. You broke the rules."

"Rules? Ha, there are no rules. At least I did something. I controlled this world for many years until the populace disappeared. But it didn't matter, I had The Chamber, the last chance, and I had the other universes, the closed ones. With The Chamber I could access them, go back to before Hexads became common technology, live in countless pasts, explore more than one man could ever grow bored of, and it almost all came to nothing. I was so close, and almost failed, but now..." Cray smiled, a madman, his prize almost ready.

"Almost failed?" Dale knew he wasn't going to like the answer.

"Yes. This idiot, this old Cray, he was to get everything ready, I was to come as I did now, in here we could meet without fear of a paradox, but he miscalculated, we needed three when there were only two, and the two here are pathetic specimens so the third needs to be very strong. What better than the original? The true source of all of this?"

Dale knew what he was talking about, Amanda didn't seem to be following what Cray was saying. One thing he was sure of: Cray was genuinely insane. He was talking too much, telling them things, this wasn't how Cray in his right mind would act — he was always tight-lipped. He obviously thought himself unstoppable.

"Amanda." said Dale.

"Amanda," said Cray. "The final piece of the puzzle, the last drop of power needed to send The

Chamber and all it touches, its machines to make it function, everything, wherever I want in time, where I can begin again, let the paradoxes unfold and a whole new world of Amandas will be there to power me on to the next and the next."

"Why?" came the simple question from Amanda. "Why this? Why this madness?"

"Because he loves you," said Dale. "This was to be his life, once he knew he was above the restraints of the effects of time travel, once he had what he wanted from all the Amandas to power this thing, then he was going to live here, live amongst countless Amandas, forever. Right?"

Cray nodded, almost shy with his movements. "Don't you see Amanda? You are the most special woman that there has ever been. You are the changer of worlds, the creator of universes, the reason why The Chamber exists, the whole point to the whole future of humanity. This is all for you." Cray swept an arm, indicating The Chamber. "You did this Amanda, you brought me Hexads, you set this path, you brought the universes into being. I just wanted to share it with you."

"No, no, no, no, no. It's not my fault, it isn't. I'm not to blame. I just want to go home. I don't want this."

"You'll see, we will jump to a new world, full of Amandas on countless paths and we shall populate The Chamber and make it as it once was. We shall have a beautiful life together. All of us."

"No," said Dale.

"No? You think you can change this? The path has already been set Dale, this is the future, this is here, this is happening, and I will have Amanda, all of her."

"No, you won't."

Is it Love?

Time Unknown

I can't believe I missed this all along. He loves her and he's done all of this just so he can be with her, all of her, all the versions of her there have ever been. But he's ruined it, he's already used so many of her to produce Hexads, and to get this insane Chamber ready, and now he's gone completely mad.

"Don't you see?" said Cray, almost pleading. "You're so special Amanda, I knew it the moment I set eyes on you. Just like the other me told me I would before I got rid of him to ensure things worked out the right way. Just before I ended his life he told me how beautiful you were, how special. I almost didn't believe him, myself, until I saw you, then I knew. I've always known. It's you. And me."

"No, you're mad. You can't think that I want anything to do with you after what you've done. Do you?"

"You'll see, give it time. And anyway, there have already been countless Amandas that felt differently. Many that have stayed here have been more than happy to spend time with me." Cray almost leered, and was lost in memories of Amanda for a while by the faraway look in his eyes.

"I'm sure they were quite mad then. You locked them up in this strange place, created it so this is where they would appear, or where you could bring them, and what choice did they have?" said Dale.

"There is always a choice. Always," said Cray defensively.

"And I've got choices too. I will never be yours. Never." Amanda stared into Cray's eyes and Dale knew he found no uncertainty there.

She was resolute; what else did he expect? Had Amandas really given themselves to this man? This monster that kept them locked up for his own amusement, that created their prison by what he did to them? Creating more and more Hexads so more and more people jumped and caused more and more worlds to be created where more Amandas got caught in paradox after paradox and vanished from the world, ending up inside The Chamber?

Cray was insane, totally and utterly insane.

"You will be mine," shouted Cray, one arm shooting out and grabbing Amanda roughly by the neck. Amanda began to go purple, blood flow cut off, her breathing coming in gasps, rattling like she was coughing on smoke.

Dale moved to release her but Cray stared at him and said, "You make one more move and she's dead. Gone forever."

Dale was full of uncertainty. What should he do? Would Cray really kill her? Now, when he needed her more than ever? He doubted it, but was it worth the risk? Surely he wouldn't?

Cray loosened his grip, still clutching her tight, but Amanda was at least able to breathe. She took in deep lungsful of air as her color faded, hands clawing ineffectively at the steel grip still pushing into her delicate flesh.

Cray moved his gun from where it was digging into her side and lifted it to her head, fingers leaving deep marks on Amanda's neck as he let go, taking a step back.

"I will shoot her Dale, you too. Don't test me, you'll regret it if you do."

"Okay, okay. This is pointless you know? It's not going to work."

"You have no idea what you're talking about. You think I don't know what I'm doing? I've worked too long and too hard for this to fail. Countless Crays have worked for endless years to make this a success, and if it wasn't for this idiot," Cray kicked the body on the ground, "then it would all be ready right now. But it doesn't matter, there's still time for everything to work out. There's always time."

Cray waved them off to the right, the direction of the foul machine and the two Amandas that still remained. Amanda understood instantly and tried to run, fear overcoming everything but the need to get away.

There was nowhere to go; there was no escape.

"Stop," said Cray calmly. "If you run I'll shoot him Amanda. I may do it anyway, just because he's so damn annoying."

Amanda turned and looked at Cray, then stopped. She walked back meekly, like a puppy that knew its master would punish it if it disobeyed.

"It's okay, you'll be okay," said Dale, pulling Amanda close, putting an arm around her waist.

Amanda didn't speak, couldn't. She was terrified, knowing what Cray wanted.

Dale reached for her knife.

"Please," said Cray. "You really think that's going to work?"

Dale just shrugged; he had to try.

"Take your weapons off Dale, and drop them," ordered Cray.

Dale did as he was told, it had been a long shot anyway. He felt more vulnerable than he'd ever felt in his life.

"Now, move," ordered Cray, stepping behind them and prodding Dale forward with the gun.

~~~

Time went into free-fall for Dale; everything became hyper-real. He could feel every beat of his heart — surprisingly slow considering he would normally melt down at the thought of danger to himself, let alone Amanda.

Each footstep was like a lifetime, senses acute, awareness expanding to take in not only his own thoughts and emotions but to notice as if for the first time everything around him too.

This was the clarity he'd heard about when people were in extreme situations, like the fabled life flashing before your eyes, or when mothers get superhuman strength when it comes to their children being in danger and they do whatever it takes to save them. Dale may not have felt superhuman, but he became more aware of himself and his environment than he had ever been in his entire life.

The hum of the dome became almost overpowering, as if it was getting louder and more insistent, rather than Dale simply focusing on it more. Watching his own feet move reluctantly forward felt weird, like he was seeing them for the first time and they weren't really his, moving of their own volition as he certainly didn't want any part in what was unfolding in the heightened reality he found himself now living in.

Cray pushed Dale hard in the back with the barrel and he had to let go of Amanda. "No more cuddling, stay apart. And keep walking."

Amanda turned to Dale, the fear so visible he was amazed she could actually walk. He knew he'd be on the floor, a gibbering wreck. His eyes focused on a pale freckle on her neck, pulsing quickly where the carotid pumped blood fast. He felt like he could see the adrenaline surge through her body so she could cope with the nightmare. What must be going on in her head? The things she knew had happened to all the other Amandas, and now were going to happen to her as well. It didn't bear thinking about.

How had it come to this? This bizarre situation where life didn't make any sense, where nothing made sense? Worlds created at the press of a button, the ability to travel through time and where megalomaniacs think nothing of ripping apart reality just because they can and they want to see what's on the other side?

The Chamber? That had to be the weirdest of the lot. Cray had gone to immense effort to build such a thing — Dale couldn't even begin to imagine how it was constructed, or the vast machinery involved, hidden behind the bedrock. They were probably devices larger than The Chamber itself, there to turn the massive arms that created the spin. Let alone its function: to house Amandas that were created in other universes, just so he could keep them, perpetuate the cycle until now it had all come to an end, Amandas used up. Gone.

"Stop," said Cray.

Dale realized he'd been lost in thought and hadn't noticed they were now getting close to the terrible room.

They were stood by the old woman, still involved in her digging. Cray bent down and helped her to her feet, with genuine affection too, it seemed. He treated her gently, like she was his family, as if he'd been a part of her life for a long time. Maybe he had, maybe he'd seen her as a young woman and made sporadic visits to her as she grew older, or one of him at the very least.

Damn, the other Amanda inside the room, I didn't tell her about her. Dale glanced at Amanda, who mouthed a silent "What?" clearly seeing the worry in his eyes even though he tried to hide it.

"There's another one, a woman inside the room. She's not right Amanda, don't take any notice." This was going to be hard for her to take, seeing a version of herself reduced to such a pathetic creature, begging for the foul machine to perform its terrible act on her. Wanting it, needing it. And then it would be her turn, she was to be taken by the machine too. Drained of her life, a little bit less of a person afterward.

What could he do? How could he get them out of this mess? Dale had felt strangely confident until now, somehow believing that all would be well, that they'd get out, get away, leave victorious. Now he wasn't so sure. He hadn't consciously thought it, but he supposed he'd believed that he'd do what he'd done before: promise to make a jump and repeat what he did to allow them to get away, but so far nothing had happened. Was that just because he hadn't actually turned such vagaries into a proper conscious thought?

If so then now was the time to get the hell out before things got any worse.

"Dale. Dale! What other Amanda? What happened to her?" Amanda was even more terrified, maybe he should have kept quiet? She might not have to see the woman anyway.

"Quiet," ordered Cray, pointing the gun at them, helping the frail woman move. She was unsteady on her feet, muttering about worms, and she looked even more skeletal, if that was possible, now she was walking. Her legs seemed like they were nothing but twigs — matching her ineffective digging implement.

"Who's in there? What have you done to her? How could you let her," Amanda pointed at the old woman, "get like this? You're a monster."

"I didn't do it," said Cray, voice sharp. Yet there was a hint of pleading, like he didn't want to be seen as the bad guy. It was ridiculous. "It wasn't me. I told you that the other me let things go wrong, he didn't keep on running everything how he should have."

"Or maybe the whole place is just winding down," said Dale. "It's unstable Cray, can't you see that?

This isn't natural and it can't go on working perfectly forever."

"It can, and it will. I can deal with any problems. But after we finish this, after you give of yourself Amanda. In there." Cray pointed.

Amanda collapsed to the ground like she was made of air and it had suddenly escaped through her mouth as she moaned with fear.

She was out cold as Dale bent to help. Her head was clammy, her hands were icy, eyes were shut and her breathing was shallow.

It was too much for her, it was as if she'd simply gone into shock, shut down as she couldn't face what was about to happen.

Dale began to panic, when he knew it was the last thing he should be doing. He had to get them out, and fast. Otherwise, he feared for Amanda's sanity, especially once she met the other woman inside the room — her fragile state meant it might send her over the edge. That or the machine itself could kill her.

Or Cray. Once he got what he wanted who was to say he wouldn't just get rid of them all? Wipe the slate clean and start again with his new access to countless Amandas from all the up-until-now closed-off worlds?

"Move. Now," ordered Cray. Dale stepped back reluctantly as Cray bent and felt for a pulse. Then he slapped Amanda hard across the cheek, color springing to her flesh like a bubbling geyser.

Amanda reacted instantly, sitting bolt upright, hand moving to her face. She looked terrible, but at least she was conscious.

"Okay, enough of this, time to make your little sacrifice. It's time to visit the machine."

"No, no you can't. I won't. You can't make me."

"Is that right?" Cray stepped back and before Dale knew what was happening his face felt like it was on fire. He put a hand to his cheek and it was pouring blood — Cray had ripped his flesh open with a quick swing of the gun.

"Stop it, just stop it. I'll do it, all right? Just leave him alone." Amanda stood shakily, while Dale tried to stop focusing on the pain so he could think of a way out.

Think Dale, just think. Okay, what if you jump and just power this damn thing down? No, because then we'll all die as who knows where we'll go flying off to inside this place. What about if—

"I said move, are you deaf?" Cray jabbed him hard with the gun then lifted it, arm moving back for another swing.

"Okay. We're going." Dale reached for Amanda's hand and said, "Are you all right? You gave me a bit of a scare then."

"I'm fine. Well, I'm not, but you know...?"

"I know."

"That looks bad," said Amanda, moving Dale's blood-stained hand away from his cheek.

"I'll live. Hopefully," said Dale grimly.

"Faster, walk faster." Cray jabbed Dale again, and with no other choice and no time to think of a way to get them out, Dale and Amanda, with Cray and the old Amanda behind, walked up the path.

Amanda squeezed his hand tightly, eyes focused on her feet.

Just trying to will them to move. She's braver than me. Think Dale, get out of here.

Time Unravels

Time Unknown

They reached the door.

Amanda tried to run, leaving Dale behind, but he didn't blame her, how could he? She was petrified. This wasn't just about her though, Dale could tell that much. Neither of them could avoid thinking about the consequences if The Chamber really did make a jump. Dale couldn't even imagine what kind of an effect it would have on reality if Cray was successful; he doubted Cray did either.

There was a strange silence as they stood outside. Amanda was next to Dale again, a few paces back from the door, Cray and the old Amanda were to their left, the old woman quiet, waiting. Cray was smiling, clearly anticipating what was to come.

Then the quiet was broken by a shriek of panicked excitement as the Amanda inside the room came to the door and spotted Cray.

"It's broken, it's not working. Are you going to fix it? Fix it, fix it, fix it."

"Yes Amanda, I'm going to fix it for you. Do you want to give of yourself, give to the machine?"

"Yes, yes, yes. Give to the machine. Give Amanda to the machine, make everything all right again. Bring everyone back, give Amanda someone to talk to. Amanda wants friends. Amanda needs more Amanda. Amanda is lonely."

"Don't you worry my dear, you won't be alone for much longer. I'm going to fix everything, just you wait and see."

Cray nudged Dale again, while the crazed Amanda danced around them excitedly, singing, "Give to the machine, give to the machine," before she ran back inside, then peered out, saying, "Hurry, hurry, hurry."

They went inside.

Amanda was lost in a daze of panic and confusion, not able to keep up with what was happening, the new Amanda an obvious shock. Dale should have told her about the crazed woman, but he hadn't thought things were going to go this far, this wrong.

Cray directed them over to an empty corner, then carefully moved the old woman to the ground, where she sat happily, humming something tuneless in a dull monotone, stick stabbing at the tiles. All the while the crazed Amanda hopped about excitedly, unable to contain her pleasure at the anticipation of the machine working again.

Dale watched as everything became hyper-real once more. He watched as Cray moved over to one of the large black stacks and took a small key from his suit pocket, then inserted it in a tiny keyhole. Once the door was open he flicked a series of switches and as he locked the door up the machine hummed into life, reminding Dale of a printer starting up. Once the machine had configured itself it went silent, the insane Amanda almost beside herself with excitement and anticipation, eyeing the machine greedily, wanting to give herself.

The sight of someone so far gone made Dale sick to his stomach. What had she been through for this to be the result?

"You did this Cray, look what you've done to the woman. You okay with that?"

"No, I'm not okay with that, but it wasn't me," said Cray defensively, "it was that idiot outside. He did it all wrong. I'm sorry." Cray was looking at Amanda, apologizing, utterly sincere. Amanda's eyes were glazed over, she couldn't cope with it and had retreated somewhere deep inside to escape the horror.

"You going to make her mad too?" asked Dale, watching as Cray lifted the old lady from the floor like a stack of brittle kindling.

"It has to be done; we all have to make sacrifices. This is too big to not see it through to the end Dale, you know that."

"I know nothing of the sort. I know that you're a monster, sick and twisted and utterly insane. You think I'm going to let you do this? Let you ruin everything?"

"What choice do you have? You move and you're dead." Cray half-undressed the old lady carefully then shuffled her into the machine, calming the hyper Amanda with promises that she could go next, that she would have her turn soon enough. She pouted like a child, but calmed a little, hanging her head like she'd been chastised.

The old woman stood in the machine, not moving, letting herself be wrapped in its metallic embrace without seeming to even notice. Dale watched in horror as the arm swiveled out from the recess and a soft pneumatic sound began. All too quickly the needle approached the naked upper body of the woman, her skin-covered skeleton waxy and blotchy under the stark white light.

She smiled as the needle punctured her spine, going in deep. Dale watched the precious fluid trickle down the tube as Amanda gasped next to him, eyes darting around the room like a cornered wild animal, returning to the old Amanda, drawn by the horror.

"Don't watch. This isn't happening Amanda, not really."

When it was over Cray dressed the woman, attention moving from her to Dale and Amanda, the gun trained on them almost constantly. Dale knew he'd never make it across the room to Cray even if he was distracted, and knew that if he was dead he'd never get Amanda and him out of The Chamber.

Next was the turn of the ever-so-eager insane Amanda, her naked upper torso already bared, ready for the promise of cold steel puncturing her skin, ice-cold metal sucking away what little reality she had left — if any.

As she hopped into place, surprisingly calm and moving sedately after her manic actions just a moment ago, Dale noticed a change in the background noise of The Chamber. The blue light coming from the outside, where the door was still open, seemed to intensify, and Dale wasn't sure but it felt like he was a little heavier, like The Chamber had begun to speed up, increasing the gravity.

"It's beginning, the energy is powering up The Chamber, soon it will be The Hexad, the largest time travel machine to have ever made a jump, and we will be a part of it. We'll be free to move through new universes, where there will be countless new Amandas with every subsequent jump." Cray was smiling like Dale had never seen before, lost in anticipation of what he saw as the perfect life waiting for him.

"You're mad," said Dale, hand numb where Amanda was squeezing it so tightly.

"Am I? I don't think so."

"I give myself to the machine," said the insane Amanda as she was held tight by the metal bands and the needle pushed against her skin before piercing it. She let out a blissful moan as it went deeper, eyes rolling back in her head in pure ecstasy.

We have to get out of here.

Dale was beginning to seriously panic. What was wrong with him? Why couldn't he think straight, do something to get them out? Was it from the blow to the cheek? Dale put a hand up instinctively, wincing with the pain as he felt the large gash with fingers coated in dry blood. No, it wasn't that, it was... It was The Chamber, the fact he wasn't supposed to be inside. He was fading, becoming less than a full person, already losing parts of himself to the nothingness he was going to become if he didn't act fast.

What could he do? He needed to do something to save them, before it was too late. There were no hatches apart from the one far away, not as far as he knew anyway, so what other way was there to get out? There were the large access points for the staff that had come and gone long ago, but none of that was any use, even if he could have opened them somehow as another version of himself. He needed something to do right here and now, a way to stop this before Amanda was taken by the machine and they all jumped away forever.

Something changed again; this time Dale felt lighter than ever, the burst of heaviness gone. A moment later and it felt normal once more.

"Your turn Amanda. Come on, it isn't so bad," said Cray, smiling as the world changed and the buzzing inside The Chamber grew louder and louder. The insane Amanda was dancing around again, buttoning up her blouse after giving of herself, skipping to the door, before moving outside, growing more and more manic as the buzzing increased.

The light grew bright, the blue seeping into the room, casting its glow on the white interior.

"Can you feel it? It's going to happen. Give to the machine and then we shall be gods, out of space and time, untouchable. Forever."

"No, no, you can't make me. You can't," shrieked Amanda.

Dale focused with every ounce of his being and shoved Amanda to the side, towards the door where she stopped, unable to run and leave Dale behind. "Go," shouted Dale, lunging after her as she ran outside, Cray right behind them. "Keep going," shouted Dale, as Amanda stopped again, knowing Dale would be killed if she tried to escape.

"I can't, he'll kill you."

"Just go, trust me."

Amanda ran down the path, Dale close behind, but Cray shouted, "Stop."

Dale knew what he had to do, he just needed a few seconds. The buzzing increased, the gravity pitched low once more right as Cray shouted above the noise, "I warned you Dale," and fired.

Dale prayed, and when he found he was still alive, he leapt at Cray in the temporarily lowered gravity, thinking to reach him before he fired again. His instincts had been right, the changing gravity fields as The Chamber got ready to jump meant that the aim of the gun could never be calculated — as soon as the bullet left the chamber it was skewed by the warped gravity, veering well off its mark. But close to Cray it wouldn't matter, especially not if the gravity returned to normal.

Dale's leap brought him near to Cray, but not near enough. Cray took aim again.

This was it, he couldn't possibly miss, then Amanda would be all alone and he'd be dead. Normal gravity returned even as the buzzing increased and the light from the end of The Chamber began to pulse rhythmically. Dale stared into Cray's eyes and knew this was the end.

A blur of movement streaked from the right and Cray went down in a confusion of limbs. It was the insane Amanda, she'd attacked Cray out of nowhere — nobody had given her a thought, Dale certainly didn't think she would do such a thing, and Cray definitely believed her to be harmless.

"You were going to force her, make her give herself when she didn't want to," screamed the Amanda, arms flying wildly, hitting at Cray's face, trying to bite him and kick him as they rolled on the floor.

"No worms, need worms," screamed the old Amanda, now crouched down again, digging futilely with her stick.

The buzzing got louder, the blue pulsing faster and faster as Dale ran for the prone figures, praying once again he didn't get shot.

"Get off me, get off!" shouted Cray, trying to get away from the Amanda that had morphed into a berserker, frenzied and relentless.

"I'm the one. I'm the special one," she screamed, tearing at Cray's clothes with her teeth, out of control and truly lost.

But not quite. Dale understood with a flash of insight that the real Amanda was still in there somewhere, still able to understand what was happening on some level, and had reacted instinctively to stop Cray, albeit in a rather delayed way. Maybe it was the locked-down memory of when she first had to give herself to the machine, the memory surfacing, hate boiling over.

It didn't matter. Dale grabbed for Cray's arm holding the gun that was being used to hit the demented Amanda over the head — she didn't even notice the blows. Dale caught a finger, and twisted viciously, a satisfying crack the result. Cray howled in pain while Dale prized the gun out of his hand, standing just in time as Cray finally managed to roll the Amanda off him, who seemed to suddenly lose herself once more and just sat on the floor, rocking back and forth, cradling her head, moaning as blood trickled out of her ear, her face a mess of scratches and already beginning to bruise from the fight.

Cray moved to stand, dazed from the attack, totally unprepared for the onslaught from such an unexpected source.

"Stay right where you are," said Dale, pointing the gun at Cray in a reversal of roles. Dale looked around and saw that Amanda was moving back up the path fast. "Okay, inside," Dale ordered Cray, as Amanda finally got back to him.

"What happened?" asked Amanda, out of breath, staring in wonder at the mess that was Cray, standing and glaring at his attacker with hate.

"She went crazy at him," said Dale, nodding at the insane Amanda. "I think it must have finally hit home what he was about to do to you. She saved us."

Amanda stared at the woman, who looked anything but a fearless attacker. "Well, that was close."

"You can say that again, but it isn't over yet. Not quite." Dale turned his full attention back to Cray, and said, "Move," once more, indicating the room. "Inside."

Cray walked silently towards the open doorway, grimacing in obvious pain from the swollen finger poking out at a weird angle.

"Dale, what are you doing?" Amanda looked confused, but Dale knew what he had to do and wasn't going to waste any time.

"Wait here, I'll be back out in a minute. Just keep an eye on her." Dale indicated the insane Amanda. "She's not stable." Dale gave Amanda a kiss, the contact giving him the resolve he needed, then pushed Cray into the room once more.

Payback

Time Unknown

"Take off your jacket," ordered Dale, every word sending pain shooting through his head. "Now!" he barked, when Cray didn't instantly do as ordered. Cray carefully pulled the sleeve over his mangled hand, then dropped it off the other, letting it fall to the floor. "Now your shirt."

Realization hit home and Cray panicked, looking around the room as if there was something that would save him.

"Take it off."

Cray unbuttoned the shirt; Dale kept the gun firmly aimed at his head.

"You can't do this, you don't know what will happen if you do," pleaded Cray, panic building, his usually gravelly voice rising in pitch.

"I think I know exactly what will happen, and I think it's not even close to the punishment that you deserve," said Dale, motioning for Cray to take off the unbuttoned shirt. Cray fumbled with the buttons on his left cuff, wincing with the pain — he finally managed it before then undoing the right arm. Cray let the shirt drop to the floor. Dale noticed with satisfaction the dark stains under the armpits — it was about time it was someone else doing the sweating.

"Now, get in."

"No, I won't."

"You have two choices: either you get in, or I shoot out your kneecaps and I drag you in myself."

Cray stared at him full of hate, but moved into the machine that he had made countless Amandas from endless worlds enter before they gradually closed down on him and he was left with an ever-dwindling population.

The machine sensed his presence, maybe there were pressure pads in the floor? The uncaring metal bands held Cray fast.

"You're going to regret this," spat Cray.

"Not as much as you are buddy," said Dale. He walked out of the room as the needle pierced Cray's skin.

~~~

"Right, now we just need to run, really fast," said Dale.

"Where to? There's nowhere to go. What did you do in there Dale? What's happened to Cray?"

"I put him in the machine. Right about now he'll be having the fluid sucked out of him, so we won't have long before, um..."

"Good, he deserves it. He deserves worse," said Amanda, looking nowhere like it was enough punishment for all that he'd done.

"Yeah, but I'm not sure what's going to happen now. He needed you as the last offering to get The Chamber to jump to a new universe, or create its own, but now I'm not really sure what it will do. We need to get out of here and we need to change wherever it was Cray set The Chamber to go to. It needs to jump back before any of this madness happened, so everything goes back to normal."

"You think it will?"

"Honestly? I'm not sure. Come on, we have to run, fast."

"Where?" asked Amanda, running beside Dale as he picked up speed.

"The same way we left before. Down the hatch. I just pray that what I'm thinking really does happen by the time we get there. Let's go. Faster."

They ran like their lives depended on it, which Dale suspected they did, heading for the spot where the hatch was the last time. Dale focused all his attention on hoping beyond hope that what he prayed he would do would actually come to pass. If not...

"There, it worked," said Dale, panting hard, his face throbbing with every footfall, a cramp in his side threatening to stop him dead in his tracks. But up ahead the hatch was opening and the top of a hat could be seen rising from the welcome sight of the hole in the ground.

As they got closer the buzzing inside The Chamber grew louder and louder — Dale understood that they wouldn't have long before it either jumped, or exploded. He really had no idea what it would do now he'd hooked Cray up to the machine rather than it being Amanda.

Damn, the other Amandas!

In their rush to get away Dale hadn't given them a second thought. It was too late now, and they couldn't go with them at any rate — outside The Chamber the paradoxes would build in a way Dale didn't want to imagine, but still, it felt wrong. He glanced back as they got close to the hatch; Amanda caught him doing it.

"Don't worry, it's what I would have wanted. There's no other way. It's just us now."

Dale nodded, smiling as The Caretaker's head popped up through the hatch; he didn't look happy, not in the least.

"This was not part of the deal Dale," said The Caretaker, before his head disappeared below ground-level. Moments later he re-appeared. "Oh, hello Amanda, do excuse my manners, but someone," he gave Dale the daggers, "has been rather rude and interrupted me from some very important work." He was gone again.

Dale just shrugged and helped Amanda down the hatch onto the steps. He was right behind her pressing the button so it closed behind him.

The buzzing was much louder outside of The Chamber, almost deafening, and he knew it would be impossible for them to talk. Dale just pointed down the corridor in the direction of the exit; The Caretaker and Amanda nodded.

They ran, the sound of their footsteps lost, the buzzing getting unbearable, gravity feeling skewed, as if it was lighter at Dale's head than at his feet. The coriolis effect, he'd heard of it, and it was almost as confusing as time travel, but not quite. Nothing was.

As they ran, with The Caretaker and Amanda in front, Dale could tell they were having the same issues with the gravity. Both were moving strangely, battling on but it was as if their bodies were trying to lean back, twisting to the side. It was completely disorientating and utterly exhausting. Dale just hoped they had time.

They moved as well as they could, no time for talking, but made it to the door. Tellan, a.k.a. The Caretaker, pulled it open without hesitating and said, "Hold on," as he pulled out a Hexad and slammed the blue dome into the bare concrete wall.

Dale definitely didn't have time to make his time travel noise, nor did he have the inclination, before all three disappeared.

~~~

"Wow, this is going to get messy really fast," said Dale, trying to take in the space The Chamber was housed in. It was different to the previous one they'd encountered and Dale wondered where they were, when, too.

The rock was dark, almost obsidian, although the huge cavern that housed The Chamber was just as devoid of life as it had been at the end in the alternate one.

But that wasn't what was giving cause for concern, it was the fact that the entire massive space was bathed in sickly blue light, shining off every surface, lighting the black to blue in ever-increasing pulses in sync with the strobing and buzzing of the dome of The Chamber. It was speeding up too, rotating along its axis slightly faster. The gravity inside would have been getting uncomfortable by now.

"Sorry about this Tellan, I honestly didn't want to do this, but I hope I did. Can we get to the actual machine room that controls how this thing jumps? Did I already ask you to find it? See what we have to do?"

"You did young man, and I must tell you that this is far from how I do things. I'm The Caretaker, not your lackey."

Wow, he really is pretty annoyed by this. But if it saves our skin then I'll live with it.

"Sorry, I ran out of ideas. Things were getting desperate."

"So you told me, will tell me. Gosh, I really do dislike this time travel business immensely, it's why you were supposed to clear up all this nonsense."

"I know, I know. Now, the machine room?"

"Hang on, and stay close, it's pretty cramped where we need to be. I don't want anyone fusing into the machinery."

Amanda looked lost, unable to keep up. "Hey, what's happen—"

They jumped.

Please Explain

Time Unknown

"Can someone tell me what the hell is going on here?" shouted Amanda, her voice almost drowned out by the incredible noise of machinery that towered above them like crazed mechanical beasts.

Dale took a second to take in his surroundings, acutely aware of just how close they had come to ending up ground to pulp in the monstrous cogs that reached far up into the room. The place made sense — it wasn't as large as the cavern housing The Chamber — but it was still a ridiculously huge space, crammed full of machinery large and small.

Punching through much of it, probably after coming through a lot of bedrock for stability, was the central pole that secured The Chamber and from which the numerous bands stabilizing it emanated. Dale had thought them there merely for the purpose of spinning The Chamber, but once they'd realized it was a huge time machine in the waiting then the image in his mind held a different kind of information: as well as functional in terms of maintaining the spin, they were also the dials that could be set to make the co-ordinates for The Chamber to make its jump.

The smell of oil permeated everything, coating the inside of Dale's nostrils like petroleum jelly. The pole was thick with grease and the mess of machinery around them glistened with black oil. The dull metal moved relentlessly as it had for more years than Dale cared to think about.

Now they had to change it, and fast, before the whole thing came crashing down, or wiped them out of existence aligning itself.

"Dale! Answer me."

"Sorry," shouted Dale, face feeling like it was splitting apart, his voice and the pounding machinery ringing like a church bell that had been relocated to inside his skull. "There's no time, we have to do this now." Dale turned to Tellan. "Do you know how to change it?"

Tellan shook his head. "No, that's not what you asked me to do. You asked me to find where it was located and to come open the hatch. Now, if you will excuse me, I do have other matters to attend to." The Caretaker doffed his hat to Amanda, gave Dale a rather curt nod, and disappeared.

"Damn. Looks like it's just you and me kiddo." Dale had hoped Tellan would have known what to do, but it seemed like he'd had different ideas. What could have been more important than this? Dale supposed he probably didn't want to know.

"Dale, please?"

"Amanda, I jumped, or I will jump, and I went to Tellan's home, that horrible place, and asked him to come help. Well, he did, now it's down to us. Look, you're better at this than me, can you please take a look at the controls and figure out how we change where The Chamber is going to jump to? Do you think it still will, now I, you know, put Cray in that machine?"

"I don't know, probably, although if it's fluid from me that makes Hexads function, and this is one helluva Hexad, then it might just skew it a little... Or a lot."

Amanda eyed the machinery cautiously, then sidestepped around Dale so she could see what he'd been frowning at with such incomprehension. She stared at him like he was mad. It looked like a retro games table from the early eighties, like a Pac-Man machine gone rogue, all shiny dark glass, switches and even a roller ball.

Dale watched as Amanda touched the reflective glass and small images appeared on the screen, looking like icons for various apps. That was where the similarities ended though, it was nothing like the modern tablets and computers they were used to using, this was something else entirely. Amanda cautiously fiddled with the machine, the touch screen extremely sensitive and super-fast. As she tapped a few icons she smiled and Dale felt relief wash over him.

"You can figure it out? Can you send The Chamber, the damn Hexad or whatever it is, somewhere far away, and stop all this?"

"Sure, it's simple," said Amanda, fishing in her bag, pulling out a Hexad.

"What are you doing?"

"This is all just diagnostic stuff, more for the running of The Chamber than for time travel. But there is an interface, look." Amanda pointed at a simple depression at the top right of the angled glass, a hole the size of the base of a Hexad. Dale peered into it, seeing a series of gold connectors and a small criss-cross bump of metal right in the center — it matched the strange shape in the Hexad's base he'd always wondered about.

"Genius!" Dale kissed Amanda on the forehead and she smiled back at him, the hope in her eyes the same that Dale knew was showing in his.

"Let's do this," said Amanda, and placed her Hexad into the ring. It held fast with a metallic click, faint because of the surrounding machinery, but they heard it as they were practically on top of the Hexad they were peering at it so closely. It sunk slightly in the ring, then turned once, popped back up, and the diagnostics changed on the screen. Amanda glanced at them, then paid them no more mind.

She paused for a moment, thinking, then adjusted the concentric rings around the Hexad before letting go, shoulders relaxing once she seemed content with her settings.

A 6 flashed on the blue dome, and with a nod to each other Amanda placed her hand on the dome. Dale placed his on hers, and pressed down as he went, "Whooooooooooooooooooooosh."

They jumped.

Seriously?

70 Years Past

"Okay, we have exactly five minutes to get out of here before we, well, before we can't."

"Um, okaaaaay. Why do I have a bad feeling about this Amanda? A very bad feeling."

"I might have panicked a little," said Amanda nervously, pulling the Hexad out of the ring. 5 blinked on the top.

Dale couldn't tell if they'd actually jumped anywhere, the machinery was still working, the room was the same, but the touch-screen interface was practically screaming at him, flashing a red warning symbol it was impossible to ignore: the universal red-bordered triangle with an exclamation mark in the center.

As they'd been touching the Hexad, and the Hexad was thus connected to everything else, then the whole lot had jumped with them, a feat so far removed from Dale's experience with jumping to date he wondered what else had come with them too.

The housing clearly had, so maybe his impression it was a man-made housing, maybe a hollowed out mountain that contained The Chamber, may just have been wrong. The whole lot had jumped with them, as well as the room that contained The Chamber.

"Bloody hell."

"Yeah, I know. Right? Come on, we don't have much time. Leave all your Hexads, and I mean all of them. This is it Dale, time to end this." Amanda dumped her bag, just threw it away like it was trash, not containing the most valuable commodity there had ever been in the entire history of countless universes, so Dale rather reluctantly did the same. All that was left was the Hexad in Amanda's hand, the 5 pulsing regularly.

"Let's move, now." Amanda grabbed Dale's hand and they ran for all they were worth, weaving through the cramped space, heading away from the controls, hoping, praying, that there was a simple exit to the room, and that they could get to it quickly.

"What date did you set?" panted Dale, weaving between the machinery, trying to keep hold of Amanda.

"August," said Amanda, glancing at him then looking away.

"Year?" Dale had a bad feeling.

"Nineteen forty five."

"Month?"

"August. Like I just said."

"And, ugh, the day?" *She wouldn't, would she?*

"The sixth, all right?"

"You are not going to also tell me we are—"

"A door, there's a door. Quick, come on."

"Why don't we just jump, from in here?" asked Dale, dreading Amanda's answer to where they actually were.

"Because we can't. We have to know if The Chamber is destroyed, and we can't do that unless we watch. But I don't want to watch from here, do you?" Amanda reached the door first and turned a simple handle, opening up to a world more insane than anything Dale had experienced in what had become a rather terrifying life so far.

~~~

"You did, didn't you? You jumped us to bloody Hiroshima the day they drop Little Boy. Are you insane?"

"No, we have to make sure, we have to be certain that The Chamber is obliterated."

Dale looked around him. It was eerie, everything was still as it would have been. No buildings were burning, nothing had been bombed by more conventional means. He knew the history and knew that Hiroshima had never been targeted right up until the atomic bomb was deployed — the powers-that-be wanted to be able to evaluate its effects properly.

He knew that at the center of the explosion the heat had destroyed everything in a fairly small circumference, but the explosion itself had a much wider reach, not to mention the radiation that killed the survivors slowly and painfully.

"Are we right at the epicenter of this?" asked Dale, as they ran as fast and as far away as they could. Dale ignored the chaos that was happening all around them, caused by the sudden appearance of a huge edifice that was miles long, impossibly high, and had jumped right where many buildings were.

The further they got, the more Dale could see, and it was clear that many buildings were now fused through The Chamber and its support structure — from the outside nothing more than a series of gigantic boxes of different sizes, the rooms necessary for the maintenance of The Chamber itself. But The Chamber was devoid of the space it had occupied, it was exposed to the air and all the more impressive for seeing it out in the open. Parts of it were fused too, but the ceaseless momentum of the machinery was still turning the poles, ripping away the buildings it was fused to, turning them with it.

They kept running, both constantly turning back to see what was happening as they moved further away — however far they got through the maze of buildings they were still too close to really take in the magnitude of The Chamber and what made it spin.

"Not quite, no, but look, it's starting."

The machinery was groaning as it strained to support the pole that spun the Chamber, and in less than a second something malfunctioned and The Chamber, spinning fast and off-kilter, began veering to the side. The buildings it had fused to, not to mention whatever was going on in the machine room itself, meant there would have been countless malfunctions and the gravity was warping, the spin out of control.

Dale heard an almighty crack from behind as they lost sight of the pole. It must have snapped as The Chamber rolled, smashing into the floor like the bomb had already gone off. Buildings collapsed in all directions as The Chamber rolled away, the spin giving it huge momentum, its size destroying anything in its path like they were nothing more than buildings in miniature.

All Dale could think of was Godzilla movies and how the beast paled into significance against The Chamber.

Dale's head was buzzing. He didn't know if it was from the pain, the sound of The Chamber, or maybe it was the sound of an atomic bomb hurtling towards earth that would kill countless people but would help end the Second World War. It got louder and louder. Something wasn't right, he could feel it in his bones. Dale looked at his watch, they still had five or so minutes before the explosion, and as he looked up at Amanda he knew she was feeling the same thing he was.

"This isn't right, is it? It's like I can feel the future changing just by us being here."

Dale shook his head. They were clearly both in-tune enough with such a momentous invasion on reality that they were both getting the same bad vibe. "No, it's very, very wrong. We just killed I don't know how many people by jumping here, all those buildings crushed."

"I know, but there's going to be a bomb dropped here, so it won't make any difference."

"But does it? What about for us? We just killed people. I know they would be dead anyway, but it's still murder, isn't it?"

Amanda was struggling as much as Dale: where did you draw the line? He could see it in her eyes. Time travel was making a mockery of the morals they had believed in their whole lives. Was it murder if people would be dead anyway? Or murder if what you did resulted in people having never existed in the first place? What about the bomb? Shouldn't they be using time travel to stop such catastrophic events from ever happening? It was something he'd thought of a lot, but seeing the result of interfering with the way things happened meant it was simply too dangerous to meddle.

"Do you think we've done something bad?" asked Amanda, interrupting his dark thoughts.

"I think so. What if they don't drop the bomb now, because they've seen this? The Chamber may be broken but it's still here. And what about the war? We might have changed the entire course of human history. We need to put things back how they were."

"Dale, I can't stand this, I really can't. I don't want to do this anymore, I want to go home. Why do we have to make such decisions? We're here, where they drop the first atomic bomb and people die horrible deaths, and we could stop it."

"And be responsible for maybe millions more deaths? That's not a decision I want to make. This is an impossible situation, we need to change it." Dale was resolute.

Amanda nodded.

She pulled out the Hexad, the 5 flashing. "Where to?"

"We jump back to just before we first enter the machine room, and we make a different jump, one where we can get rid of The Chamber without it interfering with anything. It has to have never existed in the future, Hexads need to have never existed."

"Okay." Amanda adjusted the Hexad, said, "Ready?" and as Dale nodded they jumped.

The bomb dropped.

Try Again

Time Unknown

"What are we doing Amanda?" said Dale, standing by the familiar touch screen in the machine room.

"What do you mean?" she asked, as she repeated what she'd done before and set the screen again, ready to take the Hexad, now flashing 4.

"I mean is this all necessary? Taking this whole damn thing away? Isn't there another way? To make it so it has never existed, that Hexads never existed? Something simple. This is getting ridiculously epic. Atomic bombs, crushing cities, can't we just, um..." Dale had no idea what to do, how to stop it.

"Give me a minute, okay?" Amanda brushed dirty hair away from her face — she looked terrible. "Hey, don't forget what you have to do, you know, jump to The Caretaker, get him to come help us in The Chamber? Do that now, so I can think. Okay?"

Damn, I nearly forgot. What will happen if I don't make that jump?

"Right, good idea." Dale took the Hexad, made the adjustments, found he could get into the zone quickly where he was able to direct the Hexad to that awful place that he'd jumped before to find Tellan, and gave Amanda a kiss on the forehead before jumping.

~~~

A few seconds later he was back. He stared at the Hexad, 2 flashing accusingly. They were almost out of jumps, and this was their only remaining Hexad now. Dale realized they were out of options, and part of him wished he had an endless supply of the terrible devices, just for a little peace of mind.

No more room for mistakes.

"You weren't gone long, I haven't had time to think," said Amanda.

"Sorry, didn't want to risk it. The other us, and Tellan, will be here in a minute, so we have to do this now. But I told him, so that's all set up. Let's do this."

"What though?" Amanda was panicking; they were out of time.

Dale's face dropped as realization dawned. "Oh."

"What? What is it Dale?"

"I'm sorry Amanda, I really am. I love you."

"Dale?"

Amanda was alone. Dale had jumped.

A Simple
Solution

2 Days Past

What if none of it had ever happened? That was what they were striving for, wasn't it? Making it so the whole insanity of the last few days had simply never been, that life was just normal, getting up on a Saturday morning, feeling hungover, having a fry-up and mowing the lawn, wishing that you'd bought the snazzy Bosch rather than the budget own brand mower from the out-of-town DIY store.

Normal.

Realization came to Dale like a bolt out of the blue as he stood in a machine room that powered an artificial world that warped reality and made a mockery of living one's own life as it was meant to be lived.

Dale knew the answer, knew how to set things right, allow a single reality to play out as it was meant to: linear, the past and the present affecting the future, not all mixed up so all of it meant little.

So he paid the ultimate sacrifice. Dale jumped back to where he knew he had to so that reality would be normal, things would work out.

Dale smiled down at the sleeping form of Amanda and smiled.

I love you.

Dale pressed down on the flashing 1.

~~~

As his thoughts faded and his eyes closed Dale had only one regret: he never did get to say goodbye to Amanda. Not properly.

There was one final act. Dale set the Hexad, the 0 flashing accusingly, then slammed it into his chest, or rather, the mess of flesh that was this him and the him that in the reality that would have been if all this hadn't happened was standing in the kitchen at the fridge reaching for the milk to put in his first cup of coffee of the day. Feeling rough while Amanda had a lie-in.

He'd understood the truth of the situation just in time: it wasn't Amanda that had been the cause of the production of Hexads and all that ensued, it had been the existence of her *and* him, so he took the burden, doing what he had to do to ensure none of it, not any of it, would ever come to pass.

Dale was soon to be no more, and as the mess of flesh that was two Dales winked out of existence, jumping with a Hexad that flashed -1 before it too vanished, Dale wondered what would happen, not to him, but to the one reality he was leaving behind.

Hopefully it would turn out all right in the end.

If not then it would all have been for nothing.

Still, it had been a wild ride, and, if he was honest, it beat mowing the lawn.

He hoped Amanda remembered to feed the birds.

Dale and Dale vanished.

A Strange Awakening

Present Day

Dale opened his eyes with a start, as if something had woken him. He turned to check the clock but it was still too early for the alarm, and besides, it was Saturday wasn't it? It wouldn't go off anyway. He tried to recall the dream he'd been having, but it was already gone, elusive and fading as they always seemed to do.

Amanda stirred beside him and opened her eyes sleepily, looking sexy as hell with disheveled hair, smiling at him like he didn't look mad with his hair sticking up as usual. It wasn't fair, she looked hot in the morning, he looked like he'd been dragged through a hedge backwards.

"Morning honey," said Dale.

"Morning."

Dale snuggled back down, sinking into the pillow, pulling the covers tight, one arm exploring Amanda beneath the sheets. "Mm, you smell nice," said Dale, sinking his face into her hair, taking her scent in deep.

"Haha, I haven't even had a shower yet."

"Doesn't matter, you always have this lovely smell to you."

Amanda turned on her pillow and smiled, then sniffed deeply, making fun of him.

She shot upright, eyes wide with fear, looking completely terrified. "Who the hell are you? What's going on? Where's Dale? DALE!"

"Amanda, it's me, it's me. What's wrong?"

Amanda crawled out of the bed, then backed away heading for the door. Naked and terrified, she shouted, "You're not Dale, you're not him. You don't smell anything like him," as she ran for her life before the monster in her bed had the chance to do anything at all but sit there nonplussed, wondering what kind of a nightmare she must have had to wake up acting so strangely.

Hopefully it would pass.

But what if it didn't?

The End

Book 3 in the series is **Hexad: The Ward**

Sign up for the author's newsletter for new release announcements and flash sales at www.alkline.co.uk

52483157R00220

Made in the USA
Charleston, SC
20 February 2016